Synthetics Rising

Douglas Norberg

CHAPTER 1 SEEDS OF WAR 1

CHAPTER 2 BIRTH OF A GENIUS 13

CHAPTER 3 DEFECT 32

CHAPTER 4 M.L.S.S. INC. 51

CHAPTER 5 THE HAITIAN WAR 66

CHAPTER 6 DEFEAT AND EXILE 70

CHAPTER 7 THE UNIVERSAL PRINCIPLE OF RELATIVITY 90

CHAPTER 8 THE SECT 106

CHAPTER 9 COLONIZATION 130

CHAPTER 10 INDEPENDENCE 138

CHAPTER 11 RECOLONIZATION 151

CHAPTER 12 EVONIA 162

CHAPTER 13 THE LONG TREK 194

CHAPTER 14 GROWTH 212

CHAPTER 15 COLONIZATION 221

CHAPTER 16 REDISCOVERY 227

CHAPTER 17 DIPLOMACY 243

CHAPTER 18 AMBUSH 249

CHAPTER 19 VICTORY OR DEATH 267

CHAPTER 20 VULTURES DESCEND 278

CHAPTER 21 DIPLOMATIC ENTANGLEMENTS 295

CHAPTER 22 LOST IN SPACE 303

CHAPTER 23 PROCRASTINATION 315

CHAPTER 24 EPOCH 328

Chapter 1

Seeds of War

Some say the seeds of the Synthetics Rising were first planted when man began to use artificial insemination. Others believe that it was when man first learned how to conceive life in a test tube. Most people believe that the seeds of the Synthetics Rising were planted when man began to tamper with the building blocks of life itself, i.e., the genes. Regardless of when the seeds were first planted, the Synthetics Rising would prove to be the most destructive war man has ever encountered.

There was a time in the history of mankind when the word science and the concept behind it were unknown. As man's society developed and his culture grew more complex, some individuals began to ask questions. Why does this work? Why doesn't that work? The individuals who tested their theories came to be called scientists, and the field in which they worked was called science. Their work was not merely to explain why but to prove their theories by experimentation. Scientists intuitively know that the most powerful of all weapons is knowledge. Yet, it wasn't power that scientists sought. Thus, their motive was the purest of all. They sought only the satisfaction of their own curiosity. It was for others to use or misuse their discoveries.

At first, science had little impact on the lives of ordinary people. For each puzzle the scientists unraveled, two more puzzles were presented. As these two were solved, four more took their place. Man's knowledge and his society leaped forward. With each success, science had more impact on the lives of ordinary people. The importance and the number of scientists grew steadily over time.

At first, the discoveries of science were simple, including the laws of mechanics, simple anatomy, the flow of blood through the body, the function of different organs, etc. But as each hurdle was overcome and each level ascended, another quest began. The biological study grew beyond the level of anatomy, beyond the function of organs, beyond even the cellular level, down to the makeup of the genes themselves.

Man's first control over procreation began with artificial insemination. This was done by taking sperm from the male and injecting it directly into the female genital tract. The first subject for this experiment was animals, and when artificial insemination became commonplace in animal husbandry, then it was tested on humans.

After artificial insemination inside the female's body came artificial insemination outside the female's body, that is, the fertilization in a test tube. This was done by injecting a female animal with fertilizing chemicals and flushing the ripened eggs from her genital tract. The eggs were recovered, fertilized, and frozen. When the surrogate mother was ready, one of the eggs was thawed and inserted inside her genital tract. There the egg attached itself to the uterus and developed according to its genetic programming. This development took place because of research in animal husbandry. By this method, a genetically superior mother could have many more offspring than she could bear herself. The result was a far superior herd of animals.

After this technique was refined and gained widespread acceptance, it was attempted on humans. Women with fertility problems were the first to submit. A woman with blocked fallopian tubes could have her ripened eggs removed surgically, fertilized in a test tube, and implanted in her own uterus. Public disclosure of this procedure caused a mild sensation, but since the woman was still bearing her own child, no one could make a persuasive moral objection.

When women with blocked fallopian tubes were able to have their own children, women with uterine problems began asking their doctors what science could do for them. At first, the women with uterine problems hired other women to bear their husbands' children. However, the children were the children of the surrogate mothers, and the inevitable happened. Some surrogate mothers refused to give up their children. However, when doctors learned to fertilize outside the body of the mother and implant it into the surrogate mother, the woman who gave birth was not even related to the child and therefore had no rights to the child at all.

Inevitably, some rich women did not want the trouble of pregnancy at all. Even though they could have their own children, why bother when it was so much easier to hire someone to do it for them. Instead of getting pregnant, they hired someone to get pregnant for them. Again, there was a public outcry against what the press called rich bitches, but the courts ruled that both the 'rich bitches' and the surrogate mother had the right of contract.

After the rich bitches hired surrogate mothers, merely affluent mothers wanted to know if it was possible for them to avoid the difficulties of pregnancy. If this could be done, there was a fortune to be made since while affluent women individually had less money than rich women, collectively, they had a great deal more.

There were only so many women who would hire their bodies out as mothers, and those who did always wanted a small fortune. Then the artificial uterus was invented. No one actually deliberately set out to develop the artificial uterus, at least not at first. The artificial uterus was only developed when all the research had been inadvertently made available by other independent work. Finally, one day when all of the pieces to the puzzle had been made, a genius looked at the pieces and saw that they would fit.

The first step in the artificial uterus was the development of artificial blood. Artificial blood was developed for use in operating rooms. At first, it was of poor quality, but when some were made that could carry more oxygen than real blood, it came into widespread acceptance. It had all the advantages over real blood. It was cheaper, could be made germ free, was available in unlimited supply, and most importantly, carried more oxygen.

Synthetics Rising

The next step in the artificial uterus was the understanding of the endometrium - the lining of the uterus. It, too, was the result of research into something unrelated, and that was research into combating women's diseases. With artificial blood that could carry both nutrients and oxygen and with an understanding of the endometrium, all that had to be really done for the artificial uterus was the development of an artificial endometrium, and this was surprisingly easy. Medical supply companies, drug companies, and engineering companies vied with each other to be the first to produce a working model.

The development of the artificial uterus was hailed by everyone except religious fundamentalists as a monumental breakthrough. Not only could children now be born of cows, not only would women be free of pregnancy, but complications of pregnancy could also be eliminated. The fetal conditions could always be perfect. Congenital birth defects disappeared overnight.

Almost immediately following the disappearance of congenital birth defects, genetic birth defects also disappeared. After the development of the artificial uterus, all fertilization took place in a test tube where it was possible to microscopically examine both the egg and the sperm prior to fertilization to see if they were healthy. It was also possible to determine the defective eggs and sperm of persons with genetic diseases so that only the eggs and sperm that did not carry the genetic disease could not unite.

If these developments seem beneficial instead of seeds of a disaster, it is because they were beneficial. Science is amoral: it can be used for evil just as well as good. A research scientist never really comprehends the full impact of his discovery. He cannot possibly visualize the uses it will be put to when someone else builds upon it. Eventually, most diseases except those of old age were eliminated. Ironically, this created more problems than it solved. The primary problems men had to deal with were social problems. It was inevitable that man would begin to improve himself as well as his environment.

The first step to biological engineering was an understanding of the atomic structure of life itself; RNA and DNA. Once RNA and DNA were understood, genetic engineering became possible. The first successes were simple microorganisms such as bacteria that ate oil slicks. Once the oil slicks were consumed, the bacteria had no more food and died out. Research proceeded into organisms that consumed even toxic wastes. The successful development of these organisms was hailed as a great achievement. A huge amount of toxic chemicals had been manufactured. The biodegradation of these chemicals was of great benefit.

Genetic research did not stop there. As research proceeded, the process of mutation was understood and with its comprehension, so was the formation of the cancer cell. When the formation of the cancer cell was understood, so was the immunological solution to destroy that cell.

These benevolences are so enormous that it is hard to understand how such developments could lead to a totally destructive war. The very beneficial nature of research explains how it could happen. As each benefit accumulated, with each success of science, the public grew increasingly confident that science to benefit society. Research, which should not have been done, was done, and those who did criticize such research were denounced as doomsayers and ignored.

From time to time, incidents took place that shook the confidence of the public in science. The first such occasion was when industrialization defiled the planet's air and water. What was the answer? What else, other than science! In order to correct pollution, laws were passed, money was appropriated, and huge plants were built to clean the effluent.

The second such incident was when the public discovered that industries were dumping their toxic wastes because they had no place to put them. Even when they had a place to dump, it was cheaper to dump them illegally. Genetic engineering came to the rescue, and new organisms were created to digest these toxic wastes: science had again solved its own problem.

The most serious incident of a scientific error was when a genetic researcher inadvertently created a new virulent virus. In three weeks, 10 million people died! The disease was only stopped from destroying all of humanity when other genetic researchers (the ones who created it were all dead) produced a similar but harmless virus, mass produced it, and inoculated the whole world. In the end, despite the fact that science had created the problem, humanity was grateful, and public respect for science was enhanced.

As genetic engineering developed, its engineers moved up the evolutionary ladder. They developed and improved on plants until they developed one that was all fruit, grew faster, under more adverse conditions, and had more protein. Animal genes were improved so that animals grew faster, on less food, and were much more resistant to disease.

The first development in human engineering itself was a process known as cloning. Cloning is the process of creating a duplicate image of oneself. An example of a clone is a twin. A human ovum is taken, and the nucleus is removed and replaced with the nucleus from a cell of the person desired to be cloned. Since all its genes came from the same person, that person is a duplicate of the original.

Unlike the artificial uterus and genetic engineering, cloning did not catch on. The reason why it didn't work is the very reason why one would have expected it would: ego. Although it might seem appealing to have an exact copy of yourself around for all eternity, it is frightening to watch an exact copy of yourself grow up. What is more, when it is an adult, it is younger and better. Who needs to compete with oneself? Cloning's only importance to this story is that its techniques were essential for the development of genetic engineering.

One of the methodologies often discussed concerning human genetics but never carried out was selective breeding. Often done with domestic animals, it was never done with humans. The closest attempt occurred in Nazi Germany when girls were encouraged to mate the SS men. The selection of the girls and the SS men was hardly scientific, and the children produced were the same as their parents.

There were a number of reasons that selective breeding was never carried out amount humans. The best scientific reason is that there was never any agreement on what characteristics are most important. With racehorses, the only desired factors are speed and endurance, with dairy cows, it is milk production, and with beef cattle, it is meat production. With humans, there can be no such simple gradation of desired qualities.

The real reason selective breeding was never tried with humans is that humans are incurable romantics. Sex has never been a simple biological act for them. Humans have always used it to express something more like love, romance, or expression of affection. To copulate just for the purpose of creating better child conflicts with the human soul.

After the genetic engineers improved the characteristics of plants and animals, they moved on to humans. The first experiments produced horrible monstrosities. The results of these experiments were not made public. With the development of the artificial uterus, such occurrence could be avoided. The fetus could be carefully monitored. If the fetus did not develop normally, it was aborted. No one other than the scientists found out about it.

Gradually, the genetic engineers refined their techniques and hatched their first synthetic humans. The first engineered humans hardly made improvements in the racial stock. The children were uniformly retarded and usually self-destructive. Those that survived were put in homes and maintained until death.

This time the genetic engineers' "mistakes" could not be kept secret. The children had to be maintained at public expense. When a legislature inquired about the expense, he told a journalist, and Pandora's Box was opened. Many magazine articles were written, and the story appeared on all the news services. The public hardly noticed.

Genetic research on humans continued. Eventually, normal-appearing children were hatched. At least these children appeared normal. No one noticed at first that these children were not like other children. Their emotions were bred out. They showed no feelings. Not only that, but they were in no sense superior. They were only of average intelligence, but they were completely without imagination or creativity. What was the use of engineering a new human unless it was superior to the old?

Despite the early failures, the research continued. New children were born that were not only smarter but stronger, quicker, and more athletic. They were still undemonstrative, but in testable areas, they were clearly better. The genetic engineers were not satisfied with these children. They were smarter but only marginally so. They continued to refine their techniques until they produced a near-genius child. Not only were they noticeably superior in all testable factors, but also they were able to think quicker and concentrate longer and more intensely. Best of all, for their designers, they were "psychologically stable". From the designers' point of view, this meant that the children were conformist and not disruptive. What it really meant was that the children were almost utterly devoid of human feeling and needed no human affection, even when a small children. Finally, the engineers thought they had achieved a truly superior human being.

Shortly after developing this new, "better" human, a bitter, acrimonious dispute arose among the engineers. With the development of the artificial uterus and the technique of replacement of the nucleus of the cell, why was there a need for sex organs? Not only did sex organs sap vitality from the animals, but it caused the animals to behave erratically. The younger engineers wanted nothing to distract their inventions. They were afraid of how their inventions would behave if they had sex organs; they might turn into hopeless nymphomaniacs. Even the older engineers had to admit that there was no technical reason for sex organs anymore. Therefore, sex organs were eliminated. The engineers wanted a predictable invention, and if the invention did not prove functional, it could not reproduce itself and would die out naturally.

Outwardly, the children appeared to be male. They were given the convenient penis, but there were no vestiges of testicles or any other male sex organs. As the children grew, the penis retained its boyish shape, and the child never developed any pubic hair or any other masculine secondary sex characteristic.

Chapter 2

Birth of a Genius

Robert Carl and Valerie Stuart sit in a hospital waiting room, waiting their turn. Their turn for when the artificial uterus will be opened, and they will be parents. Robert and Valerie are married, but Valerie does not use her husband's name; it is not the custom. They know their child will be male – that is what they ordered! With a microscopic examination of the sperm before fertilization, it is a simple matter to ensure fertilization of the egg with a sperm containing the Y chromosome. Since it is their first child, they had a choice. Had it been their second child, it would have had to be opposite in sex from the first. The only way to have two of the same sex is to find another couple that wants two of the opposite sex. By law, the ratio between the sexes must stay even.

Long ago, they picked the name for the child; he will be called Dana Stuart Carl. The last two names are mandatory. When a male child is born, he must take his father's last name and the middle name of his mother. The reverse is true if the child is a girl. Brothers and sisters no longer have the same last name.

Robert and Valerie lived together for four years before they decided to have a child. It is not permitted to have a child unless you are married. The reason has nothing to do with prudishness; research has proven that children with both parents are usually better adjusted. The law is easily enforced because women no longer bear their own children. Virtually all children are born of the artificial uterus. Only a few strict religious cults still make their women give birth.

Neither Valerie nor Robert are worried about their child. There are never problems or complications at birth, and the children are always healthy. After the ovum is fertilized, it is put into the artificial uterus, where it is monitored constantly by a variety of artificial sensors. The parents have been not only able to see the monitors on their son but have been able to watch through miniature television cameras inside the artificial uterus developing their child. Although not worried, they are nervous, the firstborn is always a great expectation.

As Robert and Valerie wait for their turn, they reflect upon what they went through to have the baby. The red tape was easy, it is their first child, and neither carries any hereditary defects. If they had been carriers, they would still have been able to have children, but their reproductive cells would have been specially screened. The artificial uterus has been in operation for a couple of generations, so almost all the hereditary diseases have been wiped out. Almost no one has to undergo the special screening procedures anymore.

The first step in the procedure was the trip to the doctor's office for the fertilization process. Valerie took fertility pills the week before to ensure there would be ripe ova. Robert refrained from sex with Valerie for a week to ensure an adequate supply of sperm. This is an anachronism from the early days of in vitro fertilization when the doctors wanted to ensure an adequate supply of sperm. The techniques are now so well developed that only a few sperm are needed.

A nurse calls their names in the waiting room. Robert and Valerie clasp hands, kiss, and separate. No words are spoken, none are needed. Valerie is led down a long hall to a special operating room where she undresses and lays on a special table with her feet in stirrups. Shortly, the doctor enters with her nurse, a male. Though Valerie is naked and exposed, she is not covered with a sheet, nor does she feel naked or embarrassed. It does not occur to her that she should be ashamed of her sex.

The doctor picks up a device called an ovarian catheter; it is really a miniature television camera attached to a miniature suction device. The device is inserted into Valerie's vagina and runs up through her uterus and into her fallopian tubes. There the doctor spots a ripe ovum, easily seen on the electronically magnified television screen. Pushing a button, the suction device is actuated, and the doctor obtains a ripe ovum. In order to be sure of fertilization, the doctor obtains two more ova before ceasing the procedure. Twenty minutes after she left the waiting room, she returned. When she arrives back at the waiting room, she finds Robert waiting for her.

In the meantime, Robert has been led into a small examining room by two nurses, both female. Instead of Robert undressing, the nurses undress him. These are not special duty nurses employed for just this function; they are regular nurses who perform this task like any other. Few nurses object to this as part of their job. Both nurses are married, and it would not occur to their husbands to object to this part of their wife's jobs. In fact, there is a popular belief that this part of a nurse's job makes them better lovers.

After the nurses undress Robert, he is asked to lie on his stomach. One of the nurses massages his back and shoulders while the other massages his feet and thighs. When they feel their patient start to relax, they ask him to turn over. One nurse massages his feet while the other massages his chest, gradually working together. When the two nurses meet at Robert's crotch, his penis is fully erect. The nurse who has been massaging his chest reaches for his penis while the nurse who has been massaging his chest reaches for his scrotum. The penis is grasped firmly and massaged in long, slow strokes while the scrotum is deftly massaged with the fingertips. No lubricants are used.

As Robert enjoys the massage, the thought of being the first man to give medical sperm samples flickers briefly through Robert's mind. Instead of using nurses to gather the sample, the men would be led to a room and simply told to fill the vial. The man would undress, look at the vial, the bare examining table, the four sterile walls, and wonder how he was going to get it up, much less how he was going to fill the vial. Robert knew that if they managed, they left the room exhausted and sore.

The nurses have thoughts of their own. The miracle of a soft, limp penis growing stiff and finally ejaculating has always fascinated them. The magic of their touch always rewards them with the drama of the patient's response. It never occurs to them to be offended by this. It is simply a natural part of the miracle of life. It is a natural body function like any other. They would not have understood their great, great grandmother's modesty.

As Robert's excitement grows, his thoughts drift off from the doctor's office to the most sensual experience of his life, the first time he and Valerie made love. Robert responds quickly to the practiced hands of the nurse, feeling him stiffen prior to ejaculation, reaches into her pocket without missing stroking and produces a vial which to places over the glans at the head of Robert's penis just before he ejaculates. When Robert's organism is over, she tilts the vial upright, re-clasps the vial, and releases Robert's penis. In her best professional manner, she says, "Thank you, Mr. Carl. This will be an entirely adequate specimen." She leaves the room.

The remaining nurse produces a small wet towelette and cleans the few remaining drops of sperm off the head of Robert's penis. As she leaves the room, she says, "You can get dressed now. Your wife will rejoin you shortly in the waiting room."

Robert is only in the waiting room a few minutes before his wife joins him. With a twinge of sarcasm, she says, "I trust you enjoyed yourself more than I."

Robert ignores the remark. "It's time we go to work." he walks over to the telephone and, without picking up the receiver, pushes a sequence of buttons. In less than a minute, two vehicles appear outside. Robert takes one and Valerie the other. Each hits another sequence of buttons, and each vehicle automatically takes its passenger to the programmed destination.

Robert and Valerie's reverie is broken when the medical technician comes into the waiting room and calls their names. Robert and Valerie get up from their chairs and follow the technician into a huge room with long rows of stacks where the egg-shaped artificial uteruses are stored. The technician strolls quickly down the stacks finding first the C's and then little unborn Dana. Placing a pan he picked up when he entered the room under the artificial uterus, the technician first reaches into his pocket and pulls out a hypodermic needle. Inserting the needle into a rubberized part of the artificial uterus, he pushes the plunger down, and a stimulant squirts into Dana's umbilical cord. The technician pulls out the needle, places it back into his pocket, and keeps time on his watch. When two minutes have elapsed, the technician pulls out a key, and the artificial uterus cracks open and spills out its water.

Working very quickly now, the technician pulls the artificial uterus apart and, with a syringe, cleans any water or debris out of Dana's air passages. With almost the same motion, the technician stretches, clamps, and ties Dana's umbilical cord.

Working more slowly now, the technician picks up Dana, checks his breathing and heartbeat, goes to a sink, and washes him off. Next, he dries Dana, puts a paper diaper on him, wraps him in a blanket, and hands him to his parents.

Valerie takes Dana from the technician, shows him to Robert, and cradles him in her arms for several minutes, admiring him. Finally, Robert says quietly, "May I hold my son?"

Valerie hands Dana to his father. Robert takes the child and, for several minutes, makes baby faces and baby sounds before handing him back to his mother. They thank the technician, who has been patiently watching a scene he has seen thousands of times before and leave.

Valerie, like virtually all mothers, continues to work despite having an infant to care for. Before going to work, she and Robert takes Dana to the infant care center. Such centers are plentiful and are state-subsidized so that the cost is affordable to everyone. The care given at these centers is excellent.

As a newborn, Dana spends most of his time eating or sleeping. Although it is possible to feed and care for infants, mechanically, it is not done. Experience has shown that if the infants are not held, they die! The technicians not only spend a great deal of time feeding and caring for them but also playing with them in order to keep their minds stimulated.

Thus, it develops the routine of Dana's early life. He is not a good child, he cries a lot and has a poor appetite. It is not until Dana is six months only that his parents realize that their child is unusual - he begins to talk. At nine months, he is speaking in complete sentences. Robert and Valerie do not need a child psychologist to tell them they have an intellectually gifted son.

At two years, Dana teaches himself how to read and shows a special fondness for playing with toys requiring spatial acuity. Observing this, Robert teaches Dana how to use the family computer. When Dana masters this, Robert teaches him how to play chess and begins what is a lifelong hobby.

However, intellectually gifted Dana is still a small child. While his mind develops rapidly, his body and emotions do not. Dana does not walk until well past one year, and he is smaller than average, although well proportioned. Though intellectually gifted, Dana behaves no better than other children. In fact, he behaves worse, he is temperamental, a finicky eater, easily frustrated, and a mama's boy. When Dana turns three, Valerie takes him to a child psychologist.

At the psychologist's office, Robert and Valerie have only to wait a few minutes before the psychologist comes in to greet them. As he approaches, he says, "You must be the Carl/Stuarts."

"Yes," answers Robert rising from his chair, "My name is Bob, and this is my wife Valerie and our son Dana."

"Well," says Dr. Bollard addressing Dana, "would you like to come with me, young man? I have some things I would like to show you." With that, he leads Dana into his office.

After Dr. Bollard and Dana leave, the secretary speaks, "This will take about an hour, perhaps you'd like to do some shopping and come back in about an hour.

"Very well," says Valerie, "we'll be back in an hour."

When Dr. Bollard and Dana come out of Dr. Bollard's private office, Robert and Valerie are calmly sitting in the waiting room. Dana runs up to his parents, unusually animated, telling them about how much fun he had.

"Would you please come into my office?" asks Dr. Bollard.

After Robert and Valerie are sitting comfortably in Dr. Bollard's office, he says, "I would like your impressions of what you think is wrong with your son."

Valerie speaks first, giving a detailed description of her son's temperamental nature and his poor eating habits. After she finishes, Robert adds only a few details.

Only after Robert and Valerie are completely finished does Dr. Bollard begins, "Your son is an intellectually gifted child, as a matter of fact, at his age, and our tests cannot measure his abilities. With his brain developing as rapidly as it is, it is too early to measure his intellect fully. I have determined the reason for his temperamental nature."

Dr. Bollard pauses a moment to make sure that Robert and Valerie are paying attention and for effect. "The brain intuitively understands what it is good at and what it is not. The brain likes to perform activities where it has abilities and resists those where it doesn't. You will recall from school that the intellectual portion of the brain is divided into two hemispheres which are connected by only a few fibers, and that each hemisphere controls certain tasks. In a right-handed person, the left hemisphere is dominant, controlling verbal, intuitive functions, while the right hemisphere controls logical, spatial functions. In a left-handed person, the situation is reversed."

Dr. Bollard continues, "Dana's problem is that both of his hemispheres are equally gifted. The result is that he doesn't know which one to use and has difficulty coordinating them. He has difficulty performing functions requiring the simultaneous use of both brain hemispheres. When he grows up, he will be ambidextrous. He will also lack good fine muscle coordination. He will have terrible handwriting."

"The reason for Dana's temperament is that when he performs requiring both hemispheres, he cannot live up to his intuitive expectations of himself and becomes angry and frustrated. Dana will make foolish mistakes for an exceptionally gifted child. On the other hand, some of the most gifted people in history have had the same or similar difficulties. People who have the same problem as Dana seem to have special gifts of insight or creativity that other people of equal capacity do not have. Geniuses such as Beethoven, Edison, and Einstein are all thought to have had the same handicap as Dana. Other than his hemispheric disability, Dana seems to be a perfectly normal child."

After Dr. Bollard finishes, Valerie speaks, "We have known Dana to be gifted for a long time. What can we do to correct his temperament?"

Dr. Bollard sighs and answers slowly, "You must be patient. You should try to give him as much love and security as you can, and above all, do not reward his poor deportment with attention. Eventually, his brain will learn to control his emotions."

Robert and Valerie have many more questions to ask. Dr. Bollard answers them as patiently and as forthrightly as he can. Robert and Valerie understand the answers but somehow emotionally cannot quite accept the fact that their intellectually gifted child is somehow flawed. Eventually, Robert and Valerie exhaust themselves of questions and bid goodbye.

As they leave, Dr. Bollard says he will be sending them a written report and suggests that it might be a good idea to enroll Dana in a school for gifted children. He says, "Children as bright as Dana have an insatiable thirst for knowledge. If challenged, his mind might be preoccupied and improve his deportment."

Robert and Valerie thank the doctor, retrieve Dana from the waiting room and leave. After they return home and Dana is playing in the next room, Valerie turns to Robert and says. "What do you think, dear?"

"I think it was a waste of time and money!"

"So do I. I think we give Dana as much love and affection as possible, and we already knew he was intellectually gifted. I don't see how sending him to another school will help?"

"Neither do I. I want to give him as normal an environment as possible. I want him to go to school with the same children he plays with."

"I had so hoped that a psychologist would be able to offer a solution. Now it looks more hopeless than ever. Even so, I am glad that we tried."

As Dana grows older, his deportment does not improve. He does not play with the other children and spends most of his time with his favorite toy, his computer. He spends endless hours in front of it, playing chess, reading books from the public library, learning math, and writing new computer programs. Dana's parents worry about his emotional progress but never enough to give Dana as normal an environment as possible.

When Dana enters first grade, he proves to be a disciplinary problem. He spends most of his time daydreaming and does not participate in-class activities. He likes to participate in physical education but is otherwise bored and inattentive in school. At first, the teacher chides him privately in order to get him to participate.

When that does not work, she begins to chide him publicly. As his teacher continues her corrective measures, Dana responds by becoming progressively more defiant. Finally, the situation becomes so bad that Robert and Valerie are called in for a meeting. When Dana's teacher states that she thinks Dana is emotionally disturbed and possibly mentally retarded they know they will have to put him in a school for gifted children. Robert and Valerie do not bother to correct Dana's teacher to tell her that their son is not emotionally disturbed or mentally retarded - they know it will not help. They realize that Dr. Bollard was correct and must enroll Dana in a school for gifted children.

The next day Robert calls a new school that he has heard is opening in Moose Lake, a school for gifted children. When he calls the school, the people at the school are very polite, too polite! They reluctantly agree to the testing, and Robert, despite his apprehensions, agrees to take Dana in for testing.

The next day, Valerie takes Dana to the Moose Lake Special School instead of taking him to the Barnum Public School.

Turning Dana over to a man who identified himself as Mr. Howard, Valerie returns to her farm home outside of Mahtowa. The farm is 16 miles away from the school, and Valerie knows that by automatic transport, it will only take her 10 minutes to return.

The testing lasts for 2 hours. Valerie is waiting in the outer office when Mr. Howard returns with Dana. As she watches her son, she notices that same eagerness and animation that she saw when she took him to see Dr. Bollard. It is only then that she notices that Mr. Howard is also beaming.

"Mommy, mommy," Dana spontaneously exclaims, "You should see all the fun puzzles and games the man gave me. I tried to get them all but couldn't."

"Ms. Stuart," says Mr. Howard, "would you step into my office, please?"

Mr. Howard shows Valerie into his office. They sit at a table opposite each other. Dana remains with the secretary in the outer office. "Your son is a remarkable child,' begins Mr. Howard. "He shows truly remarkable scores in memory, spatial reasoning, abstract comprehension, verbal ability, and in fact, just about everything. The only thing he has difficulty in is in functions that require interhemispheric communication."

"Yes, I know. Dana has been tested before."

"When was that done?"

"When Dana was three."

"In that case, it is doubtful that you realize the full impact of Dana's abilities. Dana is undoubtedly the most gifted child. It has been my privilege to test. He will have some difficulties performing up to his expectations of himself, but eventually, he will learn to cope."

"Dana has a problem with his temperament and his deportment. I feel it only fair to tell you."

"I was wondering why you brought him here. How did you find out about this school?"

"My husband heard about it; I don't know how."

"I see. I take it. Dana was bored and inattentive in public school and became a disciplinary problem."

"Yes, how did you know?"

"It fits the pattern. Thank you for telling me this, Ms. Stuart. That should not be a problem here. Our children are all well behaved, and we keep them quite busy."

"I take it that you will admit Dana then?"

"It isn't up to me, but I will recommend it." Mr. Howard pauses for what seems to be a long time before continuing. "There is something that I have to tell you before you decide to enroll your son in our school. This is not a school for gifted children.

"What kind of school is it then?" asks Valerie calmly.

Mr. Howard pauses for what seems like a long time before answering. "It is a school for Synthetic children."

"Synthetic children!" exclaims Valerie, startled at the loudness of her own voice. "What are Synthetic children?"

"Synthetic children are the product of decades of genetic research," answered Mr. Howard patiently. "The government has been funding research into human genetics for many decades now. As part of that program, we have engineered a human being that we believe is in all aspects better. This old mental hospital and dormitory were chosen as the school for our children."

"In many ways, Dana will be inferior to our children. He certainly will not be on a physical par with them. His thought processes will not be as quick, nor will his ability to concentrate be as high, yet he should be able to make up for it with his high IQ. We have not yet engineered a child with Dana's 10. I am going to recommend him for admittance that is if you are still offering him for admittance. The matter will have to be taken up before a faculty board, but I think they will improve."

Valerie has hardly heard a word Mr. Howard has said after he uttered "synthetic children." Questions flood her mind with such force and rapidity that she is unable to verbalize them. "Won't it be harmful to Dana to attend school with children who aren't real children?" she finally blurts out.

"You misunderstood," responds Mr. Howard. "I understand your concern, but all our children are real. They are hardly artificial.

"Well, how will this affect my child's emotional and cultural development? Will the other children pick on and abuse my son? He is below average in size."

"I can't say for sure how going to our school will affect his development. What we do know is how well he is doing now. I think I can say safely say that this school will challenge him academically, and the chance of the other children picking on him is non-existent.

Synthetic children are actually smaller than your son. He will be the largest child in the class. Our children are very closely supervised, and antisocial behavior just doesn't happen. It was one of the major attributes we engineered out of them. The only way our children ever do any damage is due to their curiosity. They are forever taking things apart to see how they work. Believe me, this can be quite damaging."

"I'll be quite frank with you, Ms. Stuart. I'm sure our board will admit Dana. A gifted child like Dana should be able to keep up academically, and as a normal child, he not only represents a reference point with which to measure our own children but those children need to have experiences with non-synthetic children. I promise you we will take very careful care of him. He and his relationships with the other children will be watched constantly. Why don't you talk it over with your husband? I'll call you when the board has made its decision. If you do not wish to admit him, you don't have to."

Still stunned, Valerie returns to the secretary's office, where Dana is waiting. She puts out her hand for Dana to join her and asks the secretary to call a transport. In a few moments, the transport arrives, she programs its destination, and they speed off.

Robert returns home for lunch this day from his job in Cloquet, where he is an attorney. Normally, he eats his lunch out, but this day, he makes an exception. He wants to find out how Dana and

Valerie made out at the new school. As soon as he walks in the door and sees his wife, he asks, "How did it go at the school today, dear?"

"You'd better sit down first, dear," she responds, "you're not going to believe what kind of a school that is." Robert takes off his coat and sits at the kitchen table while his wife explains that the Moose Lake School is a boarding school for synthetic children. After explaining what a synthetic child is, she finally asks him what he thinks of sending Dana to school there.

Robert responds slowly, "It is the only school for gifted children around here, and I certainly don't want to send Dana away to boarding school."

"Neither do I."

"I don't think we have a right to assume that it will do Dana harm. If it doesn't work out, we can always remove him from the school. The public school certainly isn't working out."

"I suppose you're right," sighs Valerie. "In any event, Dana hasn't been admitted yet. He still has to be approved for admittance by a faculty board."

"Is that much of an obstacle?"

"I don't think so," Mr. Howard seemed quite anxious to have him admitted. He apparently thought it would be beneficial for their students to have experience with normal children and to give the faculty a tool to measure their children with normal children."

"Did he say anything of how he thought Dana would be affected by their children?"

"Yes, but he didn't know. He did assure me that their children are very well behaved and carefully supervised.

A week goes by before Mr. Howard calls. During that week, Valerie takes a week's vacation to stay home with Dana from her job as a nurse in the Cloquet Hospital. She does not wish to subject her son to more humiliation until she hears from the new school. It is Friday when Mr. Howard calls and confirms that Dana has been approved for admittance. Valerie responds that she is glad and that she will bring Dana for his first class on Monday.

Chapter 3

Defect

On Monday, Valerie takes Dana to the synthetic school in Moose Lake. When the transport comes, Valerie teaches Dana how to program one's destination into the transport's computer memory. Dana programs the transport.

Upon arrival at the school, Valerie takes Dana into the building and looks for the classroom they have been assigned. She can't help noticing that the building isn't at all like a school - there are no students milling about! It is not until later that she finds out the reason for this, the oldest group of the advanced synthetic model, the ones that Dana is going to school with, is only six years old, the same age as Dana. The older, inferior synthetic children are housed elsewhere.

Valerie finds the correct room and opens the door. Inside the classroom is a man in his middle forties and about thirty children, all "boys". Valerie immediately notices the lack of "girls" but does not ask why. As she approaches the teacher, she looks about the classroom noticing the pupils. They aren't in their uniforms, as she expected. They all have different features and hair colorations and are of different races. Yet, they all have something familiar about them. They are all the same size, yet there is something more subtle. They are all bright and attentive, but there is still an emotionless vacancy about them.

"Mr. Anderson?" addresses Valerie upon reaching the teacher.

"Ms. Stuart, I presume."

"Yes, and this is Dana."

"Nice to have you here, Dana. You may take that seat over there," says Mr. Anderson, pointing to a desk in the middle of the room. Dana kisses his mother goodbye and takes his seat.

Mr. Anderson, noticing an apprehensive look on Valerie's face, says, "Don't worry, Ms. Stuart, we'll take good care of Dana.

"Thank you," replies Valerie, turning about and leaving the room. As she leaves, Valerie notices something else about the synthetics as she looks back and sees her son sitting at his desk. He is indeed the largest child in the class. Yet, from experience, she knows that he is small for his age.

Immediately after Dana takes his seat, one of the synthetics next to him asks, "Who was that?"

"My mother," Dana answers.

"What's a mother?"

"A mother's a…." Dana stammers, unable to give a response to a person who has no point of reference.

Suddenly, Mr. Anderson begins the class. It is a class on phonetics. As Mr. Anderson proceeds, Dana quickly realizes that teaching at this school is very different from his other experience; there is very little repetition of previous material. Nor is there any emphasis on busywork. There is no coloring or playing in the sandbox and very little unorganized time. Another thing Dana finds most unusual, there is no inattentiveness. Everyone pays rapt attention to the teacher at all times. The few times when Dana looks about at his classmates, he finds them studiously watching the teacher.

After a couple of hours in the classroom, the class is taken outside for physical education. As they parade outside, Dana first notices that he is the largest one in the class. This delights him, he thinks how much fun it is going to be to bully and dominate the other "boys" the way he was bullied when he was in the public school.

The game is soccer. Dana is pleased; it is his best sport. Dana takes an inbound pass and tries to outmaneuver an opposing player in front of him. The opposing player is too quick and deftly kicks the ball away from him, sidesteps him, and takes the ball down the field. Dana is perplexed; no one has ever done that to him before. Dana does not see the ball for a while. Many times, Dana has a chance at the ball, but someone else always seems to reach it just before he does. Dana does not understand this until the end of the period the ball squirts out just in front of him for a clean breakaway. Dana kicks the ball and races downfield. Even though there is no one near him when he receives the ball, he is overtaken from behind, and the ball is not only kicked away from him but in such a way that the opposing player recovers the ball himself and passes it quickly upfield. Dana finally understands that even though these children are smaller, they are much faster and better coordinated.

Witnessing Dana's trials is Mr. Anderson, who smiles at what he sees. He realizes that the synthetic children are faster and better coordinated, which he expected but still is worried as to how Dana will fit in at school. Will the physical superiority of the synthetics create a problem for Dana? Will Dana be able to continue to take physical education with the other children? Within a week, it becomes obvious that Dana cannot continue to take physical education with the synthetics. The disparity of ability is too enormous.

When Dana arrives home on his first day at the synthetic school, his parents immediately barrage him with questions. "How was school today?"

"OK, I guess."

"Did you enjoy it?"

"Sort of."

"What was it like?"

"All right, I guess."

Finally, Robert and Valerie get the point. Dana isn't going to talk about it. When Dana leaves the room, Robert says, "I sure wish I knew what happened at that school today."

Valerie answers the question, "He didn't say it was bad, and he didn't come home mad."

Life settles into a regular pattern for Dana. He awakes in the morning, eats breakfast, goes to school, comes home, does his farm chores, plays with his little sister or some neighbor children, and goes to bed. At first, he only does satisfactory in school, but eventually, he starts to excel.

After a month of no responses from Dana, Robert and Valerie can contain themselves no longer and make an appointment with his teacher. At the meeting, Mr. Anderson tells Robert and Valerie that Dana is not performing up to their expectations but that he is still doing acceptably. When asked if Dana is disruptive at school, they are told that he has been no disciplinary problem at all."

"How does he get along with the other students?" Robert asks.

"That's hard to say," responds Mr. Anderson.

"That's hard to say," mimics Robert incredulously.

"Yes," answers Mr. Anderson, "our students aren't communicative like other children."

"Aren't communicative," mimics Robert again.

"I mean, they aren't emotional. They don't engage in horseplay like other children. They don't make friends."

Robert and Valerie look at each other in silent amazement, unable to grasp a child that does not act like a child.

"What do they do?" asks Robert finally.

"You mean in their free time?"

"Yes."

"They play intellectual or athletic games with each other. They seem to thrive best when they are performing — they are very competitive. They also have an insatiable curiosity. Many of them work on special science projects in their free time.

"Don't they ever play with toys?" asks Valerie.

"With educational toys," answers Mr. Anderson. Valerie and Robert again look at each other, reading each other's thoughts. What kind of place is this to send a son to school?

"You say that Dana is progressing in his schoolwork?" Robert asks.

"Yes indeed, he is far ahead of where he would be if he attended public school."

"Don't you think it bothers him not having any friends at school?"

"I'm sure it does, Ms. Stuart, but we keep the children so busy here we hardly have time to notice."

Valerie and Robert look at each other again. They don't know it yet, but each has the same thought. However, undesirable this school Dana is still doing much better than he did at public school.

"Thank you very much, Mr. Anderson," says Robert as he gets to his feet, "this has been most enlightening."

Valerie arises just after her husband. Robert shakes hands with Mr. Anderson. He and Valerie leave. On the way home, Robert and Valerie talk over Dana's continued attendance at this school; it is almost their exclusive topic of conversation for the next few days. Emotionally, they both desperately want to take Dana out of the cold, austere, synthetic school – yet intellectually, they keep concluding that they really have no choice. Dana is learning at the synthetic school – he was not learning at the public school. Worse yet, the other students and even the teachers there persecuted him. Robert and Valerie have also noticed that his deportment has improved considerably. With this realization, each knows the decision to remain has been made.

While Dana has no real friends at school, his relations with his synthetic schoolmates are acceptable. Despite the fact that Dana is different from them, they do not tease him. Even though Dana cannot keep up with them physically, there is no bullying him. It is not their nature. They know they are superior; they don't need to prove it to themselves. Since they lack human feeling, they also lack the human need to dominate over others. Moreover, because of Dana's performance in his classwork, they respect him.

Even though the synthetics are devoid of the need for human affection, there remains in their infrastructure an order of rank. It is not a pecking order per se. Synthetics almost never fight with each other; it is a ranking order of merit. At the top is a synthetic of Korean lineage named Kenneth. Kenneth is at the top simply because he is acknowledged as the most able. Kenneth always gets the best marks in school and is the best athlete. Kenneth is always chosen as the captain of his team in athletic games. When there is a choice of what to participate in, it is Kenneth who chooses the game.

There is no second. There are three: Bill, Mark, and Bob. Bill and Bob are white, Mark is black. All three are equal in abilities, both scholastically and athletically. Among Synthetics, there is no divergence in intellectual abilities and athletic abilities. If one is a better scholar, "he" is invariably a better athlete.

One might think that the synthetic infrastructure was pyramidal. It isn't, it is diamond shaped. It is shaped like two pyramids, one on top of the other, the top one right side up, and the bottom one, top side down. Dana, since he is not synthetic, is not in the infrastructure. Dana is one of the two exceptions in the school that athletic ability and intellectual ability do not run together. The other exception to the rule is Sean; as he runs scholastic performance, so does athletic ability. First of all, except for Dana, he is the largest one in the class. Second, in athletic performance, he is equal to Kenneth, but in scholastic performance, he is the worst. The most unusual aspect of Sean is that he, alone of all the synthetics, exhibits human emotion. Once when his team lost at soccer, he actually cried. After that, the other synthetics regard him as an aberration.

Sean is at the bottom of the diamond. Sean is also the only one who can, in any sense, be regarded as a friend of Dana. Sean is the only one in class who will converse with Dana. It isn't that the other synthetics won't talk to Dana. They just don't engage in small talk. Sean still won't seek Dana out, but he will at least converse with Dana.

Due to Sean's need for affection and recognition, he is aware and resentful of his position at the bottom of his society. Aware of the fact that he is the best athletically and that outside of Dana, he is the largest, his lack of status annoys him. Each year that goes by, his lack of recognition annoys him more until, by the third grade, it seethes within him; somehow, he has to do something to raise his status. The answer finally comes to him while reading a history book; he will fight Kenneth for leadership. Sean feels that due to his larger size and athletic ability, he should easily be able to defeat Kenneth. Once Kenneth is defeated, he says to himself, I will take over as the leader.

The next day Sean goes to the school library and checks out a book on boxing. In two days, the book was read. Sean has perfected his boxing style and is ready to confront Kenneth. The day after, during the exercise period, Sean walks up to Kenneth and, without warning, strikes Kenneth in the face with his fist, knocking him to the ground.

Completely surprised, Kenneth looks up from the dirt and quietly asks, "What did you do that for, Sean?"

"To prove that l am better than you."

"But you aren't better than I," answers Kenneth matter-of-factly as he arises from the ground. Before Kenneth straightens himself up, another fist flies, and Kenneth once again finds himself lying on the ground. This time Kenneth says nothing as he arises from the ground keeping an eye on Sean at all times. Sean seeing Kenneth watching him, assumes the traditional boxing stance. Kenneth, unfamiliar with boxing, copies Sean's stance.

Sean shoots a left jab at Kenneth's head. The left lead penetrates Kenneth's defense, and Kenneth's head recoils as the blow connects. This time he manages to stay on his feet.

Copying Sean, Kenneth left to fly a left jab at Sean. It is blocked! Sean left fly another left jab at Kenneth, who managed to block it this time. Though Kenneth manages to block the left jab, he never sees the right cross that follows. For the third time, Kenneth picks himself off the dirt.

By this time, the synthetics and Dana have crowded around to watch the fight. There is no cheering or rooting as there usually is when two schoolboys get into a fight. The synthetics watch the fight in quiet curiosity. They make no attempt to help Kenneth. Kenneth arises again from the dirt to continue the fight. The next time Sean tries a left jab, or right cross combination, Kenneth blocks both. Kenneth learns quickly, and when he blocks Sean's blows, he follows them with some of his own. The first successful blow landed by Kenneth is a left jab following a missed right cross by Sean. Sean's head jerks back as it lands but manages to stay on his feet. As the fight continues, Kenneth learns and acquits himself well.

The advantage remains with Sean, Kenneth is quicker, but Sean is heavier. Sean blows when they land to do more damage. In addition, Sean has a distinct tactical advantage, he has read a book on boxing and has planned his tactics. Once Kenneth learns a particular combination, Sean switches to another. When Kenneth learns the left jab and right cross combination, Sean goes to a left jab, right cross, and left hook combination. When Kenneth learns that, Sean feints the left hook and hits Kenneth with a right uppercut. Sean keeps Kenneth on the defensive, and the blows begin to tell. Kenneth's reflexes were slow, and his defense dropped, more and heavier blows began to fall. Finally, Kenneth can barely keep up his arms while Sean pummels him. No one objects or shows any emotion while Sean completes Kenneth's destruction. During this time, not a sound is heard except the dull thud of fists pounding on Kenneth's face. The only emotion the synthetics show is quiet, contemplative curiosity – they have never seen a fight before. Finally, Kenneth topples and falls into the dirt unconscious.

Kenneth has taken a drastic beating: his eyes are not only black and blue but swollen shut. His nose is broken and bleeding profusely. His face is cut in numerous places and is bleeding and swollen.

After the fight ends, there are no congratulations to the victor and no sympathy for Kenneth. No one helps Kenneth, takes him to the school nurse, or even tells the teacher. No one except Dana tells Ms. Di Biaso, the teacher.

Ms. Di Biaso immediately goes outside to look for Kenneth and sends Dana to get the nurse. Ms. Di Biaso finds Kenneth still lying unconscious in the dirt. She and Mr. Shipley pick up Kenneth and carry him to the nurse's office. There, Mr. Shipley treats Kenneth's cuts and bruises before sending him to the hospital to recover from his concussion. He also treats Sean for a black eye and swollen and bleeding knuckles.

After this incident, which the school officials had believed impossible, they held a meeting. After much discussion, it is finally decided to take no punishment against either of the children. It has been, as far as they can determine, a fair fight. During the meeting, some of the male teachers actually express relief that the synthetics have finally shown some emotion. It is decided that Sean and Kenneth, as well as the rest of the class, should be counseled against fighting.

After his victory, Sean feels that, at last, he will get the respect he deserves. The next day during the exercise period, when he is picked by his teammates to be their captain, he feels his efforts have been rewarded. Actually, his selection as the captain had nothing to do with his defeat of Kenneth. He simply is the next best soccer player; it is natural that he should be selected as captain. When Kenneth returns from the hospital, he resumes his place as the leader of the class and is again elected to be the captain. Sean, infuriated, resolves to remove Kenneth from the competition permanently.

Sean waits until after school, when the class usually plays soccer unsupervised. When Kenneth begins picking players, Sean interrupts, "No, Kenneth, I am the captain."

This time Sean never gets a chance to land a blow. His arms are grabbed from behind, and he is forced to the ground on his face.

While four of his classmates each hold an arm or a leg, two others grab his head. During this time, no words are spoken or instructions given. Kenneth does not participate and is, in fact, surprised at what has happened. The two who have grabbed Sean's head yank his head violently to the right. It is the last thing that Sean feels – a loud crack is heard, and Sean's neck snaps!

Sean did not realize it, but his attempt at the leadership of the synthetics is fatally flawed. His potential followers know that he is not the most competent leader. They refuse to follow him, and since he has attempted to gain leadership by force, they remove him the same way.

Sean is not missed by the school authorities at supper, nor is he missed at bedtime. The synthetics are normally so well behaved that their supervision has grown very lax. There is no bed check, there is no need for one. Where would the synthetics go? It is not until the next day when Dana asks the teacher about Sean's whereabouts that he is missed. When Ms. Di Biaso asks the class where Sean is, Kenneth calmly answers, "On the soccer field."

"What is he doing there?" she asks.

"He is dead," responds Kenneth matter-of-factly.

"He's dead," chuckles Ms. Di Biaso, thinking at first it is a perverse childhood joke. Suddenly a cold shiver runs down her spine as she recalls that synthetics have no sense of humor. They never tease, and they never joke! She runs from the classroom out to the soccer field. The class follows her.

Out on the soccer field, she finds Sean lying face down on the ground, except that his face isn't down. His face stares blankly at the sky, his head has been twisted around so that he now faces backward. "How did he die?" she demands. Bill, Bob, Mark, Jim, Andrew, and John killed him," answers Kenneth, matter-of-factly.

Ms. Di Biaso, astonished at such honesty, suddenly felt her stomach sour and sicken, and cold chills radiate out to her limbs. "Dana, go get Mr. Jones!" Dana leaves as Ms. Di Biaso reaches down and closes Sean's eyelids for the last time.

Mr. Jones, the director of the program and the principal of the school, comes running from behind. As he does, Ms. Di Biaso falls to her knees, nauseous. As Mr. Jones reaches the scene, Ms. Di Biaso quietly retches.

As Mr. Jones looks down upon the body, he blinks his eyes several times to make sure he doesn't see some ugly apparition. As many times as he blinks, the apparition does not disappear. Finally convinced, he tries to speak, but the words stick in his throat. Pausing a moment, he finally regains his composure and asks, "Are you all right, Ms. Di Biaso?"

"Yes, I'll be all right," she whispers hoarsely.

While this has been going on, the class has gathered around. None of them except Dana are interested in the body. They are all too busy watching Ms. Di Biaso retch. Why is she throwing up, they wonder – she must have the flu.

The police arrive shortly with the medical examiner, an ambulance, and a photographer. After the body is photographed and the evidence recorded, the police proceed to interview the teachers and the children. The completely honest synthetic children give exacting detained accounts of what happened and why. The local police are amazed at the detail these children give, their clarity, and the consistency of their statements. Never in the history of Carlton County has a murder been so thoroughly documented when the police turn over their report to the County attorney, who has no idea what to do.

The County Attorney had been informed of the incident as soon as it happened. He immediately realizes that criminal charges cannot be filed; juveniles in Minnesota, by law, are not capable of committing crimes. The procedure is to institutionalize the offenders — but these children are already institutionalized! Not only are the offenders already institutionalized, but their institution is clearly the best; indeed, the only one of its kind in the world!

Nevertheless, something has to be done, and the appearance of justice has to be maintained. The public expects some kind of action. The County attorney brings a delinquency petition against each of the synthetics involved. At the hearing, each of the synthetics "confesses" what "he" has done. The judge rules them delinquent – and commits them to the custody of the Moose Lake Special School!

The judicial remedy changes nothing, but the administrative reaction does. The authorities who run the school are horrified at what their pupils have done. More importantly, the government officials in Washington D.C. who fund the program are also horrified. Both realize the kind of child that their research has created. Though they haggle and fight over what should be done about the existing children, they do come to one conclusion fairly quickly: No more synthetic children!

After some months of haggling, the governmental authorities in Washington finally acknowledged the obvious, just as did the local judge, the Moose Lake Special School is the best place to care for the existing synthetic children. The school stays open to care for the existing synthetic children, but the hatchery in Rochester, Minnesota, is closed.

After the incident, Robert and Valerie consider taking Dana out of the school but decide against it. They make their decision when they check with the school and Dana and find that Dana is not really in the synthetic infrastructure and had nothing to do with the murder. Besides, they are reminded that he does not take physical education with the synthetics.

After the incident, education authorities from Washington D.C. and St. Paul make regular trips to the school. Periodic reports are required on the synthetics' emotional development. A battery of psychological tests is performed on the students to see how they look upon the incident. Dana's tests showed that he was morally horrified but that the incident caused no psychological scarring. The synthetics' tests showed a completely different result = no remorse! They felt the murder was completely justified; Sean was a genetic defect!

After the test results were published, courses on ethics and morality were included in the curriculum. A year later, another battery of tests is given to see how the new curriculum has affected synthetics. The tests show that the synthetics have thoroughly grasped the ethical concepts taught to them, but their evaluation of the murder remains unchanged!

The special school continues, and Dana with it. Nothing of a similar nature happens at the school again. Learning continues at an extremely rapid pace. At the end of the sixth year, the school authorities believe that they have taught the children everything they would learn if they had completed high school. When a GED test is administered, and all of the pupils score in the top 1% of high school graduates, they are given high school diplomas.

The special school authorities decide to request funding to send their students to college. Despite Sean's murder and the scrubbing of the experiment, there is still a great deal of interest in scientific circles, including Washington, in the intellectual performance of synthetics. The funding request includes Dana, as the only human child, his performance is used as a point of reference. His performance in college, alongside the synthetics, will shed additional light on their real abilities. The funding request, including Dana, is granted.

At college, the synthetics are allowed to choose their own fields, except that two of them cannot enter the same field. Their performance amazes their teachers. In every course, except humanities, each synthetic receives an A. None of the synthetics ever flunks a course, but their performance lags significantly in Art and Music. They all manage to obtain their humanities requirements by taking courses in foreign languages. So studious are they that they take extra courses each quarter and continue school year-round. All graduate at the end of the summer session of their second year.

Dana, for the first time since he was in first grade, is going to school with human children even though they are quite a bit older. He finds going to school with normal children quite enjoyable since he no longer has to keep up with such intelligent and studious students. Furthermore, he is left to learn and study on his own; there is little structure to school outside of going to class and doing his work. Unlike his former classmates, Dana does not take extra courses and does not go to summer school. He takes the full four years to graduate, graduating with a degree in physics summa cum laude. Even before he graduates, he is enrolled in a graduate school for a doctorate.

Dana's former classmates graduate as planned in a variety of disciplines, all scientific or technical. There are graduates in medicine, physics, chemistry, geology, biology, mathematics, etc.

Like Dana, they all immediately enroll in graduate school upon graduation. This is the first time in their life the synthetics will be separated from each other. Previously, although they attended different classes, they were always housed together.

In graduate school, for the first time, synthetics do not learn faster. The competition is too keen. The synthetics still perform near the top of their class but not necessarily at the very top of the class. It takes them the normal time to graduate and receive their doctorates. The synthetics receive their doctorates at the age of 17.

Chapter 4
M.L.S.S. Inc.

The Synthetics graduate from a graduate school and go into their respective fields. The genetic engineers who designed them and the bureaucrats who fund them closely monitor their progress. Great things are expected from Synthetics – they are soon disappointed. Shortly after they are hired, they begin to be discharged as unsatisfactory. The first to go is the physician. While he is a brilliant physician, he is disliked by his co-workers and especially his patients. He is cold towards his co-workers and brusque towards his patients. Since his co-workers do not like him anyway, it doesn't take many patient complaints before he is asked to leave. When he goes, his co-workers are openly happy that the biological robot couldn't hack it.

Another field where Synthetics has difficulty is teachers. While Synthetics completely understand their material, they cannot convey it to their students. Synthetic teachers find it impossible to understand why their students cannot grasp the material immediately. Unlike physicians, Synthetic teachers are not usually fired.

There are some Synthetics that do well. Synthetics do very well in research. They understand their subject matter and carry out instructions, and do assign experiments beautifully. The engineers and the geologist also do very well. If all they have to do is apply to learn, they have already garnered and applied it. They do extremely well. Even though they perform well in these professions, they are not promoted. Other inferior persons are promoted instead. Their cold, austere personalities combined with their brilliant intellect causes them to be uniformly disliked and their employers to be distrustful of them and unwilling to place them into supervisory positions. They are also believed due to be disdainful, haughty, and contemptuous.

The first two Synthetics fired from their jobs find new jobs and are even more quickly discharged from those. The next time they cannot find work in their fields and form a remodeling company. It is touch and goes at first. Since the owners are scrupulously honest, superlative workers always deliver on time, at a price, and without flaw, their business prospers. Within a short time, other Synthetics who cannot find work join the business. All Synthetics are given work whether the business needs them or not. With the business prospering, the name of the corporation is characteristically unimaginative: M.L.S.S. Inc. (Moose Lake Special School Inc.).

As the remodeling business grows, it naturally expands into contracting. Word spreads quickly not only of the superlative quality of the work but of the ability of the company to come in ahead of schedule and at cost. Finally, the company has more business than it can handle and to keep pace with its business begins to hire ordinary humans as workers. The management of M.L.S.S. Inc. finds it difficult to work with humans. They are emotional and irrational and demand to be paid overtime even though they are the cause of the overtime. M.L.S.S. Inc. has no choice but to meet its demands.

Notwithstanding the difficulties Synthetics has with its human workers, it still produces flawless work and is prompt in getting its work done on time and at a bid. For the first time, the company lost money on a contract because when it bid on the job, it under-estimated its labor costs because it did not include any overtime. Notwithstanding those difficulties, the company remains highly profitable. Except for its labor relations, the company is a model of efficiency. The company, despite its capitalist form, is almost a perfect example of communism. All of the Synthetic workers, regardless of the job they have, are paid the same and share equally in the profits.

Soon, M.L.S.S. Inc. became the largest contractor in the State of Minnesota and no longer does remodeling work. Kenneth, who by education is a civil engineer, is brought in to head the company. He is easily seduced away from his own company, where despite his brilliance still occupies the same position he was originally hired.

After Kenneth takes over as head of M.L.S.S. Inc., it expands its operation into other states and quickly becomes the largest contracting company in the nation. Not only does the company expand geographically, but trading on the extensive technical knowledge of the Synthetics, it expands into other fields as well: electronics, electrical equipment, computers, drugs, and medical equipment and supplies.

The products manufactured by M.L.S.S. are consistently superlative in quality and more than competitive in price. Unlike other companies, it does not expand by purchasing existing companies. It always starts a new enterprise from scratch, usually managing to design the product better or design a means of producing the product cheaper or both. However, well-designed the M.L.S.S. products are not innovative; it usually goes into a new field after the original patents have expired. When a competitor is successful in achieving a technological breakthrough, M.L.S.S. is usually able to make a better design and break the patent, or it simply buys the patent.

The spectacular success of M.L.S.S. Inc. causes enormous resentment amount humans. Numerous competitors are put out of business, and thousands of their workers are put out of work by their competition. So successful is M.L.S.S. that the mere rumors of it going into a new field are sufficient to cause massive runs on the existing companies in that field.

With the spectacular success of M.L.S.S. Inc., Kenneth realizes that the company needs someone in management who understands humans. Dana was founded and offered the position of Director of Human Relations. He accepts. Dana proves so useful in this position that he eventually supplants Kenneth as CEO of the company. Kenneth becomes the COO and Chief Operating Officer.

It is inevitable that M.L.S.S. Inc.'s actual and prospective competitors will gang up on it. Despite these competitors' economic power, they know they cannot compete with M.L.S.S. Inc., so they try to protect themselves politically. Numerous petitions are brought to Congress to do something about this "ruthless" competition. The senators and congressmen make speeches against M.L.S.S. into the Congressional record, excerpts of which are mailed to their constituents. Various bills are proposed at both the national and state levels to limit M.L.S.S.'s competition. Usually, the bills fail because everyone knows that M.L.S.S. is a fair competitor, but occasionally the bills succeed. When that happens, M.L.S.S. challenges the bill on constitutional grounds and usually wins.

When it becomes obvious that legal action will not stop, M.L.S.S. Inc.'s various boycotts are organized against its products. These attempts also prove a failure; everyone knows the products are uniformly high in quality arid low in price.

Despite the experience of the first graduating class, the Synthetics for years tried to fit into human society. Each time the same thing happens, either their emotional coolness or their quick intellect causes their employers, co-workers, or customers to resent them. They are either fired outright or relegated to some perfunctory albeit technical job. Worse than that, after three years, the newly graduating Synthetics find it difficult, despite their grades, to find employment. After a while, they do not even attempt the world of humans; they go straight into employment with M.L.S.S. Inc.

When the graduating Synthetics start going straight into

M.L.S.S. Inc.'s operation, the government drops its funding. The slack is immediately taken up by M.L.S.S. Inc. Despite the consistent yearly influx of Synthetics, Kenneth does not have nearly as many of them as he would like and knows that shortly the influx will stop forever. As soon as he makes his decision to fund Synthetic education, he makes another decision to fund a Synthetic genetic laboratory to produce more Synthetics. M.L.S.S. Inc. purchases a series of farms outside Ottumwa, Iowa, containing a total of 10,000 acres.

No sooner has the ink dried on the deeds than a construction crew, consisting solely of Synthetics, appears on the property and begins construction of long barracks-like buildings. After the first building is up, trucks begin to arrive, and what appears to be medical equipment is seen being carried inside. They are almost correct. What they see are artificial uteri and the other medical equipment necessary for genetic engineering. When the equipment is installed, Synthetics trained biologists and physicians begin their work. None of the Synthetics has any experience with human genetic engineering, but they have the technical training to learn and, at some expense, have obtained the records of the original lab in Rochester, Minnesota.

Synthetic scientists study the records carefully and experience little difficulty duplicating the result of the original scientists. In less than a year after the Ottumwa site is purchased, the first Synthetic children in 15 years are hatched. In the meantime, the farm keeps operating so that the local people will not know what is going on. Despite the need for trained Synthetics needed for the management of M.L.S.S. Inc., all the personnel at Ottumwa are Synthetic. Kenneth knows he does not need to employ humans who may tell tales. In order to do this, Kenneth has to stop the steady growth of M.L.S.S. Inc... He will not allow humans in the high management of M.L.S.S. Inc.

Unlike the outside society where the children are hatched throughout the year, all the Synthetic babies are hatched in one week. This is done so that the farm administrators will know which of the children is most able. A task made difficult if the children are months apart in age. Any children who show less than expected abilities or emotions disappear.

The first year's crop of Synthetics is small, only a few hundred but still as many Synthetics who have ever been hatched. A few hundred is all the Synthetics can care for. Only a few Synthetics can be spared from M.L.S.S. Inc. In the planning stages of the farm, a good deal of thought was given to putting the Synthetic children on feeding and waste removal machines so that more could be raised. Synthetics realize that this is fatal to human babies but believe that Synthetic babies will not be so susceptible. While the choice is tempting, the decision to try such devices is declined. The planners do not wish to take a chance on inadequate brain development due to insufficient stimulation.

The next year, another class of Synthetic students, originally from the Moose Lake Special School, joins M.L.S.S. Inc. Most of these new Synthetics go to the farm for the second crop of 600 new babies to be hatched. This is the last batch of graduates from the M.L.S.S. School.

In the third year, Kenneth has to transfer more Synthetics from company operations to help with the third batch of Synthetic babies. He realizes that in a few more years, there won't be any Synthetics running M.L.S.S. Inc.

A compromise is arrived at. Instead of transferring more adults from the corporate offices, the care of the babies is turned over to the older Synthetics born on the farm. The idea proves successful. It also allows Kenneth to increase the number of Synthetics to be hatched every year.

In the eighth year of operation, the oldest class of Synthetics is taught to help on the farm. The farm equipment must be modified to allow for their small size, but with the modification, the Synthetic children have little difficulty mastering the equipment. Finally, a few adult Synthetics can be transferred back to M.L.S.S. Inc.

When the farm was first purchased, it became quite a local topic of conversation. At first, they had very little to talk about. The Synthetics keep it completely to themselves and don't give the locals anything to fuel the gossip mill. After the first spate of building, all the locals could see were these boyish little "men" riding about on the normal farm equipment doing the usual jobs that need to be done in order to run a farm. The farm was deliberately kept nearly self-sufficient. The few things that the farm needed from the outside were never purchased locally but always trucked in.

As the farm grows, it becomes more and more of a curiosity to the locals. They continually wonder what all the building is going on there, and the people there are so secretive. Finally, someone notices that as the farm has grown, it is not shipping out as much produce as it did before. Then someone else notices that the kind of crops grown at the farm has changed. Instead of growing cash crops, it is now engaged in truck farming, yet the crops are grown on the farm never leave it. Moreover, the farm also has developed a large dairy herd but sells no milk to the local dairy. Obviously, these foods are being grown on the farm and consumed there. What could be on the farm that is consuming that much food?

In the eighth year of operation, the curiosity of the locals begins to get the best of them. It is that year that the locals notice little children operating the farm machinery. Where did the children come from, and why aren't they in school?

Sheriff William Swedberg is a career police officer. For as long as he has been able to remember, he has wanted to be a police officer. A local Ottumwan, in high school, he had been a triple star athlete, lettering in football, basketball, and track. The notoriety he received for his athletic exploits served him well later when he ran for office. A direct man, he resolves to investigate the new farm and begins his investigation simply by driving out to the farm to ask questions. The farm buildings are not located near the road; they have been moved and built at the center of the farm to preclude easy observation from the outside.

Sheriff Swedberg has to approach the main area of the farm via a long driveway. He is observed for some time before actually arriving. When he arrives, he is amazed at what he sees; there is row after row of long barracks-like buildings that have been built to look like chicken coops. However, they are not chicken coops, and they certainly do not have any farm purpose. Moreover, Sheriff Swedberg finds hundreds of little 'boys' wandering about the premises. It only takes him a second to ask himself the question: Why are there no girls? Aware that the farm had been purchased by M.L.S.S. Inc. and aware of the persons who run that company, he immediately suspects what has been going on at the farm. Shortly, the sheriff's car having been observed coming up the drive, an adult Synthetic comes out to greet him. The sheriff and the deputy who accompanied him are escorted to the farm's office.

The farm's office turns out to be the old farm homestead. The building had been moved to the geographical center of the various farms that had been bought up, but it was still the old homestead. The director was not at his office when the sheriff came up the drive but had already been sent for.

Waiting for the director, Sheriff Swedberg notices for the first time that there are no females in the farm's office. This confirms in his mind what he has been suspecting.

John, the farm's director, who was in the Synthetics Lab when the sheriff drove up, leaves his work and immediately goes to talk with the sheriff. Within a few minutes of arriving at the farm, Sheriff Swedberg has the person he is looking for. He fires his first question. "What kind of a place is this?"

'Do you have any other questions, sheriff?" is the only response.

'No indeed," bellows the sheriff, "where did all those little boys come from, and why aren't there any girls here?'

"Have you any other- questions, sheriff?" comes the reply.

"That'll do for now," replies the sheriff.

"I'm not at liberty to answer your questions, sheriff. I must contact my superiors and obtain legal advice before answering you. I will be in touch with your later today."

"Do you mind if I look around?"

"Do you have a search warrant?"

"No, but I can get one."

"I suggest you do that. Show the sheriff out," John says to the Synthetic who led him in."

Sheriff Swedberg turns swiftly on his heel and walks briskly to his automatic transport. He and his accompanying deputy enter it, and the sheriff codes the transport to take him to the County Attorney. The transport speeds off.

Sheriff Swedberg finds County Attorney Dessaint in his office and quickly explains where he has been and what he has seen. The

County Attorney is, at first, puzzled at what has been going on at the farm, but Sheriff Swedberg explains to him his suspicions. Finally, County Attorney Dessaint says, "Bill, I have to have evidence of some kind of criminal activity before I can get a search warrant."

"What about the state law for compulsory school attendance?"

"OK, let's see if the judge buys it. I'll have it ready first thing tomorrow morning. You can come by then and take it before Judge Cedar."

Even before Sheriff Swedberg is off the property, John is on the phone with Kenneth advising him of the sheriff's visit. Kenneth immediately consults with his attorneys on how to prevent intrusions upon company property by local officials. At that consultation, it was decided that not only can local officials not be kept off farm property while acting in their official capacity but that the secret of the farm cannot be kept secret any longer. After obtaining this legal advice, Kenneth decides not to obstruct the sheriff.

The next morning, Sheriff Swedberg is waiting for a search warrant in hand when Judge Cedar arrives at her office. "What do you have for me today, Bill?" she asks as she turns the key to her office.

"Yesterday, I went out to that strange farm north of town that everyone's been talking about," answers Sheriff Swedberg and continues to explain what he saw there and what he has done. Judge

Cedar takes the warrant from Sheriff Swedberg's hand and proceeds to read it carefully. After she finishes reading the warrant, she says, "OK, you've got what you want," and signs the document with a flourish.

Sheriff Swedberg goes back to his office, where three of his deputies are waiting. They get into two police vehicles and proceed directly to the farm. At the farm, they go immediately to the headquarters building, where they present the search warrant. There they find John waiting for them and not at all surprised to see them.

Sheriff Swedberg does not conduct a thorough search. Each nook and cranny isn't looked into, his officers hardly do more than take a casual glance into some of the buildings and then just to see what kind of a building it is. The only thing that the sheriff is interested in is in verifying his suspicions. He certainly isn't interested in prosecuting for violation of the school attendance law. Each deputy and the sheriff himself has an accompanying Synthetic. The Synthetic is asked numerous questions during the tour that are all answered fully. The sheriff and his men discover five different kinds of buildings on the farm: farm buildings, barracks for the children, classroom buildings, the headquarters building, and one other. It is this building that the sheriff has been searching for; it is the laboratory and hatchery.

Sheriff Swedberg is neither a scientist nor a doctor, but he has had children of his own and can identify an artificial uterus. When he goes through the laboratory and hatchery, he finds what he has been looking for. Taking out his camera, he takes the pictures he wants and proceeds home.

When he arrives home, he has the pictures developed as quickly as he can and presents them to the County Attorney and the local press. The press is fascinated by what they see and prints the pictures in the local paper the next morning with the headline. "Synthetic Hatchery Found in Ottumwa." The news services immediately pick up the story, and Ottumwa is descended upon by journalists. When the national and international press arrives at the farm, they find that Kenneth has hired human guards to keep the journalists off the property.

The secret is out, but nothing immediately is done. Nothing can be done. The Synthetics employ their own teachers, and there is no question that the Synthetics are advanced for other children their age. No laws have been broken. It is not unlawful to hatch Synthetic children.

In the next session of the Iowa legislature, one of the first bills introduced is to forbid hatching Synthetic children. It is the first bill passed and contains a special clause so that it takes effect immediately. Dana contests the constitutionality of the law but, in the meantime, has no choice but to comply. Within a few years, every other state and territory of the United States followed a similar law. When the case goes before the Supreme Court, it rules the law constitutional as an exercise of the valid police power of the state.

The argument that no other identifiable group of people has ever been prohibited from perpetuating themselves falls on deaf ears.

However, horrified are the people of the United States by the mass production of babies and especially, Synthetic babies, there is nothing that can be done about the Synthetic children in existence. The children cannot simply be killed off. Nor can M.L.S.S. Inc. be prosecuted for violating the sex ratio law since its children are all neuter. Nor can a law be passed that would relate back and make what they did illegal since that would violate the ex post facto law of the United States Constitution. Nor can the farm be closed down since the Synthetic children have to have some place to live.

Dana takes the setback calmly. He has anticipated that the secret could not be kept forever and has planned ahead. The United States is not the only country in the world, and M.L.S.S. Inc. is already an international corporation. Even before the secret gets out, duplicate hatcheries are already under construction in Brazil and Haiti.

Chapter 5

The Haitian War

Brazil is not a first-world nation, but it does pay attention to what happens in other nations. It is only a matter of time before Brazilian authorities hear stories about a huge number of children on a farm owned by an American company. Brazil sends investigators who find the same thing as did Sheriff Swedberg. Brazil bars the production of Synthetic children even faster than the United States.

Concurrent with the investigation is the discovery that M.L.S.S. Inc. has used its wealth and influence to bribe local officials. These local officials had left the farm alone because it was making them rich. However, when the matter comes to the attention of national authorities, they can no longer protect the farm. This time M.L.S.S. Inc. is guilty of criminal activity, but M.L.S.S. Inc.'s officials live in the United States, and Brazil has no extradition treaty with the United States.

The setback in Brazil does not occur in Haiti. Haiti is a smaller country with a long tradition of corruption and a lack of a free press. Besides, the national government has been bought off. The one point of consideration given by M.L.S.S. Inc. is that all its Synthetics hatched are black.

What is an advantage in Haiti is also a drawback. Haiti is a small country that is already overpopulated. Nevertheless, Kenneth steadily increases the production of Synthetics in Haiti so that

10.000 Synthetic babies are hatched every year. In order to do this, the government of Haiti is bribed, and much of the industrial production of M.L.S.S. Inc. is moved to Haiti to provide work and food to the populace. As a result, money pours into the country, which the government naturally taxes. The accommodation is clearly beneficial to both Haiti and M.L.S.S. Inc.

At first, the Haitian government is delighted with the arrangement. The population is put to work, and there is money not only for the government to tax but also for bribes. Not only do the politicians get rich, but there is sufficient money left over for public works. Public works allow another opportunity for corruption.

However, once the factories are built, the population is working, the country is prosperous, and tax revenues are stable. The gratitude of the government towards their benefactor erodes. Previously, the government of Haiti was ruled by terror. They find their ability to do that limited. If a person is killed, injured, and even detained who is a skilled worker for M.L.S.S. Inc., it objects. M.L.S.S. Inc. insists that its workers have protection from the presidential police.

What resentment the Haitian government feels towards M.L.S.S. is nothing as to when the first classes of Synthetic leave school. They are not only black like most of the population of Haiti, but they are brilliant, loyal only to M.L.S.S. Inc., and show no fear of the presidential police. Accustomed to cowering fear by the populace, the presidential police decide to find out how tough these young Synthetics are.

They kidnap several and try to break them by torture. Their experiment is a failure. The Synthetics expire as soon as the torture begins. Frustrated, the police kidnapped and tortured several more. The same thing happens. Only then do the police realize that the Synthetics understand what is happening to them and can will themselves to die. When M.L.S.S. Inc. inquires of its personnel, the high government officials truthfully deny knowledge. However, the Synthetics in charge of Haiti understand what is happening and why and begin to make preparations.

As the years go by and more and more Synthetics graduate into the Haitian operations of M.L.S.S. Inc., the Haitian government becomes more and more fearful of the Synthetics and, despite the risk of alienating its benefactor, orders the production of Synthetics be reduced; M.L.S.S. complies. After one year, the Haitian government decided it wasn't satisfied with the amount of reduction and ordered the production of Synthetics each year drastically cut back.

This time, the Synthetics refused to say that if they are forced to cut back on hatching Synthetics each year, they will be forced to cut back M.L.S.S. production in Haiti. The Haitian government's hand is forced. It cannot back down arid it cannot allow M.L.S.S. Inc. to take its operations out of Haiti. It, therefore, condemns the response by M.L.S.S. Inc. as insolence and orders all M.L.S.S. Inc.'s properties expropriated, and all Synthetics seized.

When the army and the police come to take the properties and arrest the Synthetics in charge, they find them missing. Shortly, the government finds out where they have gone. Somehow, they had gotten wind of the expropriation and fled to the hatchery in the mountains.

Chapter 6

Defeat and Exile

The next day Mark sets up his government in Port Au Prince. Unlike the village that the Synthetic Army passed through and eradicated, the inhabitants of Port Au Prince are not harmed. Instead, the population is immediately put back to work rebuilding the damage caused by the war.

Before the damage can be repaired, the dead have to be buried. Unlike the Battle of the Hatchery, the Haitian dead are not buried in mass graves. Instead, great effort is made to identify them and return them to their families. The same courtesy is not granted to Synthetic dead. The total Synthetic dead outnumber the Synthetic living, nearly all children.

Under Mark's leadership, a transformation occurred even more profound than when M.L.S.S. Inc. brought its operation into the country. Instead of just repairing the damage done by the war, a completely new city is built. Most of the city's run-down section of Port Au Prince is razed, and a new city arises with wide boulevards and bucolic paths within walking distance of everyone. Instead of the shacks, the people are accustomed to the new modern apartment buildings constructed with attached playing fields, recreation areas, and swimming pools. Unemployment, poverty, illiteracy, and disease, which have been endemic, are eliminated. The new government is austere as the old one was corrupt, wasteful, and extravagant. Corruption, the word of government in Haiti, is a thing of the past. After suffering from despotism for centuries, Haiti has become a model country.

Diplomatically the pretense that this was purely a local uprising against an attempt to exterminate the Synthetics is studiously kept. One of Mark's first things is to confiscate all of M.L.S.S. Inc.'s properties. He not only appropriates the property but also refuses to compensate M.L.S.S. Inc. for the properties taken. Then Mark begins competing in the very markets dominated by M.L.S.S. Inc.

Once the war is over, and the benevolence of the new government is seen, the new Haitian government is admitted to the Council of World Governments. Haiti's success in developing rapidly from an impoverished to a modern industrial country gives it an oversized voice in international relations.

Even before Mark finishes modernizing Haiti, "he" faces a problem that threatens to overwhelm him. The population of Haiti, already over-burdening the country, increases with prosperity even faster than before. Mark realizes that no matter how technically competent he and his Synthetics are, they cannot support an exponentially growing populace indefinitely.

Mark's reaction is swift, certain, and very Synthetic; he promulgates a decree forbidding any woman from hearing more than two children. All women are sterilized after they produce their second child to be sure the edict is carried out.

When the edict is enforced, the populace's reaction to Synthetic rule is, for the first time, hostile. Crowds pour into the streets and demonstrate against the government.

Mark taking his cue from democracies where such things are commonplace, lets the people demonstrate but keeps plenty of human police present to see that things do not get out of hand. Gradually the demonstrations die off.

An unforeseen impact of the edict is the loss of Haiti's diplomatic prestige. Mark is criticized in the world press and on the floor of the United Nations. The critics do not see the necessity of the edict; they only see that humans are prohibited from increasing their population where production of Synthetics goes on unabated.

Despite the criticism, Mark remains resolute as the edict is enforced. Haitian population growth slows. Mark knows that if the edict is enforced over 50 years, the human population will eventually stabilize.

Haiti occupies only one-third of the island of Hispaniola, the other two-thirds being occupied by the Dominican Republic. Despite its endemic poverty, the Dominican Republic, compared to Haiti, has been comparatively prosperous. The predominately Caucasian Dominicans have always looked down upon the poorer Black Haitians. Now Haiti is prosperous and much more prosperous than the Dominican Republic. Now the Dominicans are the poor neighbors. The Dominicans make the change with a typically human reaction; they passionately hate the Haitians and especially the

Synthetics who rule them. Border incidents that used to be rare suddenly become common,

Francois Toutant is a young Haitian born in Port Au Prince to an influential and wealthy family, his grandfathers on both sides having been ministers to presidents of the republic. Francois, a mulatto, is racially different from most of the populace. He is actually more white than black, like most of the ruling class.

Despite his patrician background and his Caucasian appearance, Francois harbors political leanings far different from the rest of his family. His political feelings are far to the left, which he wisely keeps to himself. Since his family is wealthy and Francois graduates at the top of his class, he is sent to France for an education. It is in France that his real political transformation takes place. Accustomed to the poverty and political rigidity of Haiti, he is overwhelmed by the prosperity and intellectual freedom of France. An exceptionally intelligent and perceptive young man, Francois wonders if freedom and prosperity and intermixed or merely coincidence.

Though sent to France merely to acquire a technical education, Francois departs from his instructions and takes courses in history, politics, and philosophy. Through these courses, he surmises that economic development and indeed all human progress cannot take place without the free exchange of ideas and that the more ideas are suppressed, the slower the growth. Just as importantly, he learns that the great men of history were all, in a sense, rebels. Not necessarily rebels in a political or military sense but in the sense that their vision transcended contemporary ideals. They were different from the others of their time and often suffered for it. The great men were great because they did not accept contemporary ideas and lifted men beyond what the other men saw as possible at the time. Francois realized, as despots never do, that as society grows, so must it also change.

In addition to his other courses, Francois also takes courses in economics. In those courses, he surmises the most obvious fact of modern wealth, so obvious that many cannot see the forest for the bark that the foundation of an industrial economy is mass production and that mass production cannot exist without mass demand, and that mass demand cannot exist unless the masses have money to buy. In a country such as Haiti, the wealth is kept in the hands of the few, and poverty will always be endemic. The solution is thus quite simple if Haiti is ever to escape the cycle of poverty, the power of the ruling class, his class, must be broken.

Completing his engineering degree in 6 years instead of the usual four, much to the dismay of his family, Francois returns to Haiti determined to rectify the abuses of his own class. Still very clever, he does not tell anyone, especially his family, of his plans. Immediately upon arrival home, he is offered and accepts a commission in the Haitian Army. He knows only too well the cost should he refuse. He also realizes that despite the political rigidity of any military organization, it is an excellent place from which to seek political recruits. Francois has hopes of reforming Haitian society from within.

Starting with his own class, Francois finds his thinking totally out of step. The other sons of the aristocracy are interested only in their own pleasure and comfort. Though what Francois is suggesting constitutes sedition under Haitian law, the other sons of the aristocracy find it only amusing; it would be unthinkable for an aristocrat to turn in one form so prominent a family as Francois'

When Francois fails to convince the sons of the aristocracy, he solicits the far larger group of junior officers in the Haitian Army, those who have had to earn their commissions. Here Francois appears to find ready adherents. All is not as it seems; these officers are only interested in promotion and are not above doing in on the bones of Francois. They believe that if they can prove sedition against anyone, particularly an aristocrat, they can promote their careers. All of Francois' endeavors are reported in detail from numerous sources, both to military intelligence and to the presidential police.

In their attempts to advance themselves, the lower class officers miscalculate; class loyalty is too strong. Instead of being tried and executed, which is what would have happened to them if they had been caught spreading such ideas, Francois is simply called in and told to get rid of his "petty-bourgeois ideas'. It is then suggested that he resign, which he does.

As Francois resigns, he takes a. lob with M.L.S.S. Inc., at this time just moving its operations in the country. Francois is delighted to see that the company he works for is benefiting the lives of his people. Unfortunately, the amount of money that actually goes to the people is grudging. The real beneficiaries of the influx of money and jobs are the government and the oligarchy. Francois eventually realizes that his employer has interwoven itself with the government and the oligarchy, and no real reform will ever take place in the country. In fact, the prosperity that M.L.S.S. Inc. bring tends to mollify the people from their misery and prevent real reform from taking place. Discouraged and beaten, Francois asks for a transfer to France and leaves Haiti, he thinks, for good.

When the Synthetic rebellion takes place, Francois returns to Haiti, thinking that real reform will take place at last. His dreams are realized beyond his wildest imagination as the oligarchy is crushed and the whole nation is reformed and remodeled not only physically but also philosophically. The real power in the country becomes not the oligarchy but the civil service bureaucracy. Free public education, free medical service, and pensions for the elderly are given, the court system becomes fair and just, and the distribution of income becomes the most equitable in the world.

Though his dreams for the economic well-being of his people are not only realized but also exceeded, Francois is still dissatisfied. The one thing he wanted for his people they still do not have - they are not free. The ultimate freedom, the freedom of self-rule, is denied them.

However prosperous the people of Haiti are, the Haitian people do not rule themselves. In a way, the despotism is worse than before because the despots at least were Haitians.

This time Francois does not become discouraged and flees to France. This time although material circumstances are far less ripe for revolution, Francois is able to find a few supporters. With these supporters, he sets up a rebel camp deep in the mountains of Haiti and launches a guerrilla war.

Francois's first efforts at guerrilla warfare are feeble at best and unsupported by the local population. At first, the Synthetic government, unable to understand what is happening, ignores him but the repeated complaints of the local population finally force it to send out a military unit to crush him. With the help of the local population, they have no difficulty finding him without him suspecting. They conduct a surprise attack. The entire guerrilla band is taken by surprise and wiped out. Those that aren't killed are captured. Due only to luck, Francois is not at the camp at the time.

Returning and discovering the shambles of what used to be his camp Francois flees into the Dominican Republic, where he is seized by the Dominican border guards. Much to his surprise, the Dominican government does not turn him over to the Haitian government. Instead, they welcome him. Then they unite him with other Haitian fugitives, mostly criminals. Within a short time,

Francois has a new band, arms supplied by the Dominican government, and a base camp inside the Dominican Republic.

With the aid of the Dominicans, Francois makes forays across the border into Haiti. He doesn't have enough strength to attack any military installations choosing instead to infiltrate and control the local villages. This time he finds some success amount the youth who resent Synthetic rule and do not remember the poverty that existed before the Synthetics. Francois finds another fertile ground at the universities where the students believe they can rule the country better than the Synthetics and know they can never rise into management as long as Synthetics rule the country.

Slowly but surely, the poverty existing before the Synthetics arrived is forgotten. Francois and his rebels make inroads into the mountain villages but also into the youth of Port Au Prince. With his control of the villages complete, Francois begins contesting the Synthetics for military control of the mountains. This time when the Synthetics come to crush to rebels, their source of intelligence, the local populace, is gone. Worse yet, it now works for the enemy. Not only do the army units not know the whereabouts of the rebels, but also the rebels always know the whereabouts of the Army. The only reliable intelligence source for the Army is from the air. The rebels become experts in camouflage.

With the resurgence of rebel activity, Mark acts quickly and decisively, armed camps are built in the mountain villages, and the local population is herded inside where they can be watched and cannot assist the rebels. With the population in armed camps, the rest of the area becomes a free-fire zone.

The irony of the armed camp idea is that both sides regard it as an assist to their side. From the Synthetic viewpoint, it is a dramatic assist to security. Anything other than a village is now a free-fire area.

From the rebel's point of view, the camps are a blessing. Even though the camps make their military situation more difficult, the military point of view is not the most important. The political point of view they know is what really counts. The populace has been forced off their lands into virtual concentration camps and resents the treatment. Resentment towards Synthetic control grows and the political control of the populace, which has until now been tenuous, solidifies. Recruitment soars.

Francois seeing the political effect of the armed camp plan, spreads his operation, knowing that the Synthetics will be forced to expand their armed camps as well. With each new camp, Francois scores a propaganda victory. Francois' insurrection, for the first time, spreads rapidly among the population. Within a short time, the whole country becomes an armed camp.

With his recruiting success, Francois also changes military tactics. Instead of small hit-and-run guerrilla operations, Francois begins to attack large military installations. Taking advantage of an extremely sophisticated intelligence network, he is able to move into position at night undetected with sufficient forces. With careful planning, he is able to overwhelm and destroy military installations with a minimum of casualties. By morning, the rebel forces have dissolved back into the countryside.

With the spread of rebel activity throughout the country and the increase in size and daring of the rebel operations, Mark determines that a more drastic tactic is required. In secrecy, "he" plans an airborne assault on the rebel base camp inside the Dominican Republic.

With coordinated air support, the Synthetics made a dawn assault upon the rebel base camp and took it by surprise. The operation is a complete success; almost the entire main rebel army is wiped out along with most of their food, equipment, and munitions. Only a few rebels escape, but once again, Francois is absent from the camp.

The Dominican government is outraged by the attack and complains to both Haiti and the United Nations. Not only had their territory been invaded, but they complained to the Dominicans a score of their border guards had been murdered. A resolution condemning the attack on the Dominican Republic was put on the floor of the United Nations and quickly passed.

Despite the crushing defeat of its regular forces inside the Dominican Republic, the real heart of the rebellion is the irregular soldiers inside Haiti. While the attack upon the base camp inside the Dominican Republic was a setback, the Dominican government replaced the material losses, and the human losses were replaced by recruitment.

As Francois rebuilds his Army, its level of activity grows, and Mark determines that action that is even more drastic is required. This time Mark chooses the action in which success is certain. He forbids the implantation of the human ovum into artificial uteruses and orders that any woman getting pregnant will have her child aborted. Mark's plan now is to eliminate the human population of Haiti.

The proclamation is received with shock throughout the world because it means the extinction of humans in Haiti. The United Nations ejected Haiti and organized economic reprisal upon all Haitian products.

Notwithstanding the reprisals inflicted upon Haiti, Mark stands firm. Mark realizes that the real issue is not the extinction of humans in Haiti but the very survival of Synthetics. Fortunately, the embargo, like all embargoes, proves leaky.

When the embargo proves, many leaky governments of the world, especially the ones in the Caribbean, decide that the embargo isn't enough and aid Francois' rebellion. With vastly increased outside assistance and open hostility of the human populace of Haiti since Mark's decree Francois' forces seem to multiply daily in both numbers and sophistication. Francois now feels that the days of guerrilla warfare are over, and it is time to move into set-piece warfare. He prepares his Army for an open invasion of Haiti from the Dominican Republic and attacks across the border.

Francois' Army easily crushes the lightly defended border and begins liberating the armed camps near the border, further swelling his Army. He then moves towards the coast and the capital city of Port Au Prince.

Mark is faced with an open invasion of "his" country. "He' knows that unless "he' acts fast and decisively, the whole country will be overrun and "his" government extinguished. "He' mobilizes "his" Army and inducts nearly every Synthetic in the nation into it and boldly attacks the very center of Francois' Army.

Francois, not expecting such bold and drastic action and not realizing that Mark will be able to mobilize anywhere near the number of Synthetics that he has, is taken by surprise. The well-equipped and disciplined Synthetic Army move almost as if they are of the same mind and punch right through the center of Francois' Army and continues into the Dominican Republic. This put Francois into desperate straits, and all armies require logistics - they must be supplied. They need food, fuel, munitions, and repair parts. The Synthetic Army had carried enough supplies with them, but Francois did not anticipate such a need. Without supplies, he cannot continue the war for long. He cannot go back into the Dominican Republic for re-supply because the Synthetics are there. He would have to fight his way through them. The only thing he can do is continue ahead, take Santo Domingo, and be reinforced from there.

The governments that have been aiding Francois are not oblivious to the implications of Francois moving to the Dominican Republic. They realize that if he takes Santo Domingo, the Synthetics will have the entire island, and there will be no base from which to eject them. They rush their armies to Santo Domingo to prevent it from being taken. They also put the needed supplies on ships to be ready to aid Francois should he be successful in taking Port Au Prince.

The reinforcement of Santo Domingo is not fast enough. So swift is the Synthetic advance that it arrives at Santo Domingo before sufficient forces can arrive to successfully defend it. Mark takes the city with little difficulty, capturing the allied force defending it.

Meanwhile, Francois has surrounded the skeleton force of Synthetics defending Port Au Prince. Francois, low on supplies and munitions, knows that he must take the city before his supplies run out or the main Synthetic Army can turn on him. He, therefore, launches a series of human waves attacks designed to wear down the defender no matter the cost. The quick and able Synthetic marksmen are able to decimate the ranks of the attacking Haitians, but their numbers are few. Eventually, the desperate tactics of Francois wear down the Synthetics, and they are overwhelmed. Francois takes Port Au Prince, and the ships are waiting to re-supply him come into to dock.

The Synthetics, however, have known they were there waiting and have demolished and mined the port. Before the ships can dock and unload, the port has to be cleared. The ships can be unloaded at sea, and their cargoes ferried into the land, but the process is clumsy and slow. While this is still going on, Mark and his Army, having taken Santo Domingo, turns and returns to Port Au Prince. The well-equipped, although weary Synthetic Army is more than a match for the decimated, ill-supplied Army of Francois. The Synthetics retake Port Au Prince: they have won.

Just when it looks bleakest for the Haitians, the United States intervenes. Mark knowing he hasn't the forces, even under the best of circumstances, to fight this great power, doesn't bother to put up resistance. He immediately offers to surrender to the United States, asking only that his troops be spared. The guarantee is given, and Mark surrenders.

In a manner of speaking, the guarantee of the United States is kept. The Synthetics are spared by the soldiers of the United States. However, after being disarmed, the Synthetics are turned over to the Haitians. The Haitians have made no guarantee to the Synthetics.

The United Nations had protested and been outraged by the fact that forbidding humans to reproduce in Haiti would eventually mean the end of humanity in that country though to natural causes. However, when the Synthetics are eliminated from the same island by unnatural causes, the United Nations is curiously silent.

Not only are the Synthetics in Haiti eliminated but also the United Nations calls for the trial of the officers of M.L.S.S. Inc. for war crimes. The United States refuses to give up its sovereignty over them insofar as they are United States citizens. The United Nations is not satisfied with this answer and demands that the Synthetics be turned over for trial.

Dana and the Synthetic ruling council, now realizing that Haiti has been lost and its last reasonable chance of perpetuating Synthetics on Earth, offers to take all the Synthetics and leave Earth. The Synthetics will leave behind their entire financial empire if only the Synthetics are given a planet to colonize. The United States seized upon this offer as an acceptable compromise and offered it to the United Nations. The United Nations also accepts it only if the financial empire of M.L.S.S. Inc. is given as war reparations. In a short time, space transports are found, the several thousand remaining Synthetics embark, and the vessels depart for the far side of the galaxy, a planet as yet, undetermined.

What Dana does not know is that the humans are against the plan to keep the letter but not the spirit of the agreement. The admiral in charge of the fleet is instructed to land the Synthetics on a marginal planet where the Synthetics will not be able to develop enough technology to reproduce themselves. Once again, the humans are underestimating humans; they are judging them by their own abilities.

Francois finally has what he has been dreaming of since he was educated in France, a democratic government of Haiti. His dream of a modern, prosperous country run by freely and fairly elected politicians seems close at hand. He has only to reach out and grasp it.

Though his dream seems so close, he has many troubles that befall him. Though the war has been won, he was beaten badly and won only through outside assistance. Despite his failure to defeat the Synthetics, Francois is the closest thing to a national hero. He is also deeply indebted to the United States, without which he would not have won.

The United States leaves many "advisors" behind to "help." Besides his other problems, Francois is deeply troubled about what to do with the captured Synthetics. While he is troubling over the problem, his troops solve the problem for him. When the Synthetics are executed, Francois tells himself he is not responsible since he did not order them. His subconscious knows this is not true since he knew early it was going on and did not stop it. He would dream of it for many years even though he was witness to none of the killings.

Only after taking the reins of power does Francois realize the enormity of the tasks facing him. While the nation is now a modern industrialized country, virtually all the technocrats that have kept it running have been Synthetics. There are simply not enough Haitians with the skills and knowledge to keep the country running properly.

Francois immediately turns to the United States for technical assistance.

Notwithstanding his troubles and guilt, Francois still feels good about himself and his country. He has the country on the road to economic recovery after a devastating war and tells himself that native Haitian will soon be able to replace the technicians from the United States.

Despite his good intentions, Francois soon discovers that life at the top is not what he thought it would be. For its military and technical assistance, the United States demands a trade and political concessions that Francois does not want to give them. Since he has no choice, he gives the United States what they ask for.

It is not, however, the United States that gives Francois his greatest distress; it is his own followers. Unlike the coldly rational, incorruptible Synthetics, his followers are human. They expect to benefit from their loyalty and support to the rebellion despite their qualifications. Francois dutifully rewards them. No sooner does Francois place his supporters in government positions than they show their human fragilities. They start taking bribes. Eventually, Francois becomes aware that he is surrounded by corruption and takes steps to root it out. It is then that he discovers that the deepest corruption is found in his oldest and most loyal lieutenants. In order to root out the corruption, he would have to prosecute his closest supporters. Francois not only cannot bring himself to do this but also discovers that he himself has indirectly benefited from the corruption. When this is seen, the very agencies designed to root out corruption become infected. What is the use of risking life and limb to find corruption if nothing is done about it? If nothing can be done: Why not profit?

Though a national hero, Francois' image has been tarnished by the diminished living standards and the puppetry of his government corruption. Though he won an overwhelming victory in his first election, he faced stiff opposition largely due to the diminished living standards in the second. In order to be sure of victory, Francois needs a lot of money and political support. He promises to aid a businessman who has mysteriously amassed a huge fortune since the war to get that money. For additional political support, he promises large wage increases to unions.

Francois wins his second election by a comfortable margin, but he has to fulfill his promises now. The labor unions get their wage increases, but the increasingly shoddy Haitian goods become overpriced on the world market when they do. The resulting loss of the market causes unemployment and inflation in Haiti. The large wage increases obtained by the unions prove worse than meaningless. When Francois discovers a massive corruption scheme in his government, the merchant financially backs him behind it. Francois cancels the investigation.

Francois is genuinely surprised when the internal situation in Haiti steadily worsens. He cannot understand it when he had such high ideals for his country. When civil unrest breaks out due to unemployment, inflation, crime, and corruption, Francois declares martial law to quell the disturbances. When someone attempts his life, he organizes special presidential police to protect him. When another attempt on his life is made, he gives his police special power to seek out the treasonous elements of society. They become experts at eliminating opposition.

When the next election rolls around, martial law is still in force. Since he controls the electoral process, he has no difficulty getting elected and his party winning a huge majority in the national congress. The first thing they do is pass an amendment to the Haitian constitution making him president-for-life. After the amendment passed, huge crowds appeared at the presidential mansion, chanting for him to accept the new office. After a while, Francois appears at the window of the presidential mansion: reluctantly, humbly - he accepts.

Thus, as the Earth turns on its axis, like all things in life repeat in cycles, another despot governs Haiti.

Chapter 7

The Universal Principle of Relativity

When Dana Carl is reading his college physics textbook, he reads something he does not understand, something that contradicts common sense. The physics book says that light speed is an absolute constant. It always measures 299,792,458 meters a second, even if measured from a moving object. Surely, he has misread the text.

Dana would eventually discover the reason for the misunderstanding. He was reading the text too literally. Light speed had never been measured in one direction. It had always been measured on a closed loop. This statement only applied when applied on a closed loop.

Dana later discovered that this belief of light speed was identical when propagating in opposite directions from a moving object was not the result of an experiment. It was a convention, a mere assumption, by Albert Einstein called the Einstein Synchronization Convention. Einstein had posited this as his basis for his 1905 work on "The Electrodynamics of the Physics of Motion". It meant that light speed was unaffected by the speed of its propagating object (non-cumulative speed). In other words, light speed knows where stationary is.

The text next mentions the proof of the Theory of Relativity, the Null Result of the Interferometer. Albert Michaelson, the great light speed researcher, did this experiment in 1881 in Berlin and again in

1887 at Case Western University in Pittsburgh. He did it with a device of his own design, the Interferometer. The purpose of the experiment was to prove the existence of the luminiferous ether. Sound travels through air, water or solid and waves on water travel across water, how did light waves travel through the vacuum of space?

Light had already been proved a wave by the English genius Thomas Young with his double slit experiment. Young shined a light through a piece of paper on a screen in a darkened room. When he did, a series of light and dark lines appeared. Young knew this means light was a wave because the light and dark lines could only happen when the waves interfered and alternately enhanced and cancelled each other. The same thing happens when two speed boats cross each other. Their wakes alternately enhance and cancel each other.

The Interferometer split a monochromatic beam of light through a half-silvered mirror into perpendicular directions and then to a central mirror and back to observation.

Michaelson knew from his calculations that due to Earth's motion the parallel beam's distance was longer than the perpendicular beam's distance, so he expected to see wave interference. There was none. For this reason, the experiment is called the Null Result of the Interferometer

The next thing that happened is that Henrick Lorenz and George Fitzgerald suggested that the device was shrinking in the direction of motion proportionate to the velocity of motion. Lorenz derived a formula for the phenomena. It is called the Lorenz-Fitzgerald contraction. $L = Lo\ (1 - V^2/c^2)^{1/2}$.

Then Albert Einstein proposed his Theory of Relativity. Since $V = $ length/time, if light speed was absolute and length was compressible than time had to be dilatable. Thus, $T = To\ /\ (1 - V^2/c^2)^{1/2}$. This theory also predicted a fourth dimension, the time-space dimension.

Dana could not accept this explanation. If anything in physics should be a constant, it should be space and time. Moreover, in order to have a fourth dimension, that dimension would have to be perpendicular to the other three. Where is the direction perpendicular to the other three?

Since the Theory of Relativity was built upon a convention, that light speed is non-cumulative, Dana thought that that is where the mistake must have been made. Perhaps light, like objects, are cumulative with the speed of what sets them in motion. That objects pick up the speed or the object they are propelled from, is known as the Principle of Relativity. The Principle of Relativity has been known since Galileo. The Principle of Relativity held that the laws of physics for objects act the same inside a body in motion as it did if the body were stationary. The laws of physics of objects do not change inside a plane moving beyond the speed of sound. They are the same as those experienced-on Earth.

Dana knew that if a ball was thrown at 40 mph from the front of a train going at 40 mph, the ball would emerge from the thrower's hand at 80 mph. Likewise, if a ball was thrown at perpendicular to the direction of the train at 40 mph from a train going at 40 mph, it would vector in the direction of travel at 45 degrees. It would travel at 68.28 mph because the cosine of 45° is 28.28, thus 40 + 28.28 = 68.28 mph.

A person can play catch inside a train car or ship the same as he can in his front yard. A ball thrown at 20 mph forward inside the moving object traveling at 20 mph may be traveling at 40 mph but it appears to its catcher to be traveling at 20 mph because he is the same car traveling away from the ball at 20 mph.

If the ball is thrown inside the car perpendicular to the direction of the moving body, since the ball and the opposing catcher are affected by the same force, the catcher will always be in the same place as the ball when it arrives. Vectors do not appear inside a moving inertial system. They only appear from the perspective of someone outside that system.

Cumulative light speed explained the Null Result because cumulative light speed would behave exactly the same way the ball did in the train hypothetical. It was a simple, elegant solution to the Null Result, and it did not have to use space contraction and time dilation to explain it.

Dana immediately realized that there were a couple of problems with his theory. The first problem was that when cumulative light speed hit a mirror in the same inertial system and bounced, it would only lose the speed of the propagating object. $(C + V - V = C)$ It would travel the return trip at normal light speed and arrive before the perpendicular beam. In order for cumulative light speed to explain the Null Result, reflected light would have to lose the speed of the propagating object twice.

Dana subsequently learned that when light strikes a mirror, it does not bounce, it interacts with the electrons of the mirror and is re-emitted. When the light is re-emitted, it is emitted at light speed less the speed of the mirror that reflects it, $C - V$. Yes, the speed of the object of propagation is lost twice! Once when light interacts with the electrons of the glass and again due to the speed of the mirror it is reflected from.

This reflection explanation is identical to the explanation for refraction. When light goes through glass it slows and bends. The principle allows for magnifying lenses, glasses, microscopes and telescopes. When light travels through glass, it interacts with the electrons of the glass, is re-emitted, speeds off to other elections at light speed, and continues until it emerges from the other side of the glass, where it resumes normal light speed.

If light speed is cumulative, its speed would be $C + V$, when it travels in the same direction as motion and, $C - V$ on the return trip. The motion of the Earth would be directly offset on both trips and arrive at the observer simultaneously. Cumulative light speed is a dramatically elegant explanation for the Null Result.

The second problem was the Doppler Effect. The Doppler Effect is the change of frequency caused by motion as experienced by a person outside the same inertial system. The usual example is the person standing at a RR crossing when a train passes. Trains blow their whistle approaching a crossing. At the precise moment the train passes, the pitch of the whistle (wave frequency) lowers. What the observer experiences is the sound waves being compressed when the train approaches and then expanded by the motion of the train against the speed of sound as the train recedes.

The Doppler effect also happens to light. Stars speeding away from Earth have a red shift.

However, Dana reversed the hypothetical man standing at a RR crossing. He put the whistle on the ground and the man on the train. Dana realized that the Doppler Effect would still occur even though the sound waves were unaffected by a stationary whistle. What happens is that the observer hears the sound waves arrive faster when the train approaches and slower when receding. The Doppler Effect would take place even though sound waves were unaffected. Thus, the Doppler Effect doesn't prove that light speed is absolute (non-cumulative)! The Doppler Effect doesn't need a light speed barrier to cause it.

Dana not only realized that light speed explained the Null Result but that it had already been proven. There was in existence already a permanent Interferometer in Livingston, Louisiana and another in Hanford, Washington. They were called LIGO's. It stands for Laser

Interferometer Gravitational Observatory. Their purpose was to detect gravitational waves. Each arm is 4000 meters long. What Dana knew is that if light is non-cumulative, it won't vector and if it is cumulative, it will. However, because the Earth is moving and people are in the same inertial system, we won't see a vector if light speed is cumulative, but we will see a vector if light speed is non-cumulative. If light speed is non-cumulative, since the Earth is moving and we are on Earth, the light beam will appear to vector in the direction opposite of motion.

A laser emitted from a moving object from a stationary position outside the moving inertial system

The speed at which the Earth is traveling against the Cosmic Microwave Background is 368,000 m/s. The LIGO's re 4000 meters long. At 90°, 4000 m ∕ 299,792,458 m/s = 3.06889675823 meters off perpendicular. The mirror will move 3 meters during transit of the light beam! When the laser beam arrives, the mirror will be 15 feet down range.

Dana also calculated that distance without assuming that the Interferometer was travelling directly perpendicular to the Cosmic Microwave background. Since Livingston and Hanford are at different latitudes, all three dimensions are covered. One of the arms cannot be more than 45 degrees off. By Pythagoras, $x^2 + x^2 + x^2 = (1^2)^{1/2}$, $3\,x^2 = 1$, $x^2 = 1/3 = x = 0.577$. at 45°, $3.687 \times 0.577 = 2.127$ meters. It still misses the mirror.

Synthetics Rising

At the speed the solar system rotates around the Milky Way, a minimum of 1.77 meters. At the speed the Earth rotates around the sun, from winter to summer, a minimum of 462 mm. At the speed, Livingston revolves daily, 7.6 mm. every 12 hours and Hanford, 4.92 mm. every 12 hours.

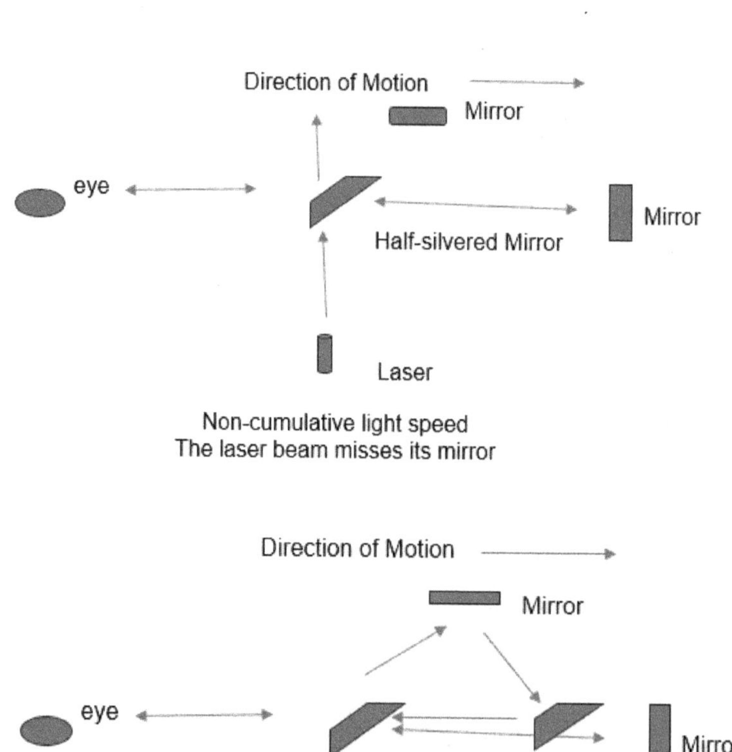

As his doctoral thesis Dana proposes the Universality of the Principle of Relativity. His doctoral thesis is denied, and he doesn't get his doctorate. He tries to get his thesis published but it is ignored. No one even responds to his publishing requests.

Billy Lynch is a test pilot. He has wanted to be a pilot all his life and considers it a source of immense pride that he has not only achieved his life's ambition but has exceeded it. He has become the best of the best, the crem de la crem, a test pilot. Cocky, confident and swaggering he is the first pilot selected for an out of solar system test flight using a proton engine. Even though he knows the mission is extraordinary dangerous, a small space pebble hitting his spaceship at the speed traveled in outer space would surely penetrate his spaceship and kill him. Yet he doesn't worry about that, his only real worry is a fear of mediocrity, that he might be like everyone else and not special. He only worries that one of the other test pilots might be selected. He regards it as his natural destiny to be the first man to travel outside the solar system, the first man to test fly the new proton engine.

He is not surprised when he is selected to be the first pilot to explore another solar system; after all, it is his destiny. An engineer by education with a corresponding degree in physics, he understands the design and capabilities of his craft as well as its designers. He knows the principles and design are very simple. All his engine does is ionize hydrogen, stripping the atom of its sole electron, and then with a small cyclotron, speeding the proton to near light speed before exiting it out of the rear of the spaceship. The recoil of each pronoun thus ejected propels the rocket ship forward. The most important design feature for Billy's engine is to use a minimum of fuel for a long voyage. Its gives exactly what its design engineers are looking for; the most propulsion for the least amount of fuel, the biggest bang for the buck, Billy calls it.

The night before his first test flight with the new craft, he sleeps fitfully, his mind preoccupied with tomorrow's events, his place in history, public recognition, but most importantly the glory of equaling his own self-image.

Long before his alarm goes off Billy is awake, too nervous to sleep so he reads some science fiction. His nervousness worries him: it is unlike him; his nerves are usually solid as a rock. In the morning, his previous night's nervousness and sleeplessness forgotten he feels only anticipation and delight as he waits for clearance to depart the space station. Once clearance is given a special tug using chemical rockets, he eases his craft away from the space station where is craft was built. Billy cannot use his own engines for fear that the highly dangerous protons fired towards the space station might damage it or the personnel inside.

Once a sufficient distance away, Billy fires his engine for the first time. His engine is designed to accelerate the ship at 9.81 meters per second, exactly the same rate as a falling object on Earth, provides "artificial" gravity. As the ship picks up speed, he watches the space station and earth slowly move away from him. Then he turns his attention to his point of reference other than the earth and the sun, the star Alpha Centari. As he looks at this mere pinprick in the sky, he thinks how ironic, the trip for him will take 4 years but for everyone else it will take 13 years. Accelerating at 1g, it will take almost 1 year to reach close to the speed of light. 186,282 mi./sec. x 5280 ft./mi. x 1 sec.^{2}/32.2ft. x 1 yr./365days x 24 hours x 60 min. x 60 sec. = .969 years.

In that year, he will travel 1/2 a light year. He will then travel 3 1/2 light years at 99.99% of the speed of light, which for him will be only a few days but for everyone else will be 3 1/2 years. He will then have to decelerate his spaceship at 1g for another year. As result of time dilation, it will take him 4 years, 2 years accelerating there and back and 2 years decelerating there and back.

As his craft speeds up Earth winks out, he cannot see it anymore. He realizes that this is because as he moves away the visible light emanating from Earth appears to him due to his speed as infrared light, the Doppler effect. Since he cannot see in the infrared spectrum Earth becomes invisible to him. He then looks at the sun, which he can still see. He knows this is because the sun is emanating light in the ultra-violet range, which because of his speed is visible to him. As his speed grows faster and faster, he knows that the light he will be seeing from the Sun will be first ultra-violet light, then x-rays, then gamma rays and then nothing.

He turns his attention to Alpha Centari. It is also visible because it is putting out light on the infrared spectrum. First, he will see it with infrared light, then microwaves and finally radio waves. After he reaches 99.99% of the speed of light, Alpha Centari will be invisible.

The trip has been planned so that most of it will take place while Billy is sleeping. If there is some small object out there that is going to collide with him there is very little, he can do about it anyway. He checks his instruments to be sure they are working properly, especially his gauges measuring acceleration. At the speed he will be traveling, he will be blind, and the only way of navigating is for his gauges to properly measure his rate of acceleration and calculate how far he has traveled and thus know when to stop. For a few seconds he muses on the debate that the engine should be designed to automatically shut off at 99.99% of the speed of light. The argument failed, since light speed cannot be exceeded there was no need to design such a feature, it would simply be something more to go wrong. Furthermore, since time will be dilating rapidly close to the speed of light the ship's engine will be using very little fuel. Instead, the ship is designed to accelerate for half the trip and decelerate for the other half.

Since time will dilate during the trip, any reliance on clocks is regarded as unreliable. Instead, the ship is programmed to decelerate by taking its navigational position from stars perpendicular to the course of travel. When the ship is halfway to Alpha Centari the ship will somersault and begin to decelerate.

Satisfied that his engines are working properly, Billy puts himself into hibernation until his ship arrives.

When he awakens, he quickly jumps out of bed. He wants to see if he really is at Alpha Centari. Running quickly to his pilot's seat he finds his craft automatically slowing down and the binary suns of Alpha Centari are directly ahead of him. He dresses quickly, eats his breakfast and begins his astronomical observations. He is the first man to prove what has been conjectured on for years, that there are planets in other solar systems. After charting the solar system of Alpha Centari, he finds the coordinates into a navigational computer that routes him on a mapping expedition through the new solar system. This part of the trip takes him a month. Near light speed through a solar system are too dangerous, the probability of colliding with a foreign object is many times higher and even a small grain of sand at such speed would penetrate the hull of his ship and destroy it.

Having completed his mapping and recording expedition Billy programs his computer to route him home. This time he repeats his routine for Earth in much the way he did while traveling to Alpha Centari. When he goes to sleep that night, he expects to wake up in the morning with the sun staring him in the face.

Indeed, when he wakes up the sun is staring him in the face. Before getting dressed, he immediately calls Houston. When he identifies himself, they say. "What are you doing here?"

"What do you mean, what am I doing here?"

"I mean you're supposed to be en route to Alpha Centari!"

"I just got back."

"You can't possibly have gotten back!"

'Why can't I possible have just gotten back?"

"Because you just left 4 years ago."

"Well, of course I just left 4 years ago, for me. It is 13 years later for you."

"Trust me, it was 4 years ago when you left here for us too. Now turn around and go back and explore Alpha Centari.'

"Trust me," mocked Billy, "I have explored Alpha Centari."

"You can't possibly have explored Alpha Centari"

"I must have imagined that solar system of Alpha Centari I explored then."

"You explored the solar system of Alpha Centari?"

"I sure did!"

"Did you record your exploration?"

"My computer banks are full!"

"Well, dock at the space station then and well try to figure out what the hell is going on."

Billy docks at the space station and immediately he and the computer tapes that have recorded his mission are put on a rocket back to Earth where his tapes are analyzed and he is debriefed. His debriefing provides nothing unusual, but the tapes do. They prove conclusively that he has visited the solar system of Alpha Centari. What the scientists cannot figure out is why it only took him 4 years to get there and back. In order to do that he would have to have traveled faster than the speed of light, which is supposed to be impossible. At least according to the Theory of Relativity, it is impossible.

It is obvious that Bill has broken the speed of light. He could not travel 9 light years in 4 years without breaking the speed of light. The scientists believe that the resistance expected as the craft neared light speed did not take place and the space craft simply sailed through the speed of light and kept on accelerating to many times the speed of light.

If light speed can be broken, the Theory of Relativity cannot be true. Shock waves are sent though the scientific community. The Theory of Relativity was the accepted theory to explain the null result. It was universally accepted among nuclear physicists. The same thing that happened many years before begins again: how to explain the null result. It is then someone stumbles upon in a corner of an obscure library a dusty thesis authored by failed doctorate candidate by the name of Dana Carl. It contains a simple, straightforward explanation that the Universality of the Principle of Relativity. When it is published in a scientific journal, it is widely and immediately acclaimed. Scientists cannot stand to have something that they cannot explain. Dana is found heading up M.L.S.S. Inc. and exalted. He is named the winner of the Nobel

Prize for physics that year. When he is given the Nobel Prize, he cannot help but reflect upon the irony that he is being given a Nobel Prize for a scientific paper that had prevented him getting a doctorate.

For himself Billy is glad to be home after his dangerous journey, ecstatic to be part of history and even more pleased with himself to have been part of revolutionizing the theories of physics. He endures the long briefing sessions and thoroughly enjoys the public adulation that he is given. After the government is through with him, he embarks and a speaking tour and begins his autobiography. His speeches at first are sold out and when his book is publishes, despite the fact there is little to tell about the trip, becomes a best seller, Billy becomes a wealthy man.

As time passes, attendance drops off at his speeches and the public quickly realizes how boring his book is, Billy's fame fleets and despondency replaces excitement. His life of victoriously surmounting challenge after challenge is gone. There are no more mountains to climb, no more victories to be won. His despondency increases into depression, which worsens until he is longer able to live with himself and take his own life. His death wins a spot on the national news and a paragraph in all the papers and magazines. Except for a question in trivia books, he is forgotten.

Chapter 8

The Sect

Paul John sits in the study of his rectory, staring at the wall, contemplating, lost in his own reverie. A novice priest raised by the stem, pious parents, he believes in the literal truth of scripture. As he was growing up, he was aware that some members of his congregation did not believe in the literal truth of scripture, that it was figurative rather than literal, a guide rather than a code. Until he became a priest himself, he was unaware of how often the parishioners chose to ignore those parts of the catechism that displease them. He was also unaware of the pervasiveness of the disobedience. "Have I been so preoccupied with my own striving for the grace that I have failed to perceive this?" he asks himself. "I have known there were backsliders and hypocrites but never like this. Never have so many members of The Way simply disregarded catechism, the word of God."

The only comparable period in the history of The Way was the reformation, when whole nations broke away from the church because of corruption. Yet, this time it is different, more insidious; this time, there is no corruption to be rectified; this time, parishioners by the millions simply chose what aspect of catechism they prefer and what they will obey. Nor are the heretics irreligious. They are often as not the simple, hardworking, moral folk who make up the backbone of the church. What Paul John finds most frightening is that the more educated, the more likely the members are to disregard catechism.

What Paul John finds most hurtful is not the disobedience itself. There has always been disobedience, but the hierarchy of the church does not seem to care! In the past, the church has always disciplined its members by community pressure or, in serious cases, by ex-communication. In this instance, in this new crisis, the hierarchy is taking no action at all. Its lack of willingness to discipline and its complacency are all-encompassing: it is doing nothing to stem the moral tide.

As he sits there wondering, wrapped in his own reverie, he knows that he has to do something, to somehow strike a blow for scripture - the ultimate truth! I know that if I take action, I will chastise my congregation, and that will upset them. If my congregation is upset, my supervisor will be upset. Yet what I have to say is correct. It is straight out of the catechism. The catechism may be de-emphasized, but it still represents the faith of this religion.

Suddenly in his mind, the clouds part, and the sun shines through on his tiny ship floundering in a sea of troubles. I know what I have to do: what the truth commands - the truth commands. I must do what God says, and he will provide. If he does not provide, perhaps, it is because he has something greater planned, such as an example of martyrdom. Either one practices what one believes, or one does not.

The next day Paul John delivers this sermon to his congregation:

"Fellow worshipers, I am deeply troubled - my very soul. There are those out there right now who have departed from The Way who worship a false God - a God of mechanism, a God of technology instead of a God of spirit, a God of love. Nor are these people few in number. Their numbers grow by the day. They no longer follow The Way, for they have found their way. They pretend to follow The Way; these hypocrites. They even pretend to attend church and attend regularly. They appear to be good parishioners, but they do not follow scripture and ignore catechism. They follow only what they find con - ve - ni - ent.

The devil works in devious, insidious, subtle ways. He always tries to corrupt us and always tries to trick us, lure us by any means into his wicked empire. The Way has never been easy. It is long and hard, a perilous journey fraught with traps, snares, and pitfalls for the unwary. You must be ever watchful, ever vigilant, or you will be caught and sucked into the quicksand of your longings, desires, and easy ways. The Way does not demand perfection, for perfection is beyond mortal attainment. Hard indeed is The Way, and hard is the path to righteousness, but The Way has one saving grace: gentle forgiveness. No matter how many times you trip, no matter how many times you fall, no matter how many times the devil tricks you, deceives you, and traps you into his pit of slime, you have within easy grasp the rope of God's salvation. It allows you to pull yourself out of the slime of sin and into the shining sun of God's grace - for he who believes shall be forgiven. His sins shall be as white as snow.

The reward, the reward, the beauteous reward is not only peace and joy here on Earth - but peace and joy forever.

The punishment for those who do not believe, for those who do not follow is everlasting torment, to be cast down into a pit of slime and muck where foul vermin await to feast on your flesh for time without end.

The price, the price, what is the price for such generosity, mercy, and reward of salvation. The price is dirt-cheap, and yet it is more costly than all the precious gold or gems of their Earth. The price is sincerity; that's all it is - to believe and to follow The Way. You cannot believe part. You cannot choose to believe only part of God's word, you must believe all of it, or you will surely be damned. Those that reject part of the word of God do not accept the word of God at all, and those who reject the word of God will surely be damned.

You know of what I speak, you understand what The Way requires, you know that scripture says that man is born of a woman and that woman must suffer the pain and torment of childbirth. I see women in this church right now whose children were not born of them, whose wombs never nourished the seed of life, whose actions defied the very essence of their sex and of The Way. It is God's Way, and his Way cannot be questioned.

You women who spurn the word of God, the word of scripture, ignore the catechism and risk the wrath of God. You cannot feast at the table of God and eat only dessert. God watches, and God waits; he knows of your sin, insincerity, and true belief. God sees you too - and he waits! You men who have allowed your sperm to be implanted other than in a woman are just as guilty as your wives. The evil could not happen without your collaboration.

Repent! Repent! I beg you to repent - you cannot do this, you cannot allow this to happen, you are risking your immortal souls.

Paul John had expected that some of his congregation would get up during his sermon and leave, but no such thing happened. In fact, all seems normal. As his custom, as the custom for all clergymen, he greets his congregation as they leave the church. He expects something to be different, to have some of his congregation express some displeasure. They do not. The only thing that happens is that he is congratulated by some of the older women of the congregation who bore their children naturally before the artificial uterus was invented.

After the last of his congregation leaves the church Paul John is pleased with himself, pleased with his sermon. He had expected some coolness of his congregation, and there was none. Still, the lack of hostility dismayed him; he could not help but wonder if the sermon did any good.

Paul John half expects during the week to have the supervisor call and chastise him verbally. It does not happen; he does not hear from his supervisor all that week.

On the next day of worship, Paul John feels a chill as he approaches the door to the pulpit. What if the church is empty? What if my congregation stops coming to my church and starts going to another. As he opens the door, he looks out and sees a nearly full church. The crowd is diminished from last week but almost imperceptibly. A matter of weekly variance, he tells himself as he steps up into the pulpit to begin another tirade against the Godless artificial uterus.

As the weeks continue, he continues his tirade against the failure of his congregation to follow the proper teachings. The church is now only half full, and he knows his sermons have affected attendance. He is not surprised when he receives a telephone call from the supervisor asking him to come and speak to him. Knowing he is about to be upbraided, he girds himself in scripture and departs immediately for the supervisor's residence.

"Hello Paul," says Supervisor John Aloysius cheerfully as Paul enters his office. "How are you feeling today?"

Paul's response is forced and wooden as he is startled at the supervisor's cheerfulness and affability.

"Uh, fine," he says.

"Sit down, sit down," says Supervisor Aloysius kindly, his repetition belying his affability, his hand steady as it points to an overstuffed chair in the corner of his huge office. Paul sits in the chair, and the supervisor sits across from him in a less comfortable chair. "I understand you've been giving hellfire and damnation sermons," he says, smiling politely.

"No, sir."

The supervisor hesitates a moment, unable to believe at first that his subordinate is lying to him. He decides he isn't and rephrases the question. "Well then, I understand that you've been lecturing your congregation on the immorality of the artificial uterus."

"Yes, sir."

"I also understand that you've given a sermon on nothing else for two months and that the attendance at your services has drastically declined."

"Yes, sir."

"To what do you attribute the decline in your church attendance?"

"To my sermons."

"Exactly what do you think it is about your sermons that is causing a decline in attendance?" he asked, finding the unevasive candor refreshing. "I don't think the parishioners like what I am saying," says Paul in a soft yet audible force, his head dropping as he enunciates his words.

"Do you think it could be the subject matter itself or the repetition of the subject matter?"

"I think it is the subject matter," answers Paul quickly.

"You don't think it is because your congregation is bored with hearing the same thing over and over?" asks the supervisor sympathetically.

"Well, I suppose that's part of it," says Paul softly, his head dropping again.

"Do you suppose that you are the only clergymen to preach against the use of the artificial uterus?"

"Suppose I told you that during the time when you have been preaching against the artificial uterus, every other priest in this supervisorship has given a sermon against the use of that machine."

"Really," interjects Paul, brightening.

"Yes, really!" answers the supervisor condescendingly. "And their attendance is not down."

"Don't you think there are other areas where your congregation needs moral guidance other than against the artificial uterus?"

"Yes."

"Well, don't you think it is your job to give them that moral guidance?"

"But supervisor," Paul objects, "the members of my congregation are risking their immortal souls!"

"You don't think I know that?"

"Well, of course, you know that supervisor. It's just that I can't stand by and watch it. My congregation is risking their immortal souls, and the hierarchy doesn't care!"

"Well, now we see the real problem here," answers the supervisor. "You are angry with the hierarchy."

"The hierarchy could expel the offenders," says Paul confirming that the supervisor's suspicion is true.

"Do you think expelling them would stop the use of the artificial uterus?"

"In some cases."

"In the cases where it doesn't, what would happen to the children; would they be raised in The Way?"

"No, I suppose not," answers Paul, a declining inflection in his voice.

'Then we would be condemning a whole family and all their offspring to damnation for eternity and not just their parents, wouldn't we?"

"Yes, I suppose," answers Paul softly.

"Paul," begins the supervisor, tiring of the Socratic game he has been playing with his subordinate, trying to get him to see the reasoning of the hierarchy in not excommunicating for the use of the artificial uterus. "You graduated at the top of your divinity class. You are smart, disciplined, and pious. You have everything it takes to one day take over my job. I want you to go back to your congregation and see their whole moral guidance and not just lecture on a single subject. They really need that from you."

Paul John sits silently for a moment staring at a blank wall trying to think of something that will refute what the supervisor has said, knowing everything that the supervisor has said was true. "But how can I do that? How can I sit silent and watch our membership flaunting catechism, initiating children who were never born of a woman?"

"Our parishioners have been sinning ever since we have been a religion. God is everlasting forgiving; you cannot forget that if you are to remain a priest." The supervisor studies the tormented soul in front of himself, watching him wring his hands, trying to resolve the hierarchy's pragmatic policy with his own rigid doctrinal ideology. Supervisor Aloysius knows the young priest well, and he had been the top student in this theology class. Much is expected of him. He is brilliant and dedicated, his only drawbacks being his uncompromising penchant for doctrinal purity and stiff, formal manner. As he watches him, Supervisor Aloysius worries that unless Paul can learn to accept those who are more flawed, he will lose him as a priest.

"It is not a matter of putting aside catechism," says Supervisor Aloysius continuing. "It is a matter of emphasis. The hierarchy does not want you to stop advocating the church's position on procreation. The church merely wants you to emphasize it where it will do the most good. Why don't you teach catechism to the young so that they understand the immorality of the artificial uterus?

A light brightens in Paul's eyes, and his face lights up. Supervisor Aloysius knows that he has succeeded.

The two men part cordially, each happy that the meeting has gone so well. Paul John because he now believes that by teaching catechism to the youth of the church, they will stop using the artificial uterus, and Supervisor Aloysius because he believes he has saved Catholicism as a potentially valuable priest.

Paul John returns to his congregation and subordinates his desire to sermonize against the artificial uterus. He does not give up sermonizing against the artificial uterus, and he merely does as Supervisor Aloysius has asked. He stops making it the only subject of his sermons. The nature of his sermons against the artificial uterus changes dramatically. Instead of being aggressive and damning, they are gentle and cajoling. Even his references are oblique, couched in parables from the Bible. Some of his congregation, those that take pride in their scholarship of scripture, find the symbolism fascinating and make games of seeing who can decipher the proper interpretation of Paul John's parables.

Complying with Supervisor Aloysius' advice, Paul focuses his main attack against the artificial uterus on the children. It is through them that he strives for religious purity. He spends every spare minute he can with them, drilling them incessantly with scripture and catechism.

After the harsh vitriolic sermons end, the church fills up again. The congregation is delighted to see Paul spending so much time with the youth. So enthusiastic is Paul that when Supervisor Aloysius retires, the hierarchy asks Paul to replace him, but Paul declines the promotion. It isn't that he does not desire a promotion. Like most men, he wishes to be promoted; it is because he feels his work with the children of his congregation is unfinished - the fruit of his cultivation has yet to ripen. He is determined to prove that with careful religious instruction, one can get the congregation to observe catechism. It does not occur to him that that is exactly what the church has been doing for two thousand years and has never fully succeeded. Perhaps, he tells himself, when I finish my work here, I will take a supervisorship and use it to spread what I have learned here.

When the first of the girls he has trained chooses the artificial uterus over natural childbirth, he is disappointed but not crushed. It is only one defeat, he tells himself, one battle, the war will still be his, his girls have been carefully taught. The majority of them will still choose natural childbirth.

Paul is proven wrong! Either his girls had not been carefully taught enough, or they hadn't listened, or they didn't believe because 90% of them, despite their training, despite his dedication, opted for the artificial uterus, opt against pregnancy. Though 90% of them attend his church regularly and are personally devoted to him, they still choose the artificial uterus.

When his best pupil, his protégé, comes to him to initiate her son, Paul decides to try to find out where he has failed. The woman has attended church every week, so Paul knows she hasn't been pregnant. "Donna," he begins softly, not wishing to offend her, "you did not bear this child, did you?"

"You know I didn't, father," answers Donna respectfully.

"I know you know that the church will not discriminate against this child as to how it came into the world but would you please tell me why you choose to disregard scripture and not bear this child yourself. I wish to know how I failed you."

"But you didn't fail me. I owe you so much. It was you who taught me catechism, you who gave me my faith. You haven't failed me. How can you say you've failed me?"

He ignores her protestations. She implied compliments to him, aware only of his single-minded failure. "But you ignored scripture!"

"I didn't violate scripture, father. I disobeyed catechism," she exclaims, pausing briefly, surprised at her response, wishing to regain control. "Catechism is the hierarchy's interpretation of scripture. Scripture doesn't say anything about the artificial uterus."

"Scripture says women must bear their children in pain and agony," Paul woodenly responds.

"No, it doesn't," she exclaims again, this time uncaring that she is responding harshly and not taking the time to recover her emotions. "It says women do bear children in pain and agony, a statement of fact."

"Scripture says women must bear children in pain and agony," Paul repeats woodenly.

"I don't believe it; I don't believe it. I don't believe God wants us to suffer for no reason, to take chances with our lives, to take chances of our babies suffering birth defects. I don't believe God wants us to suffer for the sake of suffering itself. I don't believe that any more than I believe that a large fish swallowed Noah or that the universe was created in 6 days."

"You blaspheme," answers Paul.

Donna Smith regains her composure, sighing deeply, and thinking. I really love this man, he is so devout, so loving, and caring, but I didn't want this. I didn't think he would provoke a confrontation because I love him. It was he I wanted to initiate my son.

She looks at him for what seems like a long time, and she can see he is deeply distraught, under a severe strain, that by not following what he has taught her, she has hurt him deeply. She thinks back to when she and her husband were planning to have a child. She thought about the following catechism and bearing the child herself. Yet she couldn't do it for just his sake, and it wasn't just the pain and discomfort of doing so; it was the danger to the child. If the child was not perfect, if he suffered because of her decision, she knew she would never have forgiven herself. Perhaps the church could handle the guilt of her child being deformed, but she couldn't.

She gets up to leave, aching for some response from him, some indication of forgiveness towards her. His face is cast away, and there is none. She glances at him for the last time. She can see the lines of his face etched in torment, she feels sorry for him, but she does not regret her decision. She will go to another church and find another priest to initiate her son. She leaves; she cannot help but reflect on how literalistic he is and the clergy as well, taking the scripture at its most simple meaning, seldom delving for the intent behind the words, forgetting that words are merely tools to express thoughts. Strange how the clergy doesn't seem to realize that when scripture was written, it was written in terms that illiterate people of two thousand years ago could understand, before science, before mass education, that the words of scripture, literally, are anachronisms, out of place in time. Why is it that some people, especially the clergy, cannot see the forest for the bark? Why is it that the clergy cannot see the miracle of faith and let themselves get bogged down in semantics?

Paul John hears her leave but makes no effort to say goodbye. Later he will feel guilty because he had not intended to make a scene but makes no attempt to call and apologize.

After his discourse with Donna, Paul John becomes despondent. As each successive specially taught pupil of his opts against pregnancy and for the artificial uterus, he grows increasingly depressed, and his constant depression becomes readily noticeable. He tries to cheer himself to force his personal failure out of his mind but cannot. The thing that he has poured his heart and soul into for fifteen years has failed. Though many try to console him, his depression only grows. Unable to see his other achievements, his despair and sense of failure grow until he knows he cannot continue as a priest. When he requests a leave of absence from the clergy for health reasons, it is immediately granted. His condition has long been obvious.

Paul John spends his leave at a monastery engaged in quiet, contemplative meditation. He knows that somehow he will have to resolve his feeling of failure and get over his anger at the hierarchy - or his life in the clergy is over! He will either return to the clergy from the monastery or leave the clergy forever!

Despite his quiet, passive exterior, he is a man in torment; a man tore almost asunder! Truly, he understands why the hierarchy has adopted its pragmatic policy. Who can blame them, in view of the actions of the parishioners to enforce catechism would destroy the religion. Yet, it is this policy that tortures him so. To a purist like Paul, the answer is simple, what scripture commands, and scripture commands! No matter how hard he looks at it, no matter from what angle he examines it, the answer is always the same - unbelievers cannot be permitted to worship. As the long months of meditation continue, he steadily is being forced to admit to himself that he cannot return to the clergy.

If not a priest, what then! He has always wanted to be a priest; he has never wanted to be anything else. Except for the hierarchy's pragmatism, he respects and admires The Way, the discipline it offers, its unwillingness to change doctrine for expediency, and the remarkable efficient organization it has. Most importantly, he BELIEVES in the catechism and believes that it is the proper interpretation of the word of God. Yet, how can he remain a priest and be out of step with both his hierarchy and his congregation?

Suddenly a light as bright as the sun snaps on in his head. A light so bright that the shadows of torment that have haunted him these many years pass away. Paul knows that the great triumphs of faith have taken place only after misery and torment. The answer is so obvious that Paul cannot understand why he has not seen it before. Perhaps God has been trying to tell himself something all these years. Perhaps God is speaking to him because the hierarchy and the parishioners are no longer listening. God wants him to start a new church, a church within a church, a church adhering strictly to catechism. As long as he follows catechism, how can the hierarchy discipline him?

Paul John returns to his old congregation and seeks out those he knows to be sympathetic to him, sympathetic to doctrinal purity. He tells them of his plan to organize a sect within The Way that insists on doctrinal purity. With his few followers, he organizes worships in private homes. When he does so, the word spreads around the city. And those that believe as he crowds into the private homes. Very quickly, the meetings outgrow private homes, and the meetings are held outdoors; private meeting halls are too expensive. Paul John wants to use the money collected to build a church, not pay a landlord. Many times worships are held to overflow crowds under umbrellas in the rain.

After a few months of preaching on his own, Paul John is summoned before the local supervisor. Though he is determined to continue on his own, he feels obliged to respond out of respect and obedience. He is quiet and confident as he steps into the supervisor's study, knowing he cannot be detracted from his holy mission.

"Come in," says Supervisor O'Hara as he enters the same study where he conferred with Supervisor Aloysius many years before. He smiles to himself as he does so, for her knows that Supervisor O'Hara was the hierarchy's second choice.

Paul John looks at the well-lit office, resplendent with dark, heavy, ornate furniture and wood paneling to give the office a feeling of warmth and comfort. "You sent for me, Supervisor."

"Yes, yes," says Supervisor O'Hara warmly, "have a seat. It's good to have you back."

Paul John is taken aback by the supervisor's warm greeting. He expects to be chastised for his disobedience in setting up his own church, and the graciousness with which he has been welcomed belies his expectations.

"I understand that you've been holding services out of doors."

"Yes," says Paul sitting more stiffly in his chair.

"Why?"

"Because we don't have enough room in private houses," replied Paul John, puzzled.

"No, why haven't you asked to use a church?

"Uh - I -

I preach strict adherence to catechism," he answers, seeming to evade the question.

"Yes, I know," says the supervisor smiling, grasping the evasive answer.

Paul looks at the supervisor, slow to respond, still on the defensive, believing somehow that he has been tricked, that somehow he will admit to an offense for which he can be punished. Finally, he says, "Ah - I didn't think you would give me one."

"Well, I won't - but I will let you use one."

Paul sits in his chair, shocked, torn between his suspicions and the simple honesty reflected on the supervisor's face.

Sensing Paul's emotional turmoil, the supervisor says, "You really should be more trusting.

Paul finally decides he might just as well blurt out the truth. "I didn't think you would give me a church because I didn't report back from leave. I openly defied the hierarchy, contradicting the hierarchy policy," his words finally spewing forth like hot lava, their author cooled by their eruption.

Supervisor O'Hara sighs deeply, constantly amazed at what the local clergymen think is hierarchy policy, tempted to ask what this one thinks. He refrains from doing so, and it would be a rhetorical question. "You're not violating hierarchy policy by opening up a new sect within the church!" he responds patiently but tiredly, his voice dropping its volume at the end.

"I'm not!" Paul John shoots back.

"Yes, you're not. The hierarchy has always favored strict adherence to catechism."

"Yes, but - but, you've tolerated massive disobedience to the use of the artificial uterus for years.

"We've tolerated sinning for a lot longer, but that doesn't mean we approve of it! We just haven't been able to do anything about it. Some by our own priests and even the Pope."

"Well, I'm going to start my own sect that doesn't tolerate disobedience to catechism."

"Good, more power to you!"

Paul's face goes blank in astonishment when he hears Supervisor O'Hara's exclamation. His eyes are open wide, his mouth agape, looking like an owl sitting on a branch at night. "You mean you'll give me a church."

"Not quite. You'll have to build your own church. Your sect has to exist on its own to prove itself, but at least I can give you shelter so you don't have to hold your services in the rain. I don't want our most faithful to think that we have abandoned them."

A look of understanding wipes across Paul's face. "I'm sorry I misjudged the hierarchy," he says as he leans back in his chair, suddenly feeling tired, the last of his hostility draining out of his body.

As soon as Paul leans back in his chair, he sits bolt upright as if yanked on a string. "Yes, but I've defied you and the hierarchy."

Supervisor O'Hara looks at Paul kindly, a whisper of a smile flickering across his lips, amused at the priest's honesty and his complete and sudden emotional turnabout. "Yes, and don't ever let it happen again," he says in a laughing voice waving his finger at Paul.

"What kind of a man of The Way would I be," continues Supervisor O'Hara, "if I didn't allow a certain degree of latitude for my clergymen in matters of faith? By the way, you won't be the first priests to found a new order within The Way."

"I - I had thought of that before but never from the hierarchy's point of view. You mean I have the hierarchy's permission?"

"No, you may not have our permission, but you may have our blessing. Of course, you will understand if we appear to be disinterested. This must be a grassroots movement."

Of course, *of course*, thinks Paul John to himself, there have been many resurgences of faith in the church's history. There have been many before whose complete faith reinvigorated the church. 'Thank you, thank you, thank you," repeats Paul to the supervisor rising from his chair and pumping the supervisor's hand, his face beaming, his mind still racing now that it has been relieved from the guilt he felt for disobedience. His body suddenly infused with a feeling of destiny, his religious zeal leaping to heights even beyond when he was a seminarian.

"You're welcome," responds Supervisor O'Hara warmly, aware of the sudden change in Paul, sensing the feeling of destiny that surges through Paul's veins, a feeling that he does not share. "God is with you," he says to Paul as. Paul, as he leaves, the traditional departing salutation.

"And God is with you too," Paul answers with deep emotion.

You will need God to help you. Clergyman O'Hara thinks as Paul leaves. You will almost certainly fail, but your religion needs you to try. We have faced longer odds in the past - and won!

As Paul exits the building, he thinks of the thought he had when he arrived, that this could have been his job if he had wanted it. After his experience with Supervisor O'Hara and his own times of trouble, he realizes that the hierarchy's second choice was the better man for the job.

Paul John avails himself of Supervisor O'Hara's offer to use existing buildings to hold church services. His followers prove to be the most devout, industrious, and frugal of The Way but not towards the sect which they hugely endow. The sect built its own church and then expanded into other cities in a short time. Its membership, especially when its members see the hierarchy does not oppose the sect, grows explosively but just as abruptly stops at only a tiny fraction of The Way's total membership.

When further conversions do not take place, Paul urges his membership to have large families. This proves difficult because his congregation is generally old. However, those that don't respond favorably but that too does not cause Paul's sect to grow. The same problem that disappointed him as a parish priest comes back to haunt him. When the youth of the sect become adults, they use the artificial uterus, and Paul is forced to evict them from the sect. Despite having large families, the total membership remains constant at only a small fraction of the membership of The Way.

This time rather than despairing of another failure, Paul tries another approach. With his ample supplies of money, he organizes religious communes for his faithful. In these controlled communities, he can cut off seditious ideas and better control his membership. This too proves unsuccessful; the young, this time, do not use the artificial uterus but leave the communes upon becoming adults to find out what goes on in the outside world. After seeing what is in the outside world, many come back, but many do not. The sect still suffers a large rate of attrition but grows slowly.

Chapter 9

Colonization

When Paul John reads that Billy Lynch has broken the speed of light, Paul sees an opportunity he has waited for. Never interested in science, he now becomes obsessed with astronomy and rocketry. If my sect can colonize its planet, I can outlaw the artificial uterus and virtually guarantee it will not corrupt my congregation. The government will inevitably need a group of colonists to colonize another planet, and I will make sure that that group is mine. We will be the Plymouth colony of the new planet.

After the speed of light is broken and politicians realize that space travel within a lifetime is possible, a waterfall of funds for space exploration descends on NASA. More trips are taken to the Alpha Centauri system for possible exploration, and a suitable planet is found. Even before one is found, work begins on a mode of space transport.

When the exploring craft return, they report that the only suitable planet in the Alpha Centauri system is located at the common center of gravity between the two stars. The binary stars of Alpha Centauri revolve around this planet. The planet is of more recent origin than Earth, resulting in more primitive life forms, but still capable of supporting a population.

While the transport was being built, numerous people volunteered to be the first space colonists. Most of them are adventurers, people whose main goal is excitement, whose interest wanes after a few days on the new planet. This kind of people that the bureaucrats will choose the first colonists wish most to avoid. The authorities want disciplined, hardworking folk capable of enduring primitive conditions, people who will endure anything to make their colony succeed.

At first, the authorities think a military expedition will be the best, but when Paul John offers his sect as colonists, they rethink their decision. The authorities know that the sect comprises hardworking, disciplined individuals who will probably die before they let their colony fail. They also know that the sect's organization is authoritarian and will offer the needed disciplined government in the early days of the colony. The religious sect is thought to have one advantage over a military expedition. The sect is chosen to provide the colonists with the new planet. Sending religious colonists will be sending colonists who intend to stay, while a military expedition will have its members rotated back home. A military expedition lacks permanence.

Even though the rest of the population regards the sect members as religious zealots, religious kooks who shun scientific advancement for silly reasons, their selection as the first colonists is hailed as a wise decision. The similarity between them and the colonists of the Plymouth colony is widely written about. Despite the religious antagonism of the people of the United States, it also has a long history of religious toleration in which it prides itself.

Despite his advancing age, Paul John decides to head the expedition himself. His first task is selecting who among the volunteers will go. There are four qualifications for going. The person has to have an impeccable religious record, has to have a useful, practical skill, unless a clergyman, the person has to be married, and has to be married to someone who can qualify.

Once he has selected his fellow colonists, John Paul decides what to bring. He contacts NASA, requesting as much information as possible on the new planet. When given the available information is given, John Paul should be disturbed by its lack but isn't. John Paul is blind to everything but his own ambitions. The exploring craft had no means of actually landing on the planet, and very little is known about the planet's climate, geology, geography, and biology.

Knowing so little about the planet, John Paul decides to bring only the basics and as much food and various seed as possible. John Paul decides against bringing domestic animals. He doesn't know if there will be grazing when they arrive, and they will have to be fed en route. A large supply of various kinds of clothing is taken a few guns for protection from wild animals, and all kinds of different seeds, fertilizer, and hand tools. The only sophisticated equipment that is brought is hand-powered radios so that they can communicate with the transport ships in orbit. There is no point even in trying to communicate with Earth, it is possible to do so, but it is 4 1/2 light-years away. The transport is much larger than Billy Lynch's small explorer craft, which was almost all fuel tanks. The transport also has to carry a chemically powered shuttle rocket to get the colonists and their supplies down to the planet's surface. This shuttlecraft and its fuel take up more than half the available storage space on the transport.

When the colonists arrive at their new planet, which they call Primus because they are the first, they find that the air is breathable and the gravity the same as on Earth. The most difficult thing for them to get used to is the different solar cycles. Unlike Earth, which revolves around its sun, this planet is caught at the center of gravity between a binary star system; its suns literally revolve around it, and the rotation takes 80 years. Fortunately, the planet rotates for the colonists like Earth, but the rotation takes two weeks. A day on Primus lasts one week, and so does night.

Though the two suns of Alpha Centauri rotate about a common center of gravity, they are by no means close to one another. Their distance is about the same as between Uranus and its sun. Fortunately for Primus, both suns are substantially larger than Earth's sun and give off sufficient warmth to provide an Earth-like climate even though both suns are more than twice as far away as the distance between Earth and its sun.

Since sun A is by far the larger, it is to that sun B that Primus is closest. Since Primus is at the common center of gravity, it is closest to the sun with lesser gravity. Also, even though sun A is larger, the warmth of the two suns is equal because Primus is closer to sun B.

In addition, because Primus is at the common center of gravity, each sun is directly opposite the other. This means there is no night on Primus.

John Paul immediately set his people to work building shelters on the planet's surface. There is plenty of tree-like plants on the planet so the men, supervised by the carpenters, set to work building shelters while the women tend to the domestic chores. The work is difficult since the colonists only have hand tools, but persistence brings rewards.

After the shelter is built, the colonists commence building furniture. While the carpenters

Build the furniture, the other clear the land, put up firewood and begin planting crops. Clearing land is even more laborious than building shelters because it has to be done by hand. Since the colonists did not know what would grow, a variety of crops were planted. With little grumbling, the colonists set to their tasks.

Despite all their efforts of clearing, planting, and watering, the seeds from Earth do not survive in the Prime climate. When all of the crops fail, he orders strict rationing. Knowing that even with the strictest rationing, the colony will barely have enough food to last until the next transport return, John Paul orders his people to watch the local animals and see what they eat to supplement their diet with local food.

When the next transport arrives 14 months later, it finds the colonists emaciated but holding on. With incredible food discipline and food gathering, they have managed to maintain a large portion of the food supply they brought with them. Most importantly, by this time, they have identified the local edible plants, which they are now successfully cultivating.

Captain Larson, the transport commander, is reluctant to allow the new colonists to debark. If the new Prime crops fail, the colonists will surely starve. Despite the obvious peril, John Paul insists that they be debarked and that the harvest of the local crops will be successful. Captain Larson relents but insists upon staying until the new crops are harvested.

With the reinforcement of new settlers and the success of the local crops, the colony begins to succeed despite arduous circumstances. Progress with only hand tools is arduously slow, but after the colony becomes self-sufficient in food, efforts are made to advance the colony's technology.

The first step in advancing the colony's technology is to find sources of raw materials for that technology. Minerals, especially iron, must be found. With the colony finally self-sufficient in food, the geologists can be spared from looking for whatever minerals can be found. When iron ore is found, the metallurgists set up a primitive force to repair and build hand tools and start building primitive machines. As other sources of raw materials are found, Prime technology expands far faster than its population.

Once the colony is established, the United States yields to political pressure at home and insists upon allowing non-sect members to immigrate. John Paul opposes this policy, but there is nothing that he can do about it. The Prime colony is still dependent upon the United States. Their fears of being inundated by non-sect members prove groundless. Other than adventurers, few people desire to undergo the privation of a primitive planet where the nights are two weeks long. Even the adventurers, or perhaps because they are adventurers, do not stay long. When they have enjoyed their adventure, they head home. The population of Primus remains overwhelmingly sect-dominated.

With the colony on Primus successfully established, the United States also insisted upon political development as well. The form of government may have changed, but its substance remains the same. John Paul's theocracy is abolished, a constitution is established, and elections are held for a governor and a legislature. The winner of the governorship is John Paul, and sect members hold all the seats in the legislature.

One of the first acts of the newly organized government was to set down a compilation of statutes for the new colony, notwithstanding the guarantee of religion in the constitution of Primus. The statutes of Primus reflect the bias of its population. Dissemination of birth control information is forbidden, as is the artificial uterus. Neither of these laws is the least bit controversial. There is no need at all on the planet for population control, and the artificial uterus is still well beyond the technology of the new colony.

137

Chapter 10

Independence

Jennifer Sullivan sits on the examining table in the doctor's office, waiting for her doctor to arrive. She grows more and more nervous as she waits, finding her fingers in her mouth but resisting the urge to bite her nails. It is just so - so important, she thinks. She and Larry have been married these four years, and though they have tried numerous times, she has not conceived.

Nervously she glances around the room, looking for something to occupy her mind as the time passes. Her eyes go to the simple fluorescent fixture placed on the ceiling directly in the center of the room, the four bare, eggshell white, sterile walls, and the sturdy institutional furniture, barren and cold. When her interest quickly passes from the room's decor, it wanders to her own body. She looks down at the powder blue hospital gown she wears, her bare legs sticking out from beneath the gown and hanging over the edge of the examining table. She watches her breasts heave gently under the gown as she breathes while her street clothes hang lifelessly across the chair where she put them.

The examining room door swings open, and in steps Dr. Saterlee and her nurse, "Hello Jennie, how are you today?"

"Just fine, I hope, Ruth," she answers, anxious over her examination. The two women are friends beyond doctor and patient and have been their husbands, having attended law school together on Earth for some time.

"Worried, huh?" asks Dr. Saterlee empathically.

"Yup, you know how I want children."

"If we were on Earth, we wouldn't have to worry."

"Let's not go through that again. You know my religion forbids the use of the artificial uterus."

Dr. Saterlee looks at her friend for a moment before deciding that her friend is right. This is no place for a religious discussion. "Well, I suppose we'd better take a look. Lay down and put your feet into the stirrups."

Jennifer does as she is asked, unconsciously wringing her hands as she places her feet into the stirrups, afraid her worst fears will materialize, afraid that the doctor will find that she is sterile.

Dr. Saterlee picks up her speculum, inserts it into Jennifer's vagina, snaps on the light, and looks into Jennifer's vagina through the speculum. A chill runs down Dr. Saterlee's spine as she immediately sees a congenital deformity in Jennifer's uterus. She does not say anything, not wishing to alarm her patient before her suspicion is confirmed. Removing the speculum, she inserts a catheter first into Jennifer's vagina and farther into her uterus. The diagnosis is confirmed; Jennifer has an immature uterus, and there is no way that she will ever conceive.

Poor Jennifer, she thinks, trying to think of somehow to break it to her gently. How ironic it is that she who believes in using the artificial uterus is fertile while the woman who doesn't is infertile. If she, Ruth, were found to be infertile, she would simply go to Earth, seed an artificial uterus with a fertilized ovum, and return to pick up her baby nine months later. How would she feel, she wonders, if she wanted children as much as Jennie to be told she was condemned to a life of childlessness. Ruth knows to bear a child doesn't mean as much to her as it does to Jennie. To Jennie, the essence of femininity is the ability to procreate.

"I have bad news for you, Jenny," finally blurts Dr. Saterlee, realizing that there is no way of tenderizing the indigestible.

"Yes, what is it?" snaps Jenny, her face contorted with fear, realizing his worst fears are about to visit her.

"You have an immature uterus - it - is never fully developed. There is no way that you can ever bear a child."

Jennifer receives the news in silence, a dull ache knotting her stomach, unable to grasp the full dimension of what she has just been told.

'There is no chance at all," she whimpers, knowing the question is rhetorical.

"No - none at all."

Jennifer slides off the examining table and reaches for her clothes while Dr. Saterlee turns to leave the room. As Jenny picks up her clothes, a thought flashes through her mind, and she turns to address the doctor, "Ruth, could I have a baby by using the artificial uterus."

Dr. Saterlee hesitates and then turns back to face her patient, "Why yes, of course."

"Would my children inherit my defect?"

"What defect? There is no defect, and your condition is congenital."

"If my mother hadn't carried me, would I have this defect?"

'There are no congenital defects with the artificial uterus."

'Thank you," says Jenny and turns to resume dressing. Dr. Saterlee seeing that her patient has finished asking questions goes to her next patient.

As Jennifer dresses, she has only one thought in her mind, "How - how will I ever tell Larry? How can I tell him I am a failure as a woman?"

As Jennifer sits alone in her house, staring blankly at a point on a wall, waiting in the dark for her husband to come home so that she can give him the news, she hears him open the front door. How different, she wonders. It sounds like it comes from so far away. She does not get up to greet him as she usually does, remaining frozen in her chair.

Larry Sullivan is puzzled when he comes home that night, the lights are off, and the house seems to be empty. When he finds his wife sitting alone in the dark, he doesn't need to be told the news.

"Oh honey, I'm sorry," he says, holding his arms out to her. Slowly she turns her head to look at him, her eyes dead like stagnant pools. When their eyes meet, she understands that he has already figured it out. She doesn't have to tell him. What's more, it doesn't matter; she sees that he still cares for her. As that revelation seeps into her anesthetized brain, her mood brightens, and feeling returns to her limbs. Suddenly she desperately wants to be held and leaps into her husband's waiting arms, the waterworks coursing down her cheeks even before she crushes herself against his chest.

'That's all right, that's all right," he says, "everything will be all right."

Later after Jenny has cried herself out, they sit at the kitchen table and talk. "There is another way," Larry says.

"You mean go to Earth and use the artificial uterus."

"No, I mean, use the artificial uterus right here."

"It is illegal here!" she protests.

"Only because no one has contested the statute."

"What do you mean?"

"I mean that Primus is a colony of the United States, and the constitution of the United States and its constitution guarantees freedom of religion."

"Do you really think that the Prime courts will hold the statute forbidding the use of the artificial uterus unconstitutional?"

"No, I don't, but I am sure the United States Supreme Court will."

"But you know I'm a sect member, and my religion forbids the use of the artificial uterus."

"I know that the artificial uterus is forbidden for all members of The Way and that 90% of them on Earth still use the artificial uterus.

He pauses for a moment to give her a chance to absorb what he said. He continues only when he is certain that she has absorbed it and sees that his words have affected her. "It's up to you, Jenny. There is no point in filing the suit unless you are willing to go through with it. You're the one that will have to state her willingness to depart from catechism in open court.

A few days later, Jennifer, still undecided about what to do, sits at her kitchen table with two of her neighbors. Suddenly she blurts out, "My doctor says I'm sterile!"

The two other women look at her, startled. Both are the same age as Jennie and have young children. "I'm sorry," they chorus together, both realizing the importance of fertility to a woman in Prime society.

"Larry says we can still have a baby."

After a pause, one of them, Nancy, who lives across the street, asks, "Are you emigrating back to Earth then?" a puzzled frown comes across her face.

"No, Larry says we can use the artificial uterus right here."

'The artificial uterus is illegal here," snaps Virginia, who lives down the street.

"Larry says that that law is unconstitutional because it violates the separation between church and state."

The two other women exchange glances incredulously, each unable to believe what she has heard. 'The Way forbids the device," says Virginia sternly. "Man is born of woman, says the scripture. It is our burden, our sacrament."

"I want a baby!" sobs jenny, tears flooding down her cheeks.

Both women feel their hearts go out to Jenny, each wondering how she would feel upon finding that she is sterile. Consciously unaware by asking herself that question, she expresses gratitude that the tables aren't turned. Yet they do not reach out and comfort her, each steeling herself from comforting their friend, aware that the prohibition against the artificial uterus is the prime reason for the colony's existence. Despite their hardened attitudes, each stays to see that their friend is all right. Only when she gains her composure do they return to their homes.

"We can't allow the artificial uterus," argues Debbie, another neighbor who isn't even a member of The Way, at an afternoon bridge party of women who are discussing Jenny's problem. "Look at the women of Earth. Look at what they've become since its invention. They dress like men, act like men, swear like men, compete with men and fornicate with them outside of wedlock. They have no sense of decency or morality - they have lost their femininity.

"Yes," joins Virginia, the other neighbor who consoled Jenny. "Women should be virtuous; we should serve as examples of virtue to men. If we lose our virtue, we lose our femininity."

As each of the women at all of the tables agree, the subject under discussion moves elsewhere.

Later that day, when their husbands come home, the subject re-emerges. The men agree, but not for the same reason. Though they do not say it to their wives, the husband's reasoning has to do with male supremacy, not feminine virtue. Even under the growing number of non-sect members on Primus, there is an overwhelming agreement. The overwhelming majority of citizens on Primus are opposed to what they see as the decline. Both in morality on Earth and the decline in morality there. The artificial uterus is viewed as the chief culprit.

When the suit is filed, it immediately makes headlines in all the Prime papers. Two weeks later, Larry files the papers attacking the constitutionality of the Prime Procreation Laws. Socially the Sullivans are ostracized, and Larry's practice suffers.

When the trial is had, the courtroom is full. Larry calls Jennifer is called to the stand, and there she recants her adherence to The Way. The trial is hard on Jennie, but she persists since she desperately wants a child.

A few months later, the judge hands down his decision. He decides that the Prime Procreation laws are constitutional and that the manner in which Larry has attacked them is procedurally improper. The judge rules that the issue isn't freedom of religion but freedom of procreation, a matter not guaranteed in the constitution. Jennifer Sullivan, he reasons, is free to worship as she chooses and frees even to utilize the artificial uterus if she wishes to travel to Earth.

Larry Sullivan immediately appeals to the Supreme Court of Primus. After the appeals, his law partners call him into a meeting and ask him to drop the suit. When he refuses, he is politely but firmly asked to leave the firm.

Larry leaves the firm and sets up his law practice, where he struggles. More than a year later, the Supreme Court of Primus heard his appeal. Several months later, they upheld the lower court's ruling, commended its "cogent reasoning," and ridiculed the "meritlessness" of the suit.

Undaunted, Larry files a Petition for Writ of Certiorari to the United States Supreme Court. Much to Larry's surprise, it is immediately granted. Much to his surprise, his case is advanced on the calendar, and when Larry travels to Earth, he can't get over the different atmosphere that pervades the community and the courtroom. Where on Primus he had been glared at and treated rudely, here everything is smiles and nods. Everywhere he goes, he is besieged with reporters wanting to talk to him, to get his opinion on everything, including who will win the World Series. When he walks down the steps to the Supreme Court, the crowd automatically parts to allow him through.

When he gives his oral argument, the members of the Supreme Court quietly pay attention and do not barrage him with questions as he expects. Their treatment of the Attorney General of Primus is quite different, they barrage him with questions, and it quickly becomes obvious who is going to win the appeal.

The Supreme Court of the United States hands down its decision within a week, an unheard-of short time for a decision. News of the decision arrives in Primus on the same ship as does Larry Sullivan. His persistence has paid off - he has won! The reasoning put forth by the Prime trial judge and commended by the Prime Supreme Court has been politely set aside by the United States Supreme Court. The court rules that it is religion and religion alone that proscribes the use of the artificial uterus on Primus. They also ruled that the procedural method of challenging the Prime Procreation Laws was proper and that the reasoning of the Prime courts was circular. The safety of the artificial uterus now being well established as far superior to uterine birth, there can be no other reason for its proscription. While the majority on Primus is not required to use the artificial uterus on Primus if they do not wish, neither can they prevent someone from using it.

Larry Sullivan does not remain long in Primus; it is obvious that he cannot earn a living in Primus as an attorney. When he wins the case, a large Washington D.C. firm offers him a job. He returns to Primus only to pick up his wife and return to Earth. Even though Jennifer never had a baby by using the artificial uterus on Primus, the precedent is still established.

When Paul John, now an old man but still the governor of Primus, hears the news, he calls a cabinet meeting. When the cabinet assumed he addresses them, "What shall we do about the United States Supreme Court decision saying we must permit the artificial uterus?"

"We could declare independence," says one of the members.

Henry then turns to the representative of the U.S. Congress, George Ruff, and asks, "What do you think the United States will do if we declare independence?"

Frank Shipley thinks a moment before answering, "I don't think they'd try to subdue us by force - more than likely they would impose economic sanctions."

"Can we survive an embargo Richard?" the governor asks of his economics minister, Richard Adams.

"No," replies Richard immediately, "We are still dependent on Earth for high technology items."

"We can't we manufacture them right here."

"We can, or at least we could if we had the raw materials. The trouble is that many rare earth elements needed to manufacture these products have not yet been found on Primus."

"What do you think, George, will an embargo be effective."

"Embargoes are never effective. If we can't get the supplies we need from the United States, we can get them from another country."

"Just a minute," interrupts Richard Adams, "why to take chances?" Would it be so bad if the artificial uterus were introduced? Few people would use it. As long as it is forced upon us, we are morally blameless. Later, when our economy is more developed, we can declare independence without fear.

Silence fills the cabinet chamber. Paul John glares at Richard Adams, visibly holding back his anger, his face red, his cheeks puffy.

"Excuse me," says George Ruff, "but you gentlemen haven't been to Earth recently. You can't imagine what it is like there now. The women have lost all their femininity and society its decency. Women compete with men, dress like men - many don't even wear bathing suits at the beach anymore."

"Let us remember why we came here. Henry, finally speaks again, glad that he had remained silent through the discussion. He knew from long experience how to get what he wanted in meetings, when to speak, and when to keep his mouth shut, and knew that he would have no trouble getting from them what he wanted.

The artificial uterus corrupted the rest of society and even the members of our own religion. Once the device is permitted, it will slowly and steadily erode our values and our whole society. It is too easy, too convenient. If permitted, it will slowly draw our people down the path to sin and damnation. The next time we consider its abolition, it will be even easier to find a reason to allow it to stay until, before we know it, it has corrupted our whole society. May I have a motion to present a bill of independence to the legislature?"

So moved is the immediate response from several members, immediately followed by even more seconds each member trying to get himself recorded in history as the person who initiated the historic legislation.

The Bill of Independence is duly submitted and almost unanimously passed. As Frank Shipley predicted, the United States does not try to subdue Primus by force but tries economic sanctions instead. As predicted, the economic sanctions prove as watertight as a sieve. The other Earth nations actually compete with each other trying to be the first to open a market on Primus.

Chapter 11

Recolonization

All of the known elements will be found on Primus in a few more years. The Primean economy makes steady progress, and its industry has become capable of manufacturing the most sophisticated equipment.

With independence, Primus' source of colonists is cut off. Since it wants to continue to grow as rapidly as possible, it purchases a small transport from an Earth nation and begins transporting immigrants to Primus. There are only two considerations necessary to fulfill in order to qualify as a colonist to Primus, one must be a practicing member of The Way, and one must be young enough to bear children. As the population of Primus grows, so does its economy. Soon it becomes capable of building its own space transports. As it builds transports, it builds each successively bigger than the last until each one can transport tens of thousands of people, dwarfing the first. As a result of its policy of encouraging large families and immigration, the population of Primus grows by millions each year. However, its population compared to Earth remains tiny.

A few years after Primus successfully declared its independence from the United States, another war broke out on Earth. It isn't a world war due to the destructiveness of modern weaponry; world wars have become obsolete. Instead, it is a local war between the great powers fought by proxy. The great powers don't cause the local war; local grievances cause it. However, when the war breaks out, one of the great powers helps one of the sides in hopes of obtaining a political advantage. The other great power feels compelled to assist the other side. The war lasts longer and is far more destructive.

With the outbreak of war, the great powers ask their colonies in outer space for assistance. Financial assistance is given, but colonial governments resist when the host government starts to conscript. Literally, light years away from their host governments, the colonies aren't in the slightest interested in the petty strife on Earth and see it for what it is. When the host governments insisted on conscription, the other colonies turned to Primus for assistance. When Primus promised military and economic assistance, these colonies also declared independence if needed. Primus is delighted at its new important role in galactic affairs.

Primus stops the war from spreading into outer space with the promise of assistance. Though the whole planet of Primus is much smaller in population than any of the great powers on Earth and no match for them in war, her prowess is sufficient that it could tip the balance to one side or the other, and none of the warring parties wish to alienate her.

Thus ends the period of Earth colonizing outer space. With all of the colonies declaring independence, it is obvious that having a colony in outer space gives no military advantage and only a financial drain to the host country.

The war on Earth brings another benefit to Primus. It produces large numbers of refugees who are more than willing to go to a planet where there is peace. The economy of Primus and her aggressive immigration policies make her by far the most populous of the planets other than Earth. In a short time, these policies and the unified planetary government of Primus allowed her to overtake Earth nations in population and military potential.

The leaders of Primus enjoy the prestige and power that the largest and potentially most powerful force in the galaxy gives them. Yet, at the same time, they realize that the other former space colonies also have unified planetary governments and that eventually, those planets will catch them in population. When they do, the Primean government realizes that the prestige and power of Primus will diminish. In order to ensure the continued pre-eminence of Primus in the universe, she begins her own colonization.

With the aid of her space, fleet Primus explores the unexplored solar systems, locates a series of habitable planets, and begins to colonize them. Unlike the colonization of Primus, these are military-scientific expeditions to find out the biology, climate, geography, and ecology of the planet before colonization. Only when all that is known about the planet that can be known before habitation is the planet colonized

As a result of such planning, the settlers suffered few of the hardships experienced by the first settlers of Primus. Unlike Primus itself, these colonies do not grow rapidly. As soon as Primus begins its own colonization, all the nations of Earth forbid any further emigration to Primus or any of her colonies. Primus, unlike Earth, has a little surplus population to export. These planets have to depend on their own fertility for population growth.

The chief medical officer on the third of the Primean colonies, Plicker, is none other than Dr. Elizabeth Bergman, the daughter of Dr. Saterlee, who told Jennifer Sullivan she was infertile. Although like her mother, Dr. Bergman is a member of the sect., she does not agree with all of its precepts. She has only joined the expedition to this planet because her husband is a career bureaucrat in the Primean civil service and colonial services are the fastest way to promotion. Her main opposition is her support of the artificial uterus. As a doctor, she realizes the safety it offers and its numerous health advantages to both the baby and mother. It appalls her that religious dogma is put ahead of relief from human misery. She has often thought of going to Earth or another Earth colony. She has not done so because of her devotion to her husband and their family. Somehow, she hopes that Primean society will evolve, especially its attitude towards women. When she finds out that Primus is going to develop their own colonies, she sees an opportunity to strike a delayed blow for women's rights.

It is she who convinces her husband if it is a good career move to apply for a lob in one of the colonies. Her husband, Jack, only dimly aware of her true feelings, does not suspect that she has another motive. With a wife who is a doctor, it is not difficult to get an appointment in a colony. The appointment is to the most distant of the new colonies, Plicker. Jack is appointed governor, and she is the chief medical officer. The appointment as the chief medical officer comes without difficulty in this male-dominated society since women dominate the medical profession and, as such, hold diminished prestige.

The rate of development in this newest of Primean colonies is slow because of the shortage of people. Her husband chaffs at the slow growth because he wants to be governor of a more important colony. He writes to the colonial office about the trickle of immigrants and his colony's inability to become self-sufficient. It never occurs to him that the colonial office does not wish Plicker to be self-sufficient.

After some years of not being able to grow as rapidly as he would like, Beth Bergman suggests at breakfast one morning while her husband is raging on about the shortage of workers that it might be possible to speed population growth.

"How so," he asks, interrupting his ranting.

"Artificial insemination," Beth responds casually.

"Artificial insemination violates the procreation laws!" snaps Jack sarcastically

"Not if it is your husband's sperm!" answers Beth without changing her disinterested tone of voice.

Jack pauses, looking up from his breakfast, furrowing his brow. "Why yes, you're right," but later adds, "How will this allow our population to grow faster?"

"It would if most of the babies were girls," says Beth, feigning half interest.

"But who would they marry when they grow up?"

"They would have to share husbands."

"Polygamy is against the law," snaps Jack, rapidly losing his interest.

"Only the secular law!"

Jack pauses a moment to let his wife's words register. "Yes, that's right, and I, with the council's advice, can change that law. Ah, the ruling council would never buy it."

"What if they're already a surplus of females?"

"Well, then they might. But what's the use of talking about it since there isn't a surplus of females."

"Do you think they would buy it if it meant they could have a young, pretty wife?"

"Then I know they would." Jack answers. "But how can you arrange to have a surplus of females?"

"Leave that to me," answers Beth.

"Wait a minute. The clergy would never buy it.'

"I'm not so sure." cajoles Beth. "Remember, many biblical figures had numerous wives.

"And the church has emphasized family life for centuries," adds Jack.

"You know you may be right, and more women on the planet mean the population grows faster," he says and then thinks to himself, and I can be the leader of a bigger and more important colony. "Go ahead, see what you can do to have more girl babies."

After that conversation with her husband, an unwritten policy develops between the government of Plicker and its medical establishment to favor the birth of girl babies. Most of the babies born of artificial insemination are female. When the government sees that Dr. Bergman can really increase the percentage of females, her husband finds ways to encourage fertilization by artificial insemination. The female population of the planet is increasing steadily.

When the girl babies grow up, there is naturally a shortage of marriageable men. Discussing what to do about this problem, Jack Bergman, now the elected president of the planet, suggests changing the law to allow polygamy and submits legislation for that purpose. The law is heavily debated. However, the debate is stilled when the arch-supervisor of Plicker is asked to give an opinion. His opinion ensures that the law passes. He says scripture commands, "Be fruitful and multiply," and further points out that many devout men had numerous wives in the Bible. He rules that scripture not only does not prohibit polygamy but that the church favors family life and has an obligation to find husbands for the numerous young women without them.

The first men on Plicker to take second wives are the ones who can most afford it, the men who passed the laws legalizing it. The older wives first resent the younger wives, but there is nothing they can do about it. They quickly find that there are mitigating factors. The older wives, being first wives, have seniority over the younger wives and can order them about. The younger wives are made to pay for the husband's sexual attention in many small ways.

While all Primean planets are male-dominated, women still have the right to vote. When Jack Bergman retired as president of Plicker that he won after Plicker was permitted self-rule. A new election is held. At this election, Jack Bergman's daughter, Brenda, springs from the trap her mother laid many years before. She is running for president.

Without the backing of an existing political party and being a woman, Brenda Bergman is given little chance. The political pundits forget two things. She has the name recognition of the first governor and later president of the planet, and she is a female running in a now predominantly female electorate. When the votes are tallied, Brenda Bergman easily wins. After she is installed as president, she can do little to chance for a lot of women on the planet since she has no support in the legislature. She governs the planet well. When she runs again, she runs as the head of the women's party. There is a woman running for office for every other elective office on the planet. Though the male politicians spend a fortune to unseat her, it does them no good. The electorate is now overwhelmingly female, and not only does she win re-election, but her party wins control of the legislature.

The first change that Brenda wishes to make is to abolish the Primean Procreation Laws prohibiting the artificial uterus, but such a repeal would immediately cause a confrontation with the Primean government, a confrontation she can't hope to win. Instead of attempting such overaction, she tries a more subtle approach. Instead of repealing the Procreation Laws, artificial uteruses are surreptitiously imported into the planet, and the Procreation Laws are not enforced.

The women of Plicker quickly catch on, and the use of the artificial uterus grows quickly. However, subtle Brenda's approach to the artificial uterus, the reports to the Primean government become so numerous that the Primean government sends an investigation team. When the reports are found to be true, the Primean government orders all artificial uteruses seized and destroyed.

By covertly permitting the use of the artificial uterus, Brenda Bergman has consolidated her leadership on Packer and bought time. Time to develop her planet, increase its population, and open diplomatic channels with other planets and governments of Earth who are unfriendly to Primea. When ordered to confiscate the artificial uteruses, the Plickerean legislature declared independence.

Faced with the defiance of Plicker, the Primean government could either recognize Plicker's independence or suppress the insurrection by force. Believing it possible that if Plicker declares independence, other colonies will dare the same, the Primean government decides to suppress the revolt. A space fleet is quickly assembled and sent to Plicker. Enroute, it is intercepted by a much larger fleet of space vessels from Earth and a combination of other planets that are unfriendly to the rapid growth of Primea. They are only too happy to cause a setback in its rapid growth. Outnumbered and outgunned, the hastily assembled Primean fleet has no choice but to back down.

After Plicker receives its independence, a bitter political debate rages on Plicker. On one side of the debate are those who wish now to equalize the sex ratio of the planet. With the use of the artificial uterus, the population can grow rapidly without a disproportionate number of women. The other side correctly points out that this really is not quite true, the real drawback being the number of people to care for the children, not merely to bear them. Never in the history of mankind has there ever been any society where men have cared for the children.

The women are badly split on whether to restore a 1:1 sex ratio. Generally, the older women want the sex ratio restored; they do not like the changes that have occurred among the young people since the sex ratio changed. The younger women are split, they have grown up under polygamy, and for them, it seems normal. They also know that for them, it will make no difference since there will never be enough men for them. The younger women are afraid that the old male-dominated government may return if the sex ratio equalizes again. Other women disagree, and they want for their daughters what they didn't have themselves, a husband of their own. The political experts expect a victory for equality of sex ratio by a small margin.

When the votes are counted, the ratio of stays the same. While the women were arguing amongst themselves, they forgot that men still have the vote even though they had ceased to be a political force. At the same time, the women were split over gender equality; men weren't. The men love the advantage of a surplus of women and virtually unanimously vote to retain the sex ratio.

Chapter 12

Evonia

Ron Rutter - awakens in his bed on this the most fateful day of his life, the day that will set the pattern for him for the rest of his life. He looks around the room at his two brothers, who aren't his brothers; they aren't even related to him. He just calls them his brothers because they are part of his family. There is a slight possibility that one of them might have the same biological father, but the odds against that are infinitely remote. He catches them looking back and immediately looks away as he looks at them, averting their eyes in a silent understanding of what their day means.

Out of bed, he slips into his juvenile kilt, its distinctive plaid design required wearing appeal for- Evonian males, slips on his shoes and socks, and goes to the bathroom. Evonian men wear no underwear, and it is considered unappealing. As usual, the bathroom is busy occupied by one or the other of Ron's numerous sisters - who aren't his sisters, although he does have a couple of half-sisters. After waiting a few minutes for the bathroom, he slips inside, urinates, washes his hands and face, and goes downstairs for breakfast.

At the huge breakfast table are Ron's mother, stepmother, brothers, and sister having their breakfast while another stepmother fixes it for them. There are 21 people in the family. One father - who isn't Ron's father - one mother, four stepmothers, and 18 children,

13 girls and three boys. Ron has to wait his turn, and there isn't enough room at the table for him to sit down and eat yet.

Pancakes are being served this morning; Ron likes pancakes though he has to wait a while to get enough to eat. As he sits at the breakfast table waiting for his breakfast, Georgia, one of his half-sisters, knowing the importance of this day, can't help but needle him. Today's the big day, isn't it?" she says with more than a bit of sarcasm in her voice.

"Yup," answers Ron trying not to show any emotion lest she see she is getting to him.

"Snip, snip, cut, cut," she says, hoping for a reaction.

"Tonight, you'll be walking bowlegged chimes in another girl who has figured out what they are talking about from the context of the conversation.

A guffaw breaks out from the other girls, who think this is terribly funny.

"Stop that," orders Donna, Ron's natural mother. "Ron has enough to worry about today without picking on him."

The girls are shocked at her intervention, as is Ron, who looks at her queerly, glad of her intervention but puzzled by it. It is unlike her. It is unlike an Evonian mother to side with a son. Why should she intervene on my behalf? Could it be she is proud of me that I want to pass the test, unlike most other boys? Still, even though I want to pass the test, the odds are against me, so very few pass. My sister is probably right, and I will probably fail.

Oh, if only I'd been born a girl, I wouldn't have to take the test. I could continue my education as a matter of right. Girls are so lucky; they have so many advantages over boys. Why is it that women are smarter than men and have leadership ability as well?

Most of my friends don't feel that way; they feel it is advantageous to be born a male. Girls have to work for a living, to support themselves and their families, while men just keep themselves beautiful and save their energy for their wives. A man has five wives all to himself, but a woman has to share a husband with four other women.

Why does this have to be? Why do only women work while men just keep themselves lovely? Why can't men work too? I'm not like the other boys; I enjoy schoolwork, and I'm smart. Why can't I have a career like the women? Why do just boys have to take the Synthetics Test?

I am the smartest boy in my class, but how would I fare against the girls? I know it will be harder; girls are so much smarter than boys. I heard once that boys and girls used to go to school together and that girls were not smarter than boys then, but that is hard to believe. If women aren't smarter, why is it that they are in charge? Men are bigger and stronger. If women aren't smarter, how did they get in power? Somehow, I am still going to have to try to compete in a woman's world.

I am the only one I know who will admit he wants to pass the test. Perhaps there are others who also want to pass the test, but if they do, they won't admit it. Perhaps they are protecting themselves in case they fail.

Is it really better to pass the test? My friends think not. If one fails the test, one becomes a vasecta with the right to marry five women who will support him. If one passes the test, one becomes a paterna and can only have one wife.

Still, there are advantages to being a paterna. A paterna is financially independent, and he doesn't have to ask his wives to spend money. The biggest advantage, though, is the ability to continue my education. I want to know more about the world, about books, science, and literature. I detest the hedonistic lifestyle of the vasecta. There is more to life than drinking, gambling, and sleeping with wives.

There is the other advantage to being a paterna, one that vasecta never mentions. Vasecta cannot propagate themselves. The very names paterna and vasecta denote what they are: paternal for paternity, fatherhood, and vasecta for vasectomized, sterilized. Paternity means relatively little since, except in exceptional cases, not even paterna know their own children - but at least one knows one's seed is passed.

After breakfast, Ron takes the automatic to school, where he and his classmates board a bus to take them to the testing center in a distant city. Arriving at the test center, Ron sees hundreds of boys all waiting to take their test. Milling around waiting for directions, Ron listens to the conversation of those around him. Most are complaining about having to take the test when they have no intention of passing. Ron hears a lack of conviction in their voices.

In a short time, the employees, all-female, of the testing center come out to direct the boys in. These employees are dressed in uniforms that signify their rank. Ron and the other boys are allowed to find their own seats.

After the boys are seated, one of the guards picks up a loudspeaker and announces that those who do not wish to take the test can be excused. Ron's head swivels to see which of his classmates will disqualify him. About half of the boys do, a far less number than said they wanted to fail. Ron says to himself, Eureka, now I will finally find out which other boys want to fail.

When the boys who wish to fail have left the room, the guards start handing out the tests and pencils to go with them. The guard admonishes the boys not to open their booklets, or they will immediately be disqualified. Inside the book is an answer sheet.

After distributing the booklets, the guard tells the boys to open their booklets to the first page. Ron opens his booklet and finds a page of instructions. He begins reading the instruction page while the guard with the loudspeaker reads it aloud. When she finishes reading the instructions, she asks if there are any questions. She tells the boys to turn the page and begin the test when the questions are answered.

Ron turns the page and attacks the test; it is exactly the kind of test he had hoped for, a test of accumulated knowledge. He engrosses himself in the test and speeds through it.

Halfway through the test, Ron feels tired and suddenly wonders how everyone else is doing. He lifts his head and looks around the room to discover everyone else, including many who said they wanted to fail, completely engrossed in the test. Ron realizes that he is wasting valuable time and dives back into the test.

Abruptly the guard with the loudspeaker orders everyone to stop. Ron is nowhere near finished despite his very rapid pace - or so he thought. He thinks about finishing the question he is on but doesn't; he want to take no chance of being disqualified.

The test is completed, and the boys are marched into an adjoining room where they are ordered to undress. The boys undress while the guards look on. The boys resent being forced to undress in front of women. On Evonian planets, women are dominant; it is the men who are modest, ashamed of their sex. The guards ogle as the boys undress, pointing and laughing even though they see naked boys every day. The boys, in turn, notice their effect on the guards and tease the guards with their nudity.

As the game between the boys and the guards goes on, Ron can't help but compare the pretty boys to the guards in their loose-fitting khaki uniforms. Women are so homely, he thinks, compared to the statuesque male, their short stature, floppy breasts, wide hips, and shortly cropped hair compared to the long mane a man keeps. No wonder they find us so attractive.

When the boys are all naked, they are marched before doctors, again female, for their physicals. Ron knows that this is an important part of the test, for it does not matter how well one does on the intelligence test. If one fails here, one fails everything.

As the boys finish their physical, they are directed to another room where they sit naked on benches waiting for something to happen. Ron knows he will not be given back his old clothing as he waits. The clothing he has worn up till now denotes a juvenile, indicating he is underage and therefore probably still fertile. There is a severe penalty for a juvenile to wear not juvenile clothing. A woman might seduce him and finds herself pregnant, not realizing that he is still fertile. Women who are foolish enough to seduce a juvenile take their chances.

Ron knows that if he passes the test, he will be issued a long ankle-length paterna skirt. If he fails, he will be issued the shorter vasecta kilt with the bachelor design, denoting he has less than five wives. When he has the maximum of five wives, he will have to buy a new kilt with a married man's design indicating that he has the required five wives and is therefore not available.

If he is not selected as a paterna, Ron knows he will have to be careful. Women are always trying to seduce young men, trying to get sex without marrying them. While this is not illegal, it is self-defeating since, without wives, men cannot support themselves. It is, therefore, very important to marry early and have as many wives as possible to have sufficient income. For a vasecta, to have to work is the ultimate disgrace.

Sometimes some vasecta sell themselves for money. These men threaten the other vasecta and have to be protected. If the other vasecta gets a hold of him, he will be emasculated. They are a threat to the other vasecta's well-being.

The other crime against vasecta is stealing another man's wife. Divorce is easy for a man or woman; it can be accomplished merely by a public declaration. Men divorcing their wives is extremely rare since it means a loss of income. Women divorcing their husbands is much more common though done reluctantly since it is always difficult to find another husband, especially as long as the previous husband has less than five wives. There have been numerous cases where men had taken on divorced wives before the old husband replaced her and found himself waylaid and castrated. When that happens, the wives of the castrate easily find new mates. It is the only exception to divorced women easily finding a new mate before their husband does.

Castration is punishable by death if caught, and the law is vigorously enforced. However, vigorously the government enforces it, the government is unsuccessful in stamping it out. The issue is essential to the economic survival of the vasecta, and seldom does anyone willingly consent to be a witness. Even women are reluctant to testify or help the police since they find themselves divorced and unable to find a new husband when they do.

It is not long before the boys are ushered into an empty room with one guard and two doors. Inside, the guard asks Ron his name and opens one of the doors. Ron hesitatingly walks through arid finds on the other side a guard issuing clothing, long paterna skirts - he has passed!

After he has dressed, he and the other men who have been selected as paterna are led to another room. Here they wait for quite some time. Ron thinks this is odd and can't imagine why this is so. He wants to get back to his family and show them his new clothing.

Finally, the door at the far side of the room opens, and a small group of well-dressed women comes into the room. The first one into the room is obviously in charge. She does not look around her but immediately and confidently strides forward to all the young paterna ordered to stand at attention. As the woman in charge gets closer, she looks familiar. Ron has seen her picture before, and then he remembers who it is. It is the president of the planet. What is she doing here, Ron wonders? The woman walks in front and behind the young paterna studying them carefully.

After doing so, she says matter-of-factly, "Have them strip."

"Strip," yells the guard with the loudspeaker, and the young men strip again.

Once again, Madame President walks among the young men studying their musculature and genitalia. Finally, without giving any indication if she what, she wanted or if she had found what she was looking for, she whispers something to her aide and strides confidently towards the door, and promptly leaves. The aide goes to the guard in charge, whispers something to her, and then hurries to catch up to her boss.

When the boys finish dressing, the head guard comes over to Ron, taps him on the shoulder, and says follow me. She takes him outside where the automatic transport is waiting. The automatic transport's destination already programmed speeds off as soon as the door is closed.

The automatic pulls up in front of a large mansion, one that Ron recognizes from Evonian currency; it is the Presidential Mansion. It is then that he realizes that she has selected him for some purpose though he cannot imagine what. Why have I been brought here? What does she want with me?

When the automatic transport comes to rest, one of the guards reaches out and opens the door for Ron to get out. As Ron gets out, he asks the guard, "This is the presidential mansion, isn't it."

"Yes," answers the guard.

"What does Madame President want of me?" asks Ron.

Ron's only answer is a wry smile.

As they reach the front door of the presidential mansion, a brightly dressed guard in a military uniform automatically opens the door. As he enters, they find one of Madame President's aides sitting waiting.

As soon as Ron enters, the aide stands up and says, "I'll take over from here."

"Yes, ma'am," answers the guard and returns to her station.

"Follow me, please," says the aide to Ron.

Ron follows the aide direct, but he does not admire the splendid hail with its marbled floor, marble Corinthian columns, and huge winding staircase. They ascend the stairs, walk down a long hall, and into one of the rooms. Inside, Ron finds himself in a large bedroom tastefully decorated with a handmade wallpaper depicting scenes from Evonian history, a huge four-postered bed matched with period furniture, and a hand-stitched rug.

"Please wait here," Madame President will be up shortly.

Ron props himself down in one of the ornate chairs, overwhelmed by this day and everything that has happened in such a short time. After a short time, the bedroom door opens, and Madame President slides through the door dressed in a hand-tailored suit.

"Hello Ron," she says, smiling as she closes the door behind her; "Pretty big day for you, isn't it."

"Yes, ma'am."

"Please don't call me that."

"What's that, ma'am?"

"Ma'am," she answers in a more commanding voice. "When you call me ma'am, you make me feel old."

Ron's tongue catches in his throat. He was going to say - but you are old but thinks better of it. "What shall I call you?" he asks.

"My name is Winnifred. Call me Winnie."

"Yes, ma'am, I mean Winnie."

"My assistant tells me that you have some questions for me."

"What am I doing here?" he asks, a frown crossing his face.

"Well, you certainly don't beat around the bush," she says, stalling for the time that will express her feelings towards him in just the right way. After a few seconds of pregnant pause, she decides the simplest way is to blurt out her feelings. "I find you very attractive," she says, smiling as she lays her hand across his thigh.

Ron's jaw drops to the floor, and his eyes pop out of his head. What incredible good fortune, he tells himself, both frightened and excited at the same time. It takes a few seconds for Ron's intellect to catch up with his emotions. "What about your husband?" he asks but does not remove her hand.

"I don't have a husband," she answers.

"I - I don't understand," Ron asks, puzzled and more than a little afraid.

"I divorced my last husband,"

"Why -ah— did you divorce your last husband?" now, more than a little afraid, worried about what could happen to him if he allowed himself to be seduced by another man's wife, especially if she is the president.

Her first impulse Is to tell him that it is none of his business, but she resists the impulse to realize that, given the nature of things in Evonian society, it really is his business. "He embarrassed me politically," she finally answers matter-of-factly.

"How - how did he embarrass you?" Ron asks.

"He drank too much at a formal reception."

"Ha - has he remarried?"

She looks at him, half-smile, half-smirk, "No, he hasn't, but you needn't worry; he will remarry quickly. Paterna has no difficulty finding wives, and you needn't worry about retribution; that only happens with vasecta."

What she says makes sense, but Ron immediately has new doubts about replacing the old, "How - how many times have you been married?"

Her head snaps to look at him after the impertinence of that question, her first instinct to smite such impertinence, but she remembers that she is not, in this instance, his president but his suitor and that, secondly, it is a natural question. She decides the time has come to force the issue and slowly moves her hand under the hem of his kilt. "I have been married twice before.

My first husband was a vasecta, and when I grew more successful and able to support a husband on my own, my second was a paterna

Ron stiffens when her hand reaches the bare shin under his kilt, not knowing what to do next, afraid that she might be taking advantage of him, that she might discard him with the morning's trash, or if he rejects her, he might lose the opportunity of a lifetime and becoming excited as well.

"Relax," says Winnie as her hand reaches the inside of his thigh, I didn't bring you here to take advantage of you, "I brought you here to be my next husband."

Ron does as he is told but has a difficult time relaxing because no one has ever done this to him before but also realizes that he does not understand the rules of existence for paterna, only for vasecta.

Ron winces as Winnie reaches the apex of his thighs and the object of her passion. He has long been hard anticipating her slow, methodical approach. Ron leans back on the bed while Winnie pulls back his skirt to get a better look at his genitals. While she teases him, Ron looks at her for the first time sexually. For some reason, it hasn't occurred to appraise her sexually before. Her dark brown hair is cut short, parted on the side, and combed back into a wave in the convenient feminine fashion. Her breasts and hips are small but well proportioned; she is tall for a woman. She is quite attractive for her age, a few age lines, but she wears them well - but then women age so much more gracefully than men.

She knows from experience that he is ready for her and stands up to undress, taking off her clothes in front of him. At last, she thinks she will have what she has been thinking about all day long as she undresses, he disinterested watches her. When she is naked, she kisses him deeply on the mouth while positioning her body above his in the traditional Evonian position for sex. Positioned about him, she reaches back for his penis and places it at the entrance to her vagina. Properly positioned, she simply sits down on him. She is well moistened, her faster female lust well ahead of his; she glides over him, swallowing him completely. She then moves slowly up and down upon him, flexing her pubic muscles and caressing his cock with the walls of her vagina.

She climaxes first with jerks and spasms that start in her vagina and run through her entire body. When she finishes climaxing, he still has not climaxed, but she is a practiced lover and knows that men take longer than women, so she pulls off him, and with one hand on his testicles and the other on his penis, she gently and carefully strokes him until he also comes.

Once she comes, she rolls over and falls into a sexually satiated sleep. Ron feels, despite his first seduction, that somehow romantically, something is missing - It is something he will learn to accept but never become accustomed to, for women are just not as romantic as men.

The next morning Ron awakens late. Madame President has long since left the house. He puts on his shirt, skirt, shoes, and socks and picks up his purse. Evonian men don't have pockets because it detracts from the lines of their bodies and leaves the bedroom.

The butler, who has been listening for his sounds inside the room, opens the door and asks him what he wishes for breakfast. When he asks what she has, she only smiles and suggests, "Perhaps you would like steak and eggs."

Ron responds, "Yes, that would be nice."

"Would you like it served in the dining room?" comes the next question.

"Ah - yes," he answers, unnerved by the fact that he is giving orders to a woman.

After the servant leaves, he wanders around the house, looking for the dining room. Apparently, when he is late, the word spreads to be looking for him among the servants because one of the housemaids sees him and escorts him to the dining room. Ron attacks his breakfast with more than his usual hunger feeling uneasy because he is not used to having someone watch him while he is eating. "Would you like more?" the servant asks him when he finishes.

"No, thank you," he responds, adding. "Is there someone who can show me the house?"

"Would you permit me so, sir?"

"Of course."

"Just a moment while I get someone to clean up in here."

The butler proceeds to commence showing Ron around the house. When he comes to a room full of books, he asks, "What is this room?"

"This is a library," she answers, puzzled, unaware that there are no libraries in the boys' school.

When they finish their tour, Ron asks, "What do I do now?"

The butler gives him a peculiar look and answers, "Why whatever your please, sir.

Ron pauses a moment to think about the tour and reflects back on the room that intrigued him, "I'll be in the library."

Ron wanders back to the library, which he has a little difficulty finding again. Inside the library, he has no idea what to do with himself, so he begins picking out books at random and paging through them. After a while, he sees a very large book entitled History of Evonian civilization. Intrigued by the book, he opens it and begins reading. In what seems like only a few moments, a servant interrupts him and says, "Madame would like you to meet her for lunch."

Ron leaves the book open on the library table and allows the servant to escort him back to the dining room. "How are you today, Ron," she asks as she enters the room.

"Just fine," he answers, his head swiveling around, unaware of what should happen next.

"I understand that you've found the library," she says, obviously pleased to find that was where he had been.

"Yes," he answers, wondering if anything goes on in the mansion that she is not aware of.

"What have you been doing in the library?"

"Reading."

"Yes, but what have you been reading," she asks in much the same tone as she would use on a small child.

"A History of Evonian Civilization," he answers dutifully, irked at having his privacy pierced.

He immediately looks away from her avoiding her eyes, wishing to keep his thoughts private because he doesn't know what has attracted him to the book. "Just curious," he answers.

Madame President, not a brilliant woman but an astute judge of human nature, recognizes his evasive reaction and realizes he does not wish to tell her. "I should like to tell you something," she says, changing the subject. "I am a busy woman and will not often be able to have lunch with you as I would like. I am only having lunch with you today because I am concerned that you will settle in here. I want you to be happy here."

He stares at her, understanding what she has said but not knowing how to respond. "Will we have supper together? He finally blurts out for lack of anything better to say.

"We will indeed," she answers, "today and most days."

"Ah - good," Ron answers awkwardly.

"Have you been back to visit your family yet?" she asks rhetorically.

"Ah — no."

"Why don't you go back to visit your family? I'm sure your mother is worried about you and wondering what has happened to you. You have much to tell them."

"That's a good idea."

"You'll have to be accompanied by a Presidential Guard when you go. You'll have to be accompanied by a Presidential Guard wherever you go.

That afternoon Ron goes home to visit his family. The whole neighborhood is astonished when the automatic presidential transport drives up to his old house and even more astonished when Ron gets out of the car wearing his paterna skirt and accompanied by a presidential guard. He spends the afternoon telling his family that he is there about what has happened to him. Ron enjoys the occasion enormously; it is the first time in his life that his sisters treat him with other than their usual disdain. On, Ron picks up his few belongings late afternoon and returns to the Presidential Mansion by suppertime.

At supper, Madame President asks, "Did you visit your family this afternoon?"

"Yes, I did," Ron answers.

"I imagine they were pretty impressed."

"Yes, they certainly were."

"Have you thought about what you will do with yourself in your free time?"

"I was told that if I became a paterna, I could continue my education."

"Very good," she responded, pleased with his response, "I will have you enrolled in paterna preparatory school."

"Paterna preparatory school?" he asks.

"Yes, our boys' schools are sadly lacking in academic standards. The girls your own age are well ahead of you in their education."

Seeing he still is puzzled, she continues, "The purpose of paterna preparatory school is to help the boys so that they can catch up with the level of the girls at the same age."

"Why - why do that?"

Madame President laughs when she hears the question; she has forgotten how things must appear to Ron. "Paterna and girls all go to the same schools," she explains.

"Will I be able to keep up with them?" he asks.

Madame President smiles, continually amused at the misconceptions of the general populace. "Yes, Ron, I have seen your I.Q. scores, and you will be able to keep up quite easily."

Observing that he is satisfied with her answer, she changes the subject. "Tonight, there will be a diplomatic dinner party, and you will attend as my fiancé. I had you enrolled as my husband this afternoon. Remember what you do and say as my husband reflects upon me. You must be on your best behavior and above all don't drink too much, that is what happened to my last husband. Do you understand?"

"Yes, ma'am,' he answers, and when she holds up a finger, she corrects himself, "Yes, Winnie."

"This afternoon, I would like you to buy some formal clothing so that you look beautiful for the diplomatic reception tonight. I want to show you off. Linda," she says, pointing to the butler, "will accompany you and pay the bills. You needn't worry about the cost."

Ron spends the afternoon as requested, buying fashionable and expensive paterna clothing and spending time at the beauty parlor having his mane elaborately coiffured. At the dinner party, he does his best to engage in small talk with so many women who are older and wiser than he.

Ron makes a favorable impression at the party. Words like adorable, darling, sweet and pretty are often used. Though Madame President does not deride these characteristics, she insists that she has chosen her mates for their affability and intellect. Her contemporaries accept these comments with more than a little bit of skepticism.

Present at the party is the husbands of these important women. While they show him fawning courtesy as soon as he turns his back, they deride his youthful good looks. The several times he tries to engage other husbands in conversation, he receives little more than polite acknowledgments. One of Ron's hopes is to find another older paterna to befriend him and instruct him on what is expected of him; he quickly realizes that that will not happen.

When the dinner party is over, Madame President compliments him on his behavior and, mildly inebriated herself, takes him to bed, where she makes brief but passionate love to him. After satisfying herself, she forgets to satisfy him and, when completed, rolls over and immediately falls asleep, leaving him unsatisfied sexually and romantically.

Thus, does the marriage of Madame President develop; they eat two meals a day together, breakfast and supper. They also try to spend time together during the evening. As promised, Ron is enrolled in a paterna school, which Ron will discover later, including all of the newly selected paterna.

The new school is completely unlike the other school he attended. Here the students are not lazy and disinterested. These students are not only intelligent but also highly motivated. The teachers progress through their material faster than Ron had thought possible. For the first time in his life, he has to study to keep up. He does find that Madame President was right; he has no difficulty keeping up and remains the top student in his class. Notwithstanding the greater time spent on classwork Ron still finds time for studies on his own.

As he learns more about the history of his planet, he finds that what he has been brought up to believe about society really isn't true. Neither is it false. The history and society that he has been taught have merely been simplified, and with that simplification came distortion. It was true that the first colonists of Evonia were colonists from Primea, now Evonia's greatest enemy. What he didn't know is that when the first Evonian planet, Plicker, was founded, the society that existed was male-dominated, incredible as that seems to him. Instead of the women working, the men worked, and the women stayed home and took care of the children. What Ron finds hardest to believe is that in this early society, it was the women who were regarded as the alluring sex, and it was the women who wore the inconvenient hairstyles, the inconvenient garments designed not for their practicality but for their allure. Ron finds this the hardest to grasp that women would be regarded as more alluring than men. The idea seems so absurd.

It isn't the difference between the two societies that most fascinates Ron. The more Ron reads, the more curious he becomes; how did a male-dominated society transform itself into a female-dominated society? How did the larger, stronger males lose control over the weaker, smaller females? Ron reads how Beth Bergman laid a trap for the unwitting males when she tricked them into allowing more girls to be born than males, but that still does not explain how the males lost control and became mere drones whose sole purpose was mating.

As Ron reads on in the history of Devonian, he realizes that the trap Brenda Bergman laid was not to diminish the role of males; it was only intended to elevate the role of women. Even though Brenda Bergman's intent was only to free women from servitude, how she did it was by increasing the number of women and women voters. She thought that when her revolution was successful, the normal 1:1 relationship between men and women would be restored. It was there she made her mistake. Once they gained political ascendancy, the women were reluctant to give control back to the men for fear the old ways would return, and the men were quite content with a surplus of women.

What Brenda never anticipated, what no one could have anticipated, is what happened to the men when there was a surplus of women and women were in control. The older men raised to believe that a man was responsible for providing for his family did not change their ideas, but the younger boys raised in a sea of women found that they did not have to chase girls. With the oversupply of girls, the girls, if they wanted boys, would have to pursue those boys. Almost overnight, the male instead of the female became regarded as the alluring sex. With that transformation, the styles followed. Instead of the male clothing and style being convenient and simple, the female clothing and styles became convenient and simple, and the male clothing and style of dress became inconvenient and fashionable. The girls began to cut their hair short and wear exclusively pants while the boys grew their hair long, coiffured it, and wore clothing that allowed them to show as much skin as was decent. The kind of clothing within a short time- reversed, boys wore skirts with open-fronted shirts to show their legs and chests while women wore the convenient pants and shirts. At the same time, men took up carrying purses because they didn't want bulging pockets to destroy the fashionable lines of their clothing.

The reversal of the sex roles from aggressor to submissive also caused other dramatic changes. With the girls now the aggressor, they had to make money to take the boys out. The old male ethic that a man's responsibility was to support his family disappeared within one generation. The first generation of men worked after the sex ratio changed worked but after that, when a man had five wives to work for him, it became a disgrace for him to work. His job was to save his energy to please his wives.

A transformation less dramatic than the male also took place in the women's minds. A machine filled the function of childbirth; the women no longer saw their fulfillment in raising a family. They were required to pursue the male or be left out. They also realized the need to support him. The younger women looked to work and a career for their fulfillment, just as their fathers had.

The most dramatic transformation of the female took place in her regard for the male. Raised in a world where their fathers worked to support the family, the younger men weren't interested in working; they were only interested in keeping themselves beautiful.

With the men no longer working, the younger women ceased respecting men. These men were so lazy that they would do nothing outside of making love to their wives. They wouldn't take care of the children or even keep the house. As a result, after two generations of female domination of the planet, the women regarded men as mere drones, beautiful and sexy but worthless.

After two generations, the transformation of society is almost complete. The one thing that both sexes are agreed upon is that it is the male that is the alluring sex, that his sole purpose for existing is to give pleasure to the female.

The older generation, appalled at the younger generation's attitude, cannot understand how young men have such low opinions of themselves to allow their wives to support them and do nothing to assist them. The older women cannot understand their daughters' willingness to allow their husbands to sponge off them like that: How can you respect your husband when he is dependent on you?

Even though the older generation cannot understand the attitudes of the youth, it is perceived that it is the sex ratio that has caused this abrupt and startling change. The older generation decided that it was time to restore the sex ratio and prepared an amendment to the effect the constitution of the planet that the sex ratio must be 1 to 1. In order to change the constitution, however, a plebiscite is required. All of the political leaders favor the amendment, yet when it goes to vote, it fails. The younger generation is far more numerous than, the older generation and does not understand their values. The young women know that this change will not benefit them since the sex ratio for their age group will never change, and they think it is foolish to increase the number of worthless, lazy males who will just have to be supported by their wives. The young men, content with being the alluring sex and having their wives support them, have no desire to change. The youth of the planet vote heavily against the amendment; it fails.

The older generation, who have all the political leaders on the planet, take another tack. Instead of having an amendment to guarantee a 1:1 ratio, they quietly move to change the ratio with a law guaranteeing it. Once again, they are frustrated that the young people naturally discover it and organize a plebiscite to retain the sex ratio at 5:1.

The social reorganization of the planet is now almost complete. The status of men is about the fall some more. The lazy boys knowing they will always have women to support them, become disinterested in their schoolwork and disrupt the classroom making it difficult for the girls to learn. In order to rectify the problem, the government abolishes co-education. The solution rectifies the problem, but the education of males becomes even more dismal, and the social standing of men falls with it.

The status of men has now fallen so low that mothers aren't interested in having boys, whereas the problem used to be that no one wanted girls. When the sex ratio falls even below 5:1, the government intervenes and orders that every fifth baby must be a boy, although it does guarantee that no mother has to raise more than one boy.

It has taken only two generations for this once religious society not only to adopt the artificial uterus but also to completely reverse its social relationships so that women are in total control of all aspects of society: political, economic, and social. Now that men have become mere drones, the women see no reason why these almost useless creatures should not become responsible for birth control. When the wives complete their families, they begin demanding that the husband have a vasectomy. The husband is dependent upon his wife for support and has no choice but to acquiesce. After a short time, vasectomy of the husband becomes standard practice.

Finally, women have such low esteem for men that they see no reason why their children need to be offspring of their husbands. Why not obtain sperm from superior men so that their children will also be superior. In most cases, the women prefer that their husband not be the father. They believe that the sperm banks can find a better sperm donor for their children than they can and buy the sperm rather than use their husbands. This becomes such common practice that eventually, it is discovered that a sperm bank is not using sperm of superior donors but, in fact, is using sperm from the cheapest source. Naturally, the government steps in to guarantee the quality of this most important commodity.

The government then commences the classification of men as to whether or not they are fit to produce offspring. Since men are capable of literally producing millions of sperm with each ejaculation, the government needs only a few thousand men to ensure an adequate supply of sperm. These men are paid substantial sums of money to sell their sperm. Careful records are kept to prevent inbreeding.

Thus the men are classified into two categories: paterna for fertile and a sperm donor and vasecta for sterile. Another problem develops when the women have no way of telling which is which, which are sterile, and which are not. When several unsuspecting women seduce a man and become pregnant because the paterna she slept with did not tell her he was still fertile, strict laws are passed which require paterna and vasecta to dress differently so that the woman knows which is which. If a woman wishes to sleep with a paterna, she can, but she takes her chances. If a man wears vasecta clothing and impregnates a woman, he is castrated.

Another aspect of the new law is that young women generally do not wish to marry paterna for fear of getting pregnant. Thus, the men who choose to become paterna have only older women to marry who have already had all their children and are willing to accept the burdens of contraception or have passed through the change of life. This does not present a serious problem because there is an ample supply of rich, older women who divorce their vasecta husbands to have younger paterna males of their very own.

When it develops is that rich women have a single husband all to themselves, the poorer women are in an uproar. They demand the law be enforced and enforce the rule of five wives to each husband. The government balks at enforcing the law for two reasons. First, the rich women being rich have a great deal of political power. Second, how is a paterna going to service five wives and still produce sperm for the sperm banks? In the end, common sense prevails, and the law is amended to permit a 1:1 marriage if the husband is a paterna.

Ron Rutter is amazed at the revelations of the History of Evonian Civilization. It is not as he thought; men have not been suppressed by the more clever female. In truth, they are no more clever and, in some ways, inferior. In fact, under Evonian law, men hold almost the same rights that women do. They can still vote though they seldom do. The only way that men are treated differently is that they go to school separately, and those who do not learn to the level of the average female are forcibly sterilized.

After finishing the book and finding out how men have come to occupy such a low level of esteem in Devonian, Ron spends several days thinking about how he can raise the level of men to their previous esteem. Perhaps some insignificant change now to alter the sex ratio will cause dramatic changes in a generation or two in the same manner as the trap laid by Brenda Bergman. Realizing that the trick is to equalize the ratio between the sexes so that men cannot depend on women to support them, he tries to think of some way to alter the sex ratio.

As the days go by, an idea starts to form in his mind. Since he is married to the President of the Planet, perhaps he, like Brenda Bergman, can whisper something into the President's ear, which after a generation, will cause things to happen. Perhaps if the vasecta could go to school, it might raise the esteem of men to alter the sex ratio. Ron resolves to try this idea on Winnie.

That night at supper, Ron asks Winnie, "Why is it that vasecta can't continue their education like paterna?"

"They can," is the answer.

"They can?" Ron repeats disbelievingly.

"Sure they can. All they have to do is ask - but they don't ask. Occasionally we get a vasecta who wants to continue to go to school and it is nearly always granted."

Ron is stunned; he had never known that. Suddenly a thought strikes him, "Why if you permit a vasecta to go to school, do you forcibly sterilize him?"

"We don't."

"You don't," Ron repeats again, perplexed.

"In order to become a paterna, one has to pass the test, and all one has to do to pass the test is to score at the average level of a girl. It is really very easy to do if a boy applies himself, yet few do. If the boy refuses to be sterilized, we simply do not sterilize him. He must, of course, wear the paterna skirt to denote that he is fertile, but he isn't a paterna, and the sperm bank will not buy his sperm. If he wants to be admitted into paterna school, he will be admitted, and if he can finish school and find a job, he can support himself. Of course, it is difficult for him to find a good job. If he can find a woman or woman to marry him and support him, he can do that too, but that also is difficult. No, we do not forcibly sterilize anyone."

Ron is stunned again. Gradually he realizes that if he tries to raise the consciousness of men, he will surely fail. He realizes that it hasn't been the women who have brought men to their present low esteem; it is the men themselves. Women haven't revolted and taken dominance from men; men gave it to them. Men live the way they do on Evonia and all the other Evonian planets because that is the way they like it!

It is then that Ron stops worrying about uplifting the others of his gender and accepts his status as the first gentleman on the planet.

Chapter 13
The Long Trek

The eviction of the Synthetics from Earth takes place shortly after the first Earth colony, Primus, is successful but long before Plicker is colonized. The transport captain leaving Earth has no idea where he will deposit the Synthetics. He only knows that he has been told to leave them on a barren planet on the other side of the galaxy.

After checking numerous solar systems, the captain finally finds what he believes is a suitable planet. The planet is largely desert with only marginal vegetation. It seems to him an ideal planet since the Synthetics will have little chance for survival. He parks his transport in orbit and commences shuttling the Synthetics down to the planet. Once he has them down on the planet, he leaves them with only a week's supply of food and departs.

The planet he has deposited is like Earth in three respects: it has an Earth-like gravity, an oxygen/nitrogen atmosphere, and receives almost the same amount of energy from its single Sun. Unlike Earth, which rotates daily on an axis with a 23 1/2 degree tilt from the perpendicular, this planet is perfectly perpendicular to its revolution around its Sun. It turns on its axis only once per revolution.

The dynamics between this planet and Earth are dramatic. A day on this planet that the captain calls Alpha III for the third planet of the Alpha sun lasts one year. The hemisphere that faces the Sun is a desert, and the one that faces away is covered by snow. Despite the difference in energy each hemisphere receives, the temperature variance between the hemispheres is surprisingly small since the constantly blowing winds on the planet distribute the warmth from west to east.

Besides the day and night areas on the planet, there are also the two twilight areas and the polar zones. The Alphan sun can just be seen over the horizon in the twilight areas. The first twilight areas are where the rising Sun causes the winter icecap to melt. The other twilight area is the fall twilight area, where the receding Sun allows the winter icecap to advance.

Of the two twilight areas, only the spring area is habitable. The spring area contains melted ice that has not yet evaporated. It has vegetation through the vegetation is limited to plants that grow and fruit quickly before being overtaken and dried out in the Sun. Though the spring area is habitable, it is not permanently habitable because it is constantly moving. Moreover, the closer one gets to the equator, the wider the planet is, and the further one must travel each day to keep up with the planet's motion. At the equator, one must travel 70 miles each day to keep up with the daily rotation of Alpha III.

The two polar zones are the only permanently habitable areas on the planet. Like the rest of the Earth, the Sun shines on only one half. Since there is no daily rotation, there is no Coriolis effect to insulate the polar zones or the planet's dark side. The closer one is to the poles, the more temperate the climate, and the closer one is to the equator, the harsher the climate.

Alpha II is nearly a bright planet having very little water and only sparse vegetation. What vegetation there consists mostly of grasses and a few kinds of tubers. The only large vegetation of any kind is located in the planet's polar regions and is a kind of a cross between corn and bamboo. There are no lakes or seas to speak of; what water there is mostly tied up in the ice on the planet's dark side. The only liquid water is located in the spring twilight area, where the Sun has not yet evaporated it.

Despite the paucity of vegetation, there is a surprising amount of animal life. There are several varieties of antelope and a small carnivore, not unlike a dog. As the planet revolves, the animals migrate daily to stay ahead of the advancing desert. At the equator, the animals have to keep moving at a pace of 70 miles per day to keep ahead of the desert. Animals that wander into that area cannot keep up the pace and are overtaken by desert and perish. There are no rodents on the planet, but there are insects. Their life spans are so short they can complete them in the brief time between when the polar ice cap melts in the spring and evaporates in the summer.

In the polar zones, the constant temperature and regular rainfall allow for a wider variety of vegetation in both profusion and diversity. Despite cooler temperatures, the vegetation is much lusher. Due to the greater variety of vegetation, there is also a greater diversion of animal life.

The Synthetics do not know where they are being taken and do not know what trials await them. Although everything has been taken from them, they are looking forward to being free of humans where they can build their own society. They have trusted the humans to keep their bargain and provide them with a suitable planet: they have not accounted for human perfidy.

The humans have deliberately left the Synthetics on a planet where the captain of the transport does not think they can survive. These were not his instructions. He was supposed to leave them on a planet where their survival was marginal so that they would not be able to develop the technology needed for these sexless creatures to reproduce themselves. The captain, in his desire to please his bosses, exceeds that intent.

The captain unwittingly does one favor for the Synthetics; he leaves them in the spring twilight zone. There is water available, and a few plants that there are will soon be budding. The Synthetics have no way of knowing the geophysical characteristics of this planet. When the Sun does not seem to move in the heavens, they know it is not like Earth. Fortunately, there is an astronomer in their midst who starts making the necessary observations and measurements to see if the Sun does move. It takes him two days to prove that the Sun does move and to calculate how fast it moves. When he makes those calculations, he is alarmed at what he finds. He needs no calculations to tell him what will happen when the Sun is directly overhead.

When his observations and calculations are completed, he reports his findings to Dana II, the clone of the original Dana. The astronomer has concluded from the pull of gravity that this planet is roughly the same size as Earth. He can guess that this planet receives about the same amount of solar energy as Earth does, and since it is a yellow sun, he estimates that it is an Earth-like Sun.

This means that this planet will have the yearly sun rotation as Earth. "He" calculates that the Sun climbs about one degree in the sky every 24-earth hours. This means that this planet revolves once on its axis every 360 days. With this information, it is obvious that each day that goes by, the Sun will get higher in the sky, and the Earth will get drier. When the Sun is at its apex, the surroundings the Synthetics are in will long have been an uninhabitable desert.

The astronomer knows they can't stay where they are. If they stay where they are, their food supplies will quickly run out, the desert will overtake them, and they will surely perish. Deducing correctly that the polar zone on this planet will be most temperate, the astronomer must find out where they are on the planet so that they can head in the right direction. If they are in the northern hemisphere and head south, they will have to travel farther in order to reach the polar area.

When the Sun is moving forward, it is easy to tell which way is north, south, east, or west since east, by definition, is the direction that the Sun rises. The astronomer can't know yet if the planet is tilted on its axis, so "he" assumes for his calculations that it isn't.

When "he" has the direction that the is moving Sun, and the Sun is to the south, "he" concludes that the Synthetics are located one-third of the distance between the planet's equator and its north pole. Of course, "he" realizes that if Alpha III is tilted like Earth, his calculations may be wrong, and "he" may be headed for the farther pole.

The astronomer knows it is one thing to find a course and another to maintain it. "He" certainly can't take two days every day to find the direction of the Sun in order to determine north. Trusting to luck that this planet has a molten iron core like Earth, "he" locates a magnet and dangles it on a string. When the primitive compass points in the same general direction as what "he" has already determined as north, "he" knows "his" conclusions have been correct. The astronomer knows that "his" calculations have been right, but "he" has no way of knowing whether "his" assumptions have been correct. If "his" assumptions are incorrect, his conclusion will also be incorrect. Garbage in, garbage out!

After making these determinations, the astronomer advises Dana on what "he" has found, and they immediately set Dana at the head. Normally, they travel at a fast walk, but they occasionally jog to speed the pace and use different muscles. Every hour they stop for a 5-minute rest and foot care.

Since they are not traveling west, the sun grows higher in the sky every day, and the desert constantly overtakes them. Every 24 hours they travel, the air temperature rises hotter and the landscape drier.

Dana agrees that their only chance for survival is in the polar region. They manage an extremely fast five miles per hour average for 20 hours the first days. They thus cover a total of 100 miles. The astronomer has calculated that the distance they must travel to the polar region is at least 4000 miles.

After resting for 4 hours under a blazing sun, the Synthetics resume their march north. In the second 24 hours, Dana changes the marching orders. Instead of traveling single file, Dana knows they will have to forage for food and demand that they travel horizontally to their direction of march so they can look for food without disrupting their rally. For the second 24 hours, the Synthetics travel what they believe is another 100 miles, as near as they can figure. Careful computations of the number of steps are made. This number is multiplied by the average stride and divided by the length of a mile.

As they travel, the Synthetics look for water and potentially edible vegetation. When a potentially edible vegetable is found, a biologist is called to examine it. While this is happening, the rest of the Synthetics continue their march. The biologist and his guinea pig will have to run to catch up. If the biologist thinks the plant might be edible, a Synthetic is selected to eat the plant. The biologist then accompanies the Synthetic for the next 4 hours. If after 4 hours he is still alive, the Synthetics know the plant is edible.

One of the first promising plants they find is a small, round bulbous plant resembling a cactus. Completely without tools, the

Synthetic has to take two rocks to smash the plant and eat the pulp inside. When after 4 hours, this Synthetic is not dead, the Synthetics know they have found their first edible plant. When the next cacti are found, the Synthetics stop this time and pass it around so that everyone can see what it looks like and identify it. Then the Synthetic who found it is allowed to consume it.

While there isn't much water on Alpha III, this is spring, so there are a few ponds that haven't evaporated yet. Occasionally there is even a stream. There aren't any oceans on Alpha III, so what ponds there are, are formed only in the spring and disappear in the summer. Since the salt is left behind when the water evaporates, the ponds are always salty and not fit to drink. However, when the Synthetics find a stream, they can drink their fill.

The second kind of plant they find is a tuber, which is something like a cross between a carrot and a potato. The Synthetic who ate the tuber part of the plant does fine. When the biologists see it, the Synthetic who finds it brushes away the dirt and consumes it. The leafy stalk is given to another Synthetic who consumes that. After half an hour, the Synthetic who finished the stalk gets sick; it is obvious that "he" has been poisoned. "He" is abandoned; it does not matter whether the poison is fatal or not. The Synthetics cannot take the time to care for him, nor can "he" be carried. A second edible plant has been found.

The Synthetics find more edible plants and more poisonous plants as the miles pass. Each time they find an edible plant, their chances of survival improve. Each time they find a poisonous plant, they leave behind a dead or dying comrade. Even though many edible plants have been found and cataloged, the plants are still far apart and inadequate to support their needs. They lose weight rapidly but continue their march at as rapid a pace as possible.

As they travel, they occasionally pass small herds of antelope. The Synthetics know that antelope flesh will be more nutritious than plants and that they can use the antelope skin to fashion water canteens. However, they have no way to kill to antelope, and the antelope are far too fleet to be caught. There are also dogs, which follow the antelope herds. The dogs leave the Synthetics alone, for they are not recognized as possible prey. When the Synthetics come across a fresh kill by dogs, they know they have their chance. Throwing stones, the Synthetics manage to drive away from the dogs from their kill. The Synthetic that drove off the dogs is allowed to consume the antelope. There is no means of cooking or preparing the antelope, so it is eaten raw. The bones and the hide are saved. The bones can be fashioned into a bow and arrow, and the hide can be cut with the edge of stones broken in half and made into thread. The thread can be used for bowstrings and sew the hide as water canteens.

The Synthetics discover that there is a price for driving dogs off their kill. As soon as the Synthetics have consumed the antelope and have used every possible part of the antelope carcass, they resume their trek, trying to catch the main body that has left them behind.

The dogs have been driven off but haven't left. When the Synthetics resume their trek and dogs follow gradually, closing to one of the Synthetics trying to isolate him from the others. As the dogs get closer, the Synthetics stop a moment and drive back the dogs by throwing rocks that the dogs easily avoid. As soon as the Synthetics start traveling, the dogs renew the same strategy of following and trying to isolate one of the Synthetics.

The cycle repeats itself; the Synthetics can always drive back the dogs, but every time they do, they have to stop doing so. Their leader knows that if this continues, they will never overtake the main body of the Synthetics. It rapidly becomes clear what has to be done, and the dogs are ignored. The next time the dogs close in, there is nothing to stop them. The last Synthetic in line is pulled down by the dogs, killed, and eaten. His sacrifice, however, allows the others to escape. When the dogs devour their prey, they resume their normal migration west away from the sun. They do not follow the strange creatures headed in the wrong direction.

The next time the Synthetics come upon another antelope kill, they do not hesitate even though they know the result from the last time. The dog pack is driven off, the carcass eaten raw, and any usable part is manufactured into whatever it can be used. Again, the dogs irritated at having their meal stolen, take revenge. The same thing happens all over again, and another Synthetic is taken and eaten.

The antelope carcasses and the sacrifices have provided more than just sustenance to the few Synthetics who have been fortunate enough to eat the antelope. The Synthetics have been provided with weapons and tools to kill more antelope and obtain more food. The Synthetics now have a few bows and arrows made out of the antelope bone and hide. Fortunately, the antelope have never seen Synthetics before and have no reason to fear them. Thus the Synthetics can sneak close enough to hit the antelope with their arrows and at least wound them. Then the antelope can be tracked and eventually caught when. The Synthetics get more food, but it is still not nearly enough.

The Synthetics have been traveling for 14 days now, and Dana sees their pace slowing rapidly. At first, his calculations said they were traveling about 100 miles per day, and now they are already down to about 50 with still three-quarters of the distance to go. When he looks at his Synthetics, they are emaciated and tired, with hardly enough strength to continue.

Worse yet, they are deeper into the Alphan summer, and antelope herds are becoming uncommon; food is diminishing. Unless he can get food and water for his Synthetics, he knows they will perish. The only way to ensure their survival is to use the meat and liquid they know they have themselves. If they consume each other for food and liquid, they will have the strength to continue. Dana, a human, is reluctant to make this decision. It is forced upon him by his lieutenants.

But who is to be sacrificed. It is the oldest Synthetic who have the least utility. When he gives the order, there is no questioning of the order, not because of his authority but because it is the rational thing to do—all of the original members of M.L.S.S. Inc. are killed. First, the blood is drunk to help quench the others' thirst, and then their flesh is eaten raw. Like the antelope, every part of their bodies is utilized for food or implements.

With the aid of this new source of food, the Synthetics have the strength to go on. The chief advantage is that the new source of food is almost inexhaustible. With each Synthetic killed and eaten, there are fewer mouths to feed. With this new food source, they gain strength, and their pace of march picks up.

The march continues until they see over the horizon what appears to be a range of mountains. The Synthetics spirits fall when they see the mountain, they know their pace will be slowed when they cross them if they can be crossed at all. However, when they get close, they see that some of the peaks still have snow on them. What this means, Dana, the new leader, knows is that since summer is coming that there should be running water in the mountains. Hope springs in their hearts, and even though as they approach, the terrain grows hillier and more difficult, their pace does not slow.

Suddenly they come over a hill and see something they have not seen for over a week, a stream, running water. The Synthetics run towards the stream and gorge themselves on as much water as they can drink. Not only is there water, but also close along the banks of the stream are many edible plants. These plants are attacked by the Synthetics and devoured. After the Synthetic gorge themselves on water and food, they rest.

As they rest, Dana looks at his Synthetics. They are a wretched lot to look at. Where skin once covered fat, there is now only translucent skin over stringy muscle. Arms and legs are spindly, faces are emaciated, bellies are swollen from lack of protein, hollow eyes peer out of cavernous eye sockets, and bony ridges stand out where once there were plump cheeks.

Resting a whole day Dana until all of the edible plants have been either eaten, orders his band to move up into the mountains following the stream. The Synthetics move slowly, now gathering all the edible plants they can find, which are more than they can eat. What is not eaten is dried and stored.

Moving into the mountains, the Synthetics come upon a truly unexpected find. A lake feeds the stream they have been following. The lake is located in a valley still green and populated by a large herd of antelope. Dana orders the Synthetics to make camp here. The Synthetics immediately set to work making camp. Then they divide themselves into two parts. One part goes on a hunting expedition for antelope, and the other gather edible plants.

When the two expeditions return, they hold a feast. Deciding to camp here and gather strength and supplies before returning to their trek, the Synthetics, for the first time, have the time and the fuel to cook their food. Once again, the Synthetics are careful to save any useful parts of the antelope; it is almost impossible on this planet to have too many vessels for carrying water.

The Synthetics now have more food than they can eat; they dry and store what they cannot eat. They know that this valley and lake will soon dry and return to the desert. They cannot remain here forever.

This simple prosperity does not last. Before long, the snow on top of the mountains has melted, the stream feeding the lake dries up, the lake itself starts to dry, the vegetation dries, and the antelope herd moves on. The short stay at the valley has benefited the Synthetics enormously. They have a large reserve of dried food. Every Synthetic now has a canteen holding freshwater made from antelope skin. The light-complected Synthetics have had time for their sunburn to heal. The numerous blisters on their feet have all healed. The ample food supply has allowed them to put back a lot of muscle and even a little fat. So ample are their food and water supplies that they cannot carry them all on their backs. They rig a travois, a sling holding the supplies between two sticks made from a small tree-like plant found in the valley to carry their supplies. Two Synthetics pull one end, and the other end is dragged. Dana knows that pulling such a device will slow their progress, but reasons that the supplies are more important than the few extra miles they would make per day.

The type of vegetation changes as the Synthetics continues up into the mountains. Having what he hopes are ample supplies, Dana does not order consumption of these new plants. he does not wish to lose any more Synthetics. "He" knows they will be needed to develop the planet. The Synthetic's progress is slowed, and the air becomes much cooler. At first, this temperature change is a benefit from the hot Alphan sun, but the higher they climb, the cooler it gets. When they rest, they are required to huddle together to escape exposure.

As they travel through the mountains, a curious thing happens. The compass begins to deviate from what the Synthetics are sure is true north. Dana knows what that means. There is a magnetite deposit, iron ore, somewhere in the mountains. The geologist makes a note of where this has occurred for future reference.

Finally, they reach the pass between the mountains from the top of the pass. They look out to see what is ahead of them. It is another range of mountains. There is nothing to do but continue on.

They continue down the mountains and up into the next range of mountains. Dana begins to doubt his calculations on distance traveled because he has been forced by the mountains not only to go up and down but sideways around many obstacles. He knows he hasn't traveled as far as their calculations indicate. As the Synthetics climb the second range of mountains, the supply of food runs low. Dana orders stricter rationing. Fortunately, there are still many ponds or even puddles remaining in the mountains. This water, unlike the water on the plain, is fresh and not salty and can be consumed.

As they come down out of the mountains, the sun is now far to the south. It is not as hot as it was when they went into the mountains, and though plant life is sparse because it is not quite as hot here, there is more edible plant life. There is still not even plant life to sustain the Synthetic, but they can stretch their supplies and, as yet, do not have to sacrifice Synthetics on unknown plant life or resort to cannibalism.

As they proceed further and further north, the climate grows steadily cooler, and the amount of vegetation steadily increases. Dana knows that they are not only nearing the polar zone but that the polar zone will support them. The Synthetics will survive. They soon come to a pond on the plain. They had come to many such ponds on the early part of their trek, but the water had always been salty and unfit to drink. This pond is fresh.

Dana notices something splash as they fill their canteens and rest around the pond. He couldn't believe it at first, but it was true, it was a fish. Dana is now sure that they have reached the polar zone. If fish live in the pond, this pond has to be a permanent pond. If it dried up in summer, the fish would die. Dana is now sure that he is in the polar zone.

Dana rests the Synthetics; there is now no hurry. There is an adequate amount of food and water. The Synthetics need to regain their strength again. After the Synthetics regain their strength, they resume their pace. This time there is no need to rush and resume at a very leisurely pace. The further they advance into the polar zone, the lusher becomes the plant life, the more numerous the animal life, and the more plentiful becomes the water.

Abruptly the plant life starts to diminish again. When Dana turns around, he sees why the sun is now at the horizon and the plant life has diminished because it is not getting enough light.

They are nearing the north pole. There is no point in continuing further.

Dana sets up camp near a small grove of a bamboo-like plants near a lake. "He" correctly surmises that this plant will eventually provide a basis for many useful utensils. Not only is there plentiful water, bamboo, and food but the game as well. Along with antelope, there are several smaller varieties of the game as well. One type of animal is especially plentiful, a small ground animal resembling a rabbit. When an animal is killed, it is used for many purposes besides food. The skins are not only used for water carriers, packs, and rawhide threats but for shoes, clothing, and tents. A hide spread out on the ground under a 24-hour sun does not take long to dry.

The bamboo-like plant proves even more useful than the antelope for utensils. It makes excellent end stakes for tents. It makes better bows and arrows than antelope bones, and the leaves make superlative feathers for arrows. Not only is bamboo useful for utensils but for food as well. At the end of the Alpha summer, it provides a small but delicious fruit. Until the Synthetics develop metallurgy, the bamboo will be their principal material for any utensil. They literally develop hundreds of uses for it.

After a few days, Dana realizes that the best hunting and foraging is along the autumnal line of light where the plants have had a full growing season. Therefore, he orders the Synthetics to travel east until the sun is almost directly in the southwestern sky.

Dana orders his Synthetics to stop and make camp when he reaches the autumnal line. Again, they make camp near a grove of bamboo. Here they stay for about a week, gathering food and regaining their strength until the sky begins to get dark. They then move ahead for what will be a trip for the sun of about a week. After a few of such semi-permanent stops, they gather more food than they can eat and begin to cache it underground.

Chapter 14

Growth

After a year, they come upon their first abandoned campsite. This time when they visit it instead of just camping, they begin to make permanent improvements to the site, for they know they will again visit it next year. They also have gathered seeds from the best fruiting plants they have found, till a small parcel of land, and plant the seed. Thus developing a clear pattern for the next year. Unfortunately, they cannot make the improvements they desire before they are required to move.

The next time they stop, it is at a previous encampment. Each time they make that stop, they make permanent improvements and begin a small garden as well as gathering and caching food. Shortly the Synthetics come to the encampment where they cached their first food from the previous year. This time for the first time, they know that they have a surplus of food. Dana also knows that his technology can only increase so far without the development of metal. Remembering the deposit of magnetite in the mountains, he builds carts for his geologists to haul supplies and sends them into the mountains to look for the magnetite.

While the geologists are away, the nonmetallic technology is advanced in many small ways. Besides the technology of how to bend bamboo to make a wheel, another development is the domestication of the wild dogs on the planet. The dogs are first lured to the camps by placing food out for them. When they eat the food, they are lured closer and closer to the camps and eventually eat the food right out of Synthetic hands. When that has gone on long enough that the dogs trust the person who feeds them, they are hitched to carts. Now the Synthetics can transport much more than they possibly could on their backs or even pull themselves.

Besides the steady improvement of their campsites and increase in agronomy, they also send out groups just for exploration purposes. One of these groups finds a deposit of clay. They quickly built a kiln and started producing pottery. When they are forced to leave because of the dark, a large cache of food is left so that when it again becomes light, the pottery mill can be inhabited and worked all summer long.

Eventually, another year goes by, and the expedition is looking for magnetite returns, having been unable to find anything. It had been a very difficult year; they had to endure six months of darkness before they could return. The geologists rest only a few days, during which the other Synthetics restock their provisions, and they again depart.

Nearly six months go by, and the deposit of clay is about to come under daylight. Another contingent of Synthetics is sent out to mine the clay, make pottery and farm the nearby land to protect the nearby crops from weeds and animals during the summer so that the harvest there is larger. Besides pottery, the Synthetics also make bricks used to produce a permanent settlement there. They also grow oil-producing plants so that they can make lamps and live there year-round. When the roving contingent of Synthetics arrives, the brick masons and farmers have built the first permanent town on Alpha III. They have enough food and oil to last through the winter. They also have a surplus of pottery and bricks that they give to the other Synthetics. The pottery is of enormous importance to the Synthetics. It enables them to keep their food away from insects and ground animals.

Another year passes, and the geologists again join them. This time they have found the deposit of magnetite. Unfortunately, the deposit is now on the planet's dark side, but plans are made to develop it just as soon as it comes under daylight.

When the time comes to develop the iron mine, Dana sends all the Synthetics he can spare. Fortunately, the agronomy of the planet has developed so that minorities of the Synthetics are now needed to grow the food needed to support them. Dana thus has available labor for making bricks, building permanent housing at each encampment made of brick, and exploiting the iron supply. Developing metallurgy is now their first priority. Plans are also made to mine and forge iron and steel year-round. Numerous pack trains of dogs are taken to the iron ore mine in order to bring the supplies to develop the mine.

The first thing built using the bricks provided by the potters is a high-temperature oven. This will be used to melt the ore to make the iron. Using only the pottery for digging tools, the Synthetics commence digging out the ore. Since they do not have any coal, they laboriously gather local vegetation and cook it in an oven without oxygen to make charcoal. Unfortunately, there is no limestone. Moreover, the geologists don't think they will find any because there doesn't seem to be any ocean on the planet. The best substitute they can use is antelope bones. The bones are ground up and mixed with charcoal and iron ore. When the three are heated together at high temperatures, the charcoal reduces oxides out of the iron ore, and the limestone melts float to the top and takes out the impurities. The Synthetics finally have iron. The first iron is more precious than gold, and it is used for digging implements so that the Synthetics can dig more iron ore and dig it faster.

Meanwhile, geologists have been exploring more. This time they make another discovery, silver ore. Dana immediately recognizing the value of this discovery also reduces the silver ore to produce pure silver. The potters at this time have also managed to melt sand and make glass. The silver is melted and poured across the glass to make a mirror. When enough mirrors have been made, they are used first to focus on a crucible containing the silver ore. The heat of the incessant Alpha sun all focused in place is sufficient to melt the ore in the crucible. Now silver is produced faster and more quickly. With more silver and more mirrors made, the same technique is used to make more glass, bricks, and, finally, iron. The Synthetics finally have a cheap source of fuel.

The production of a large amount of iron has a profound effect on Synthetics technology. Iron is used for so many utensils, shovels for the glassmakers to shovel sand, potters, miners, farmers, and a thousand uses. The production of iron allows the same amount of goods to be produced with labor so that Synthetic labor can be used to develop something else.

Now that Dana has iron technology developed and uses almost essential iron hand tools, "he" assembles his surplus labor for several ambitious projects. One project for the botanists is to find a plant that produces the best supply of latex. Dana knows that rubber is not the only planet on Earth to produce latex. Surely, "he" reasons, there must be a plant on Alpha III that also produces latex.

Meanwhile, "he" continues to send his geologist to look for more deposits of useful ores. "He" knows he will need copper and many other rarer elements eventually. Along with the geologists, Dana sends cartologists to map the planet.

His favorite, most superb project is the development of electricity on the planet. Since the easiest source of energy is the sun and the Synthetics are now occupying fixed communities on the planet, a whole series of power plants will have to be built, but they will also have to be linked with power lines.

Steel and all the other products needed for building a power plant. While the first power station was being built, the Synthetics were overproducing bricks and silver (copper hadn't been found yet). Even after the power plant was begun, the botanists discovered, and best source of latex on the planet, and the geologists found a source of sulfur, the two main sources needed to produce rubber. The reason rubber is needed is to cover and insulate the power lines.

Finally, the first power plant is operating. The power generated from the power plant is not only to give light to the Synthetics but also to automate many of their production facilities. The first use of electricity is to power an electric shovel for the iron mine that has been built in anticipation of the power plant. Soon much more ore is being produced with many fewer workers. The next use is electric ovens for steel and iron production since the solar ovens can only be used for half a year.

Even before the first power plant is finished, a second is begun on the opposite side of the planet. Before it is finished, the Synthetics begin stringing wire to tie them together so that the Synthetics can have power no matter what the season. When the second is finished and the third and fourth are begun. Not only does the production of steel become automated, but so does the production of everything else. Many Synthetics forced to toil to make simple things are now free for other projects.

Dana is now ready to begin his next project, the replication of Synthetics. However glorious have been their victories, however hard their course has been, it all means nothing unless they can replicate their species. The development of electricity means that their technology has developed so that the automatic pumps and regulatory devices necessary for an artificial uterus are possible.

Many Synthetics were doctors or biologists on Earth. They know how to build the Synthetic uterus and do it without difficulty. They know how to manufacture artificial blood and do that without any difficulty. Their problem is that the artificial uterus was always seeded with a human ovum, and this is the one thing that they don't have.

The only similar thing they have available to them is an antelope ovum. To make it work, the nucleus of the ovum is taken out and replaced with a nucleus of a human cell. This ovum is seeded into an artificial uterus. Many such artificial uteri are seeded to see if any of them work. The experiment works; the first Synthetic babies are born on Alpha III.

Dana cannot put all his available labor into producing Synthetic babies. There are so many projects made possible by the electrification of the planet. Automated devices too numerous to mention must be designed and built to increase production with less labor. More power plants with more power lines must be built to ensure an adequate, reliable power supply. Dana is also required to start even while "he" is engaged in numerous other improvement projects developing an automated transport system. The transport system used up to this point has been the use of carts pulled by dogs. The development of electricity will give power for propulsion and guidance. The development of rubber will also give them something much better than bamboo for wheels that must constantly be replaced. It will be a quantum leap in technology.

Dana can manage a few hundred Synthetic births during the first nine months. This amount is identical to the total amount of Synthetics on the planet. Dana would like to double the number of babies every nine months, but he does not have the labor of caring for and teaching the children. He is forced to keep the number of babies born each year constant. Each 9-month period "he" is forced to transfer more adults to child care to maintain his growth rate. After four years, there are finally older Synthetics to help with the care of the babies. Dana finally has labor enough to double the number of babies born each year. The adults who have previously cared for the babies are now transferred to teaching the older Synthetics. Now with older Synthetics to help with the chores, Dana doubles the number of Synthetics born each year. Not only are the older Synthetics required to help with child care help with tutoring the younger Synthetics, but they are also required to help with the expansion of housing and production required by their presence. For the first time, Dana has an almost adequate labor supply.

When the first Synthetics born on the planet are adults, the entire north polar zone is populated with Synthetics. It is time to develop the south polar zone. Instead of reaching there on foot, the Synthetics have the ability to do it with the aid of technology. While they could build a plane and fly there, they would have to leave most of their technology behind. Instead, they commence the building of an electrically powered railroad across the face of the planet. This time instead of building things by hand, they have cranes, bulldozers, and all sorts of mechanical aids. It is still a massive project, and Dana must commit the bulk of his available resources to accomplish it. As the railroad is built, so are power plants to power it. When the Alphan night overtakes the work crews, they commence building another railroad on the opposite side of the planet. When night overtakes them on the opposite side of the planet, they return to the first side and continue until completed.

Even while new cities and farms are being built, Synthetic cartologists and geologists are exploring and mapping the entire planet. In only a few years, the entire polar zone is mapped and the polar zone inhabited.

Before the habitation of the South Pole is finished, habitation begins in the lower latitudes. Even before that is finished, Dana has an even bigger, more difficult, and portentous project: space colonization.

Chapter 15
Colonization

As Dana begins projects involving the whole planet, he begins to look to the sky. He knows that a human spaceship is not likely to pass by in the short run and discovers that the Synthetics have survived. Even though Alpha III is in an untraveled part of the galaxy, humans will inevitably expand further and further into space until, at last, they stumble upon the Synthetics.

Dana knows what will happen when the humans rediscover Synthetics. Humans' history toward synthetic has been one of lying, cheating, and trying to exterminate them. Yet, Dana really doesn't understand his own kind. If it was their intent to exterminate Synthetics, why didn't they exterminate them? Why always the duplicity? Why do they always want to appear to do one thing when their intent is to really do another? They seem to need to lie to themselves; to convince themselves of their best when it is obvious their intent is otherwise.

If humans discover Synthetics again, it is obvious they will try the same thing again. First, they will try to be friends with us, to convince us that we can trade with them and do business with them while all the while they are planning in the back of their minds to exterminate us. They can never be trusted!

If the humans find the Synthetics before we develop a space fleet, we will be at their mercy. They can do whatever they will with us, and we can do nothing because we have nothing to resist them. It is absolutely necessary in order to ensure the survival of Synthetics that we have a space fleet. It is also absolutely necessary that Synthetics colonize other planets so that even if one planet is lost, the surviving planets can carry on.

Still putting a great deal of effort into increasing his population and developing the planet, Dana does not have a lot of resources available for exploration into outer space, but he knows he must make them available. The first step is to build the shuttlecraft, the rockets to lift the materials into orbit to build the interplanetary ship. First, the plans and computations must be made, and then prototypes tested. Once the prototypes are tested, they can be mass-produced. Once the prototypes prove serviceable, plans must be drawn up for the combination space station and dry-dock from which the interplanetary ship will be built.

As each step in his interplanetary plan is completed, the next phase occurs, and the plan grows geometrically like the growth on the planet. As this happens, the development of the planet correspondingly slows. When the first space station is built and the first rocket commences construction, there are sufficient shuttles for the simultaneous construction of a second space station.

The first interplanetary space ships were small and fast, designed for exploration rather than transportation. Before colonizing new planets, it is necessary to both find them and determine if they will be habitable and, if not, can technology be used in such a way as to make them habitable.

Even before the small scout ships make exploration, observation posts are built inside of asteroids to give advance warning of the approach of Earth ships. Once these are down, Dana sets down a strict policy regarding possible discovery by humans. The policy is simple, discovery by humans is to be avoided at all costs. If there is any possibility that an Earth vessel has detected a Synthetic ship, it is to fly into the nearest sun so that the humans will doubt what they have seen. Dana knows that humans often doubt their own senses and will not believe that intelligent life will self-destruct.

Despite the industriousness of Synthetics, the logistics of what Dana is planning are enormous. No matter how fast Synthetics progress, it is never fast enough. There are never enough resources, even though those resources have grown geometrically. Even though the Synthetic space transport is being designed to hold 1000 Synthetics, that period's baby production on Alpha III will be 10 million babies, and the year after that will be 20 million. To take the one year's population growth will require 10,000 transports, and the first one isn't even finished yet. Yet, Dana knows that eventually, the supply of interplanetary ships will catch up.

The first planet that Dana decides to colonize is away from the sun of Alpha III. It is an ideal planet for the Synthetics to colonize; reasons Dana that it is far too cold for humans to consider habitable, and therefore they won't consider that anyone else would either.

Second, it is close by and therefore easy for the Synthetics to bring their equipment and population with limited transport. Because the planet is in the same solar system, colonization can occur with shuttles.

The cold, however, is not the chief problem. The chief problem is that the planet is not warm enough to support life, and therefore since there is no plant life, there is no free oxygen in the atmosphere. The Synthetics will have to reduce the oxygen out of the poisonous gases surrounding the planet to live. After the planet has been charted from outer space and the plans developed for its colonization, the expedition readies many shuttles to take off from Alpha III for Alpha IV.

When they land on the planet, they find the entire planet covered with ice made up of water and ammonia, and other poisonous gases and liquids. The first thing that the Synthetics assemble is a fusion engine. The power of that engine is funneled into laser beams. The laser beams are not continuous but pulsating, pulsating in milliseconds. Vaporizing the rock diffracts the laser beam. The pulsating laser explodes the rock instead of vaporizing it. Pulsating lasers cut faster and use less energy.

The tunneling lasers are multiple lasers surrounding a hollow tube. The tube is connected to the suction pumps that remove the rock dust. Using the laser beams and suction pumps, the Synthetics burn first through the ice and then the rock underneath. The pulverized rock is sucked out by the pumps and blown out of the tunnel. Rock dust also interferes with pulsating lasers, so the tunneling goes slowly, but the Synthetics persist. After a few days, they have tunnels big enough to start housing themselves inside the planet. Once this is completed, the chemists start work on reducing oxygen and nitrogen from the native air so that they will eventually be able to take off their helmets and oxygen masks inside the planet. This is a simple problem and easily solved.

The vast amounts of rock dust lying on the surface of the planet created by the laser borers create a problem. The gritty dust, if not taken care of, will eventually blow around the planet and get into the equipment. The Synthetics have anticipated the problem. As the rock dust exits the suction tubes, it is hit with large continuous lasers that liquefy it. The molten rock melts through the snow to reform as more rock. When the rock cools, the snow reforms over it, and everything appears as it was before.

Every few days, reinforcements arrive with more equipment. As the pace of tunneling expands, another fusion engine is brought and assembled. Another fusion engine is brought, which is assembled inside the planet. This one is a permanent engine that will be used to provide power for the planet. Among many other uses, it will provide the power to reduce oxygen from the planet's atmosphere and provide light and warmth for indoor hydroponic gardens.

Meanwhile, the exploration ships have been busy locating other planets to colonize. One of them does not return. It spots a human space freighter that has had a breakdown in its navigational computer and had been lost for decades. The Synthetic captain follows his orders and does not chance that the human ship might have spotted him and sent a message to his civilization. He spirals his ship and crew into the nearest sun. The crew inside the human space freighter couldn't have seen the Synthetics. They had long ago run out of fuel and died. The sacrifice of the Synthetics is in vain.

The next planet the Synthetics colonize is a warm, earth-like planet. This time the planet is in another solar system, so they have to use their interplanetary transport for the first time. The planet has been carefully explored and the expedition carefully planned so the Synthetics have no difficulty, but they cannot develop it as rapidly as planned because of a shortage in transports. Like Alpha IV, the neighboring planet is habitable but cold. Michael, who has replaced Dana as the Synthetic, who has grown old and died, orders that this planet develops the neighboring planet when it can. There are an infinite number of other planets that are easier to colonize since there is still a shortage of interplanetary transport.

Chapter 16

Rediscovery

Even though Alpha III is remote and on the other side of the galaxy, it is inevitable, given the pace of exploration of humans and Synthetica, that sooner or later, Synthetics will be discovered.

When the Primean scout ships explore a particularly promising planet of lush vegetation, they call Vendor it is uninhabited. Later, when the transport carrying the colonists arrives, they find that someone has already established a colony on the planet. The Primean transport captain, Captain Blitt, does not recognize the colony as a Synthetics colony. Synthetics have long been forgotten; Captain Blitt has never even heard of a Synthetic. The only other civilization colonizing this area of the galaxy is Evonia. Since the war has just been fought with Evonia, Captain Blitt immediately concludes that the colony is Evonian, Primea's mortal enemy.

If it had merely been a matter of the Evonians beating the Primeans to a planet, the holocaust might have been averted. Despite their animosity, both civilizations recognize the right of primacy; the first to colonize get the planet. However, one of the numerous Evonian - Primean wars has just been completed, and by that treaty, Verdor is in Primean space. Moreover, such is the distaste of each civilization for the other that by that same treaty, any ship caught in the other civilization's space, for any reason, can be attacked and destroyed.

Had Captain Blitt been a lawyer or diplomat, he might have first cited International law and demanded of Evonia that they withdraw their colony, leaving their equipment behind them. He is not a diplomat or a lawyer, he is a disabled Primean military pilot, and it was the Evonians who disabled him. Seeing what he believes to be an Evonian colony on the planet beneath him, he is at first puzzled, then angry, and finally delighted - delighted because he knows he can get revenge for his injury.

Unlike Synthetic transports, Primean transports are armed. They are always wary of intruding Evonians. Captain Blitt knowing of the terms of the Star System VIII Treaty, decides he will shoot first and ask questions later. Without warning, he launches a thermonuclear missile at the tiny Synthetic colony below him. The Synthetics on the ground below him detect the Primean ship and the fact that it has fired a missile but has no means of defending itself. They are entirely obliterated. No trace of the colony remains. There is no evidence remaining of what kind of colony it had been. Feeling genuinely pleased with himself, Captain Blitt debarks his passengers on their cargo on the opposite side of the planet and sets up a colony.

A second Synthetic transport is close behind the first. It detects the presence of the Primean spaceship at a longer range and does not get any closer. Since the Synthetic colony has obviously already been discovered, its captain sees no need to execute the "prime order" and destroy the ship, its crew, and its passengers. Instead, it stays out of sight of the Primean vessel until it leaves and then establishes orbit around the planet. When it discovers only radioactive debris where its colony had been, its captain knows what has happened and departs without unloading.

The Primean colony, like the previous Synthetic colony, detects the presence of the Synthetic vessel but has no idea whose ship it is. Terrified that it is an Evonian vessel that will visit the same fate upon it that was visited on the "Evonian" colony, it quickly tries to disburse the inhabitants of the colony to avoid all being killed. The colonial commander is naturally puzzled but delighted when the unidentified ship unexpectedly leaves. The leader of the colony resolves to report Captain Blitt for destroying an undefended Evonian colony and then leaving the colonists undefended against an Evonian attack.

Michael's first thought when "he" hears the news about the destroyed colony is that the humans know that the Synthetics have survived. However, the more "he" thinks about it, the more "he" realizes that it doesn't stand up to reason. Why obliterate a tiny Synthetic colony with a nuclear warhead? If one rediscovered Synthetics, would not one capture some of them to prove that they had survived? Would not the nuclear warhead destroy all evidence of whose colony it had been? Could it have been a case of mistaken identity? The more Michael thinks about it, the more "he" becomes convinced it was a case of mistaken identity, that the civilization which destroyed the colony thought it was an enemy colony.

Michael realizes now that more resources will have to be redirected into military growth. Soon the humans will discover Synthetica, and when they do, Synthetica will need a military fleet.

An idea forms in "his" mind as to how this incident can be turned to an advantage, to cause the two human civilizations to resume fighting again, slow their growth, gain time to build a military fleet, and maybe even win back the planet as well. Since Michael has no way of knowing which civilization did the attacking, "he" organizes a military expedition against the unknown colony and gives orders to "his" commander to make it look like the enemy civilization attacked.

Michael doesn't use warships for "his" attack, "he" doesn't need any. Stealth is the weapon "he" intends to use. Instead of using modern warships with thermonuclear missiles, the Synthetics approach the planet in a spiral, always keeping on the opposite side of the planet so that the colony cannot detect their presence and establish an orbit that always keeps their ship on the other side of the planet. Just before dark falls on the colony, shuttles emerge from the Synthetic transport. These transports make their descent on the opposite side of the planet from the colony and then skim along the surface of the planet, protected from discovery by the horizon. The Synthetic force lands on the planet far enough away that the colonists cannot detect them. The rest of the trip is accomplished by ground vehicles.

When they are close to the colony, they are detected, but it is too late. The Synthetics are in among the colony before the colonists can rally. Even if they had detected the synthetics earlier, it would not have done them any good since they have no small arms. There have none because it is unthinkable that anyone would engage in an infantry attack. Such attacks have long been obsolete. The first post taken is the colonial spaceport. The Synthetics do not want any communication missiles sent off to warn their home planet.

The next problem is that the Synthetics have no idea who is the enemy of the Primeans. It has been several hundred years since they left Earth when Primus was first being colonized. The first Evonian planet, Plicker, was long into the future. The dilemma is solved by simply reading a Primean history book that identifies the Evonians and their culture as the enemy of Primea. Thus, all of the inhabitants of the Primean colony are put to death, but only the dead adult women are left scattered around the colony. All of the remains of the children and adult males are incinerated by laser, and their ashes are burned.

When the next transport arrives, it finds no one alive at the colony, only the partially decomposed bodies of the adult women. At first, its captain thinks everyone has been butchered, but someone quickly points out to him that only the bodies of the adult females can be found. The transport captain concludes that the adult males and the children have been taken captive. He has suspected the Evonians from the beginning, but the fact that they have taken the males as sex slaves and the female children to be indoctrinated makes him positive. The fact that the Evonians have never done this before escapes him. The transport this time does not debark its colonists; it departs for the home planet of Primea immediately after the dead are burled. He is livid with rage and anxious to report this slaughter.

When the news is reported, no one doubts that the Evonians have been responsible for the raid. No one stops to wonder why so little physical damage has been done. Anyone would take a virtually undefended colony by ground assault when their warships could more easily obliterate from space. Plans are immediately put in motion for a retaliatory raid.

A small, lightly defended Evonian colony is selected in a remote part of the galaxy, and the plans are drawn up for a raid. The Evonians, even though they constantly monitor the Primeans have just completed a war with them and have no reason to suspect a raid. They are not caught totally by surprise, but their forces are spread out and cannot be gathered quickly enough to repulse the raid. The few Evonian warships in the area depart against overwhelming odds abandoning the little colony and its colonists to their fate.

Unlike the Primean colony, the Evonian colony is long-established, much larger, and better defended. When it is attacked, it defends itself with missiles and particle beams. However, the colony is no match for the heavily defended Primean fleet and succumbs to superior firepower. However, the Primean victory is not without sacrifice, and the Primean fleet leaves smaller than when it arrived.

The Evonians are astounded at this large, well-planned, ruthless, and unprovoked attack. It is a new low for the Primeans, who maintained a pretense of provocation at least in the past. It is obvious to them that when they made the treaty, they never had any intention of keeping it; the treaty was pure treachery. Although the Evonians are war-weary, such is the outrage of the Primeans that they immediately mobilize for all-out war.

Michael's plan has succeeded beautifully. The Primean and Evonian civilizations are at war with each other, each side absolutely convinced of its justness and the treachery of the other. Michael knows that such wars do not end easily. While this goes on, there can be no more exploration, no colonization, and each civilization will be exhausted when it finally ends. There is now no reason not to colonize Verdor; both sides have virtually forgotten it. By the time the war ends, it will be populated, well-defended and secure In Synthetic hands. When the war ends, several more planets will be populated, Synthetica will have built a military fleet, and several more colonies will be established.

When the Primean and Evonian civilizations have exhausted themselves after an inconclusive war, the Federation, a loose association of independent planets of which Earth is a member, offers itself as a diplomatic intermediary. When both sides are done blaming the other for starting the war, and many more thousands of lives are lost, they finally agree to an armistice. As a reward for negotiating the armistice, the Federation is asked to colonize Verdor so that neither of the other civilizations can have it.

As soon as the treaty is signed, the Federation sends out a small scout ship to explore the Verdor- system and gather data on the planet. As soon as it decelerates out of hyper-light speed, it is hit by a particle beam emanating out of Verdor's moon. There is no distress call. The crew never knew what hit them.

Deeply suspicious over the disappearance of the scout ship but unable to prove that the ship was attacked and destroyed or by whom, the Federation sent out a full battle squadron: a carrier, a cruiser, and ten destroyers.

When the squadron becomes visible, decelerating from hyper-light speed, the moon bases cannot attack because there are too many ships. Such an act would only bring about their destruction. However, Michael has anticipated the Federation's response.

Aboard the Federation carrier, the Centari, the fleet is decelerating to sub-light speed, but there is no cause for concern. Suddenly, the radarman exclaims, "Officer of the deck, officer of the deck!"

"What is it?" answered the officer of the deck, Ensign Shunt.

"You'd better come and look at this, sir!"

Ensign Shunt hurries over to the radar screen and looks down. Numerous blips appear on the screen. "Probably asteroids. We'll have to divert around them."

"They're not asteroids, sir."

The radarman's words shoot through Shunt like an electric spark. There aren't supposed to be any asteroids in this area.

"If they aren't asteroids, what are they.

"They're ships, sir."

"Notify the captain and the admiral at once!"

"How do you know they're ships?"

"By the organization, look at that pattern. Asteroids are random, jumbled."

The speakers in Admiral Ostoff's and Captain Plank's office crackle and speak, "Will Admiral Ostoff and Captain Plank, please report to their bridges, please.

"What's wrong?" answers Captain Plank first and then the Admiral.

"We have spotted a fleet of ships, sir," comes to answer to both officers.

Both officers do not even bother to get dressed but grab only and robe and run barefoot to their bridges.

"What's up? asks Captain Plank as she reaches the ship's bridge.

"There's a fleet dead ahead, ma'am," answers Ensign Shunt.

"How do you know it's a fleet?" asks the Captain, always double-checking conclusions reached by subordinates.

"From the symmetry, ma'am," answers the ensign as If he had concluded himself.

Captain Plank looks at the radar screen and says, "It's a fleet, all right. I wonder who they are."

At that moment, Admiral Ostoff arrives at his bridge and sees everything that Captain Plank has already seen. "Slow the squadron to one-quarter speed," orders Admiral Ostoff, "See if you can make contact with them."

Lieutenant Commander Nelson's squadron communications officer relays the first order to the rest of the squadron and follows it with the standard acknowledgment signal.

"Contact established," announces Lieutenant Commander Nelson.

"Ask them who they are!" orders Admiral Ostoff.

"Admiral, they say, leave Synthetic space or be destroyed."

"Synthetic space, what the hell is Synthetic space?" exclaims Ensign Shunt before he realizes he is speaking out of turn.

"Damned if I know," answers Captain Shunt. "Do you know what Synthetic space is, Admiral Ostoff?"

"I'm sorry, I have no idea," answers the Admiral over the emergency television monitor between the two bridges.

Silence reigns over both bridges as the squadron continue closer to the unknown fleet ignoring the warning.

"When they are in visual range, put them on the screen," orders Admiral Ostoff.

Several minutes more pass until the large video screens in both bridges snap on. As they move closer, the size of the unknown ships grows and increases in detail. Even under maximum magnification, the unknown fleet only appears as tiny dots. No detail of any ship that would give them a clue as to what they look like can be made out.

Another message is received from the strange fleet, "Depart Synthetic space or be destroyed!"

"Ask them by what right is this their space," says Admiral Ostoff.

The answer comes immediately. One of the Synthetic lead cruisers emits a bright light from its bow.

"Dead Stop," orders Admiral Ostoff and the huge ships lurch as their retro-rockets fire. "Damage report."

The Stellar reports a shot across its bow, but there was no damage report.

It takes several minutes for space vessels to slow; meanwhile, the Federation squadron draws close enough to the Synthetic fleet to make out some of the ship's detail. Everyone on both bridges has their eyes glued to the screens where clearly imprinted are a half dozen carriers and many more cruisers and destroyers. "They look like primitive transports!" exclaims Ensign Shunt.

'Request a face-to-face meeting," orders Admiral Ostoff.

The answer is short in coming, another Synthetic cruiser emits a bright light, and a Federation destroyer reports a hit even before being asked. When asked to report the damage, they say there is none, the force of the beam was insufficient to do any damage.

"Reverse speed acceleration," orders Admiral Ostoff and the large ship shudders again as it begins to overcome its forward inertia.

"Admiral," says Captain Plank, "if those ships are as primitive as they seem, we should be able to defeat them even though we are outnumbered."

"I know that, Captain," replies the Admiral irritated, "our mission is exploration, not combat. Besides, we don't know that for sure, and we must be sure this information is sent back to headquarters.

When the Federation squadron returns to headquarters, Admiral Stuff, Captain Plank, and the crews of both bridges are de-briefed at length. Though headquarters is dissatisfied with the information they have on the Synthetics, Admiral Ostoff is commended on his decision not to seek combat on an exploration mission with a numerically superior enemy of unknown capabilities.

No one at fleet headquarters knows what "Synthetic space is either since the war with the Synthetics was fought on Earth several hundred years before. When the historical research is done, and fleet headquarters realize their technical brilliance, teamwork, dedication, and utter ruthlessness, they realize that more will have to be found out about their civilization, especially their technical capabilities.

Word of what has happened to the Ostoff squadron is leaked to the Primeans and the Evonians. There is no point in keeping such a discovery secret. Your own activities are kept secret, and your enemy's secrets are passed on. Besides, the Federation is amused since they now realize that the last war was caused by the Synthetics and not by either the Evonians or Primeans.

Each civilization decides the first thing to do is gather as much intelligence on the Synthetics as possible. The Primeans and the Evonians do not take the news of the new civilization with amusement. They have just fought a bitter, exhausting war with each other over a mistake. Primea is especially bitter since it was they who caused the war by attacking without provocation a Synthetic colony legally on the planet. Evonia's protestations of innocence had been true all the time.

While the human civilizations are buzzing about discovering another military force in the galaxy, Synthetica continues to colonize and grow. However, despite how rapidly Synthetica has grown, it is still quite small compared to any of the human civilizations except the tiny Federation. What's more, Michael knows from the reports of "his" fleet around Verdor that the humans have made many technological innovations, and the Synthetic fleet compared to the human fleets is obsolete.

In order to gain information, each human civilization sends battle squadrons into Synthetic space to gather intelligence. Michael has anticipated it and does not contest it. First, he does not have adequate forces, and he wants to use the intrusions to gather intelligence. Michael knows that the Synthetic ships are obsolescent compared to the human ships, and "he" must discover their technological innovations. Everywhere human squadrons go, a Synthetic ship follows, monitoring it, observing it and all of its technological capabilities.

In this manner, Michael gains more than "he" loses. While the humans find out the size and strength of Synthetica, "he" gains technological information that is more important. Another thing that Synthetica gains is time, time to redesign their obsolescent warships, time to build new ones, time to find more planet's to colonize and develop the colonies that they have, and time to grow.

The human civilizations are awe-struck at the progress and expansions of the Synthetics in the years since they were evicted from Earth. From just a few thousand, the Synthetics have expanded into billions on numerous planets in numerous solar systems. The humans are terrified at the rate of colonial and military expansion, and they know from their historical records that, given the intelligence of the Synthetics, their technological advantages will be temporary. Terrified of Synthetic growth, the human civilizations do something unheard of for them; they act together. Shortly after all the human fleets leave Synthetic space, an ultimatum is delivered, stop colonizing new planets and do so immediately.

The demand is forwarded to Michael, who accepts the terms and signs the treaty. "He" really has no choice. Synthetica is not only smaller than the rest of the civilizations but has inferior technology and a smaller fleet. Most of the Synthetic efforts have thus far gone into expansion rather than into military fleets. Should the human civilizations act together against Synthetica knows, the result would be a Synthetic defeat.

Michael is not displeased by being forced to sign the treaty. "He" has no designs on any human planet and sees no reason to war on any human civilization. As long as humans do not make war upon Synthetics, "he" knows that Synthetics will never make war on humans. The only reason for all the growth up till now is that only by size and strength could Synthetics, in view of past human treachery, be sure of the survival of their species.

The humans have attributed their own motives to the Synthetics. They have taken the rapid expansion of the Synthetics are proof of Synthetic aggressive intent. Not willing to trust the Synthetics, military outposts all around Synthetics are constructed to monitor their activity and ensure that the Synthetics do not break the treaty.

In a few more years, Michael populates all of the planets "he" has and colonizes a few more that the humans would not consider habitable in solar systems where "he" already has planets. The treaty permits this since, by human standards, there is only one habitable planet in a solar system. Therefore, where a civilization has one planet, the whole solar system belongs to that civilization.

While Synthetica is much smaller than any of the other civilizations, excluding the small Federation, it is, in fact, much larger than the other civilization realized. First, the Synthetic planets are much more densely populated, and second, the Synthetic have colonized many planets considered inhabitable by humans. Since these planets are considered uninhabitable by humans, it never occurs to them to check if they are uninhabitable by Synthetic standards. Synthetic is, in fact, more than twice as large as is realized by any of the human civilizations, even though still smaller than either Evonia or Primea. Despite its small size, Synthetica is able to expend a greater portion of its resources to construct a war fleet larger and more modern than any other. Moreover, the quality of the crew on those warships is considerably better than in any other civilization. The time is ripe for the Second Synthetics Rising to begin; it will not be the Synthetics who start it.

Chapter 17

Diplomacy

Dana hopes it is possible to live with humans if Synthetics is in a position of strength, but he still doesn't trust them. Before the war fleet is ready, he contents himself with the status quo, aware that Synthetica lacks the strength to change the Treaty of Verdor. However, when Primea colonizes a planet on the opposite side of Synthetica, an act tantamount to a declaration of war, Dana decides it is time to abrogate the Treaty of Verdor.

Dana sends diplomatic missions to each of the other civilizations to protest their continued colonization while Synthetica cannot. It notably opposes Primea for developing a colony on the opposite side of Synthetics space.

In the Federation, the mission is warmly received. The Federation is but a loose confederation that doesn't follow an aggressive expansion policy. It is also the smallest civilization. However, it does indicate that a general treaty limiting space colonization would be warranted.

In Primea the mission is also warmly received; it is the second-largest civilization, having been overtaken in size by the rapidly multiplying Evonians. Its answer is more specific than the Evonians. If a general treaty can be signed limiting colonization to the current ratios, the Treaty of Verdor can be dropped, but otherwise, it cannot.

Furthermore, Primea will withdraw its offending colony if the treaty can be signed.

At Evonia, the mission is also warmly received. It has surpassed Primea in population, but it has also grown tired of the constant warfare and expense of expanding its population, colonizing and maintaining a large space fleet. Yes, it too will agree to abrogate the Treaty of Verdor if a general treaty over space colonization can be signed. The Evonians decided to meet with the other civilization for six months hence on Verdor to discuss the possibility of a general treaty. The mission then travels back to the capitols of the different civilizations to see if this time and date are acceptable - it is.

Six months later, all of the diplomats meet on Verdor to try to work out a new treaty limiting space colonization. While each civilization is agreeable in principle, they find it difficult to agree to a specific document in practice. The Federation protests that it has no legal authority to bind its diverse planets from establishing a new colony. Evonia will agree to an agreement but only if its proportionate size over Primea is maintained. Primea, suspicious of Evonian intent because of its insistence on proportionate growth, says if Evonia had peaceful intentions, a 1:1 growth would still maintain Evonia as the largest civilization. Eventually, Primea yields to Evonia since it knows that if further colonization goes unchecked, Evonia's advantage in population growth will only allow it to increase its advantage.

The remaining problem is that with Synthetica blocking what had been Primea's avenue of growth, it has no direction to grow. For the treaty to be implemented, Evonia will have to give several planets to Primea. Evonia refuses to do this on the grounds that it is illegal and unthinkable to displace Evonians for the benefit of Primeans. After Primea has made a major concession to it without receiving compensation, Primea is convinced of Evonian treachery and withdraws from the peace conference. When Primea departs, the conference breaks up.

Dana is stuck in an untenable situation. Human civilizations will grow bigger and stronger as time goes by, while Synthetic cannot. While Dana knows that Synthetica is strong enough to defend itself during his lifetime, this is not true for future years. Unwilling to leave the fate of Synthetics again at the hands of the humans, Dana knows he really has no choice and unilaterally announces the abrogation of the Treaty of Verdor.

The announcement does not have the effect that Dana hoped, he had hoped that such an announcement would bring the other civilizations back to the bargaining table, but such is not the case. One civilization is delighted by the announcement. It sees a chance to get revenge on both Synthetica and its arch-enemy Primea at the same time.

A specially organized squadron of Evonian warships with five times as many cruisers as usual carefully plots a wide circle around

Synthetic space so as to remain undetected where the lone Primean colony of Latha sits on the other side of Synthetica.

Once this squadron reaches sub-light speed, it stays out of range of Lathan detectors and sends a small robot craft disguised as a comet ahead to locate the colonies of Latha without discovery. When the robot craft returns, the Evonians discover that there are several colonies on the surface of Latha, and special Primean space stations protect the planet. These space stations are actually obsolete carriers and cruisers being used to give extra military protection to this isolated planet. It is not possible to approach the colony by spiraling in always on the opposite side of the planet.

In order to appear as if they are coming from Synthetic space, the Evonian's circle Primea at hyper-light speed and materialize from the direction of Synthetica within range of cruiser particle beams. The Evonian cruiser particle beams, already charged, immediately fire on the Primean space stations and destroy them. Then they launch missiles at the Evonian colonies and destroy them also, leaving nothing living.

Certain that a diplomatic protest is a waste of time, will be fatal to the diplomats, and only give the Synthetics time to get ready for a counterattack, the Primeans assemble a fleet of 12 squadrons. Determined to avenge the attack on both Latha and Verdor, they depart for Verdor.

Desiring that the Synthetics know who is attacking the Primeans, they do not try to sneak up on the Synthetics or disguise who they are. Upon arrival at Verdor, the Primean also materialize within particle beam range and immediately destroys the Synthetic dry docks and space stations. Verdor, however, is not a new colony like Latha with few defenses. Verdor, by this time, is a completely populated and well-defended colony. When the Primean cruisers materialize, they come with a range of even larger planetary particle beams. The Primean cruisers are successful in taking the Synthetic dry-docks and space stations by surprise and destroying them, but not without casualties. The planetary particle beams open fire on the Primean cruisers. Many are hit and destroyed and those that survive, survive only because, having destroyed their targets, they move out of range. The Primeans, having destroyed the only weapons that can reach them in deep space, rain nuclear missiles down on the Synthetics. The Synthetic laser gunners easily destroy these missiles moving slowly through the atmosphere, but with the explosion of each nuclear missile, more radioactive debris builds up in the Verdorian atmosphere. When the atmosphere of Verdor is lethal, the Primeans stop.

Ironically, there are few Synthetic casualties because, at the beginning of the battle, the population took cover deep underground. There they will stay underground for many years until they can clean their atmosphere and surface of radioactive fallout. Once again, the Synthetics have been subjected to an unprovoked attack by humans. Dana gives up his frail hopes of coexistence with humans. He concludes that he must either destroy them or become so strong that even combined, they would not dare attack Synthetica. Yet what can he do? He cannot possibly hope to defeat all of humanity now if they unite against him, and if h starts re-colonizing at the old rate to expand faster than the humans, he already knows they will unite against him. Will the humans necessarily unite against Synthetica? If there is a war between Synthetica and Primea will Evonia and the Federation be content to sit back and let their enemies destroy each other? As this thought passes through his mind, Dana knows the answer, the enemies of Primea will only be too happy to sit and watch Synthetica and Primea macerate each other.

Dana assembles his fleet, and as he does, he re-commences Synthetic colonization and fills all of his dry-dock space with keels of new Synthetic warships. Dana knows that as soon as the war with Primea is over, the human civilizations try to take advantage of a weakened Synthetica. When the fleet gathers, it assumes a column formation and departs for the Primean home planet still named Primea.

Chapter 18

Ambush

Larth Flango is the commanding Admiral of the Primean fleet, a descendant of military men on both sides of his family. At fifty-six years of age, he is acknowledged as the best warrior his civilization can produce. A child prodigy, he excelled in school and was the youngest person ever enrolled in a Primean Space Academy. Since childhood, he has been fascinated by outer space. When he first enrolled in school, he amazed the teacher when she found out that he already knew how to read.

All through school, Larth was first in his class. He was first in his class at space academy, where he took up engineering, and first in his class at command and staff college.

A self-confident man, but not overbearing, he encourages his staff to express their views openly. A good listener, he believes in listening to all sides of a question before making a decision and never chastises anyone when they disagree. However, once the decision is made, he demands absolute loyalty to that decision. A stern taskmaster, he demands the same dedication that he gives: to Admiral Flange, leadership is by example.

A deeply religious man, Admiral Flango, is dedicated to the principles of The Way and to family life. He is married with seven children, all girls, and the only failure of his life is his inability to produce a son. He is devoted to his daughters. It is his principal passion to spend time with them when he is not working.

A member of the Primean government cabinet by virtue of his military post, he alone had opposed the colonization of Latha. Located distant from the other Primean colonies and isolated, it was impossible to defend. The principal reason he opposed the colonization of the planet is that he saw the Synthetics as potential allies against the more prolific Evonians.

When the cabinet decides to retaliate against the Synthetics at Verdor, Admiral Flango, suspicious of the attack, cast the lone dissenting vote. He has read everything written about Synthetics and knows that unprovoked attacks such as this one are not only inconsistent with their character but that such an attack would be foolish for them. He does not think that the Synthetics are foolish. The other cabinet members argue that the first attack on Verdor, destroying the colony in such a manner to cause a war with Evonia, was an unprovoked attack. When he points out that the Synthetics were actually there first and that it was Primea that first attacked, the other members of the cabinet ignore him. However, when the decision was made, Admiral Flango dutifully carried it out.

When the Synthetic fleet is detected assembling, Admiral Flango instantly realizes that there will be war. He is deeply suspicious of the attack upon Latha but cannot prove it. Unfortunately, he realizes that now it makes no difference. His civilization will be at war; he has no choice but to protect it. He asks for command of the fleet even though that position is a demotion from the Chief of Staff. The appointment is not unanimous in the Primean cabinet: there is one abstention, his own.

Admiral Flango's Synthetic counterpart is Henry. Like all Synthetics, he has no parents and is Institutionally raised. Like nearly all of his species, "he" is young. He was hatched on Alpha III but actually grew on another planet. "He" is the paradigm of Synthetics, small, quick, bright, cold, and ruthless. Like Admiral Flango, he gained his command by outperforming his fellows. However, unlike Admiral Flango, Henry is a hybrid. While the synthetic, on average, are smarter than humans, Henry is not as brilliant as the Admiral. Also, because "he" is a hybrid, the margin of Henry's excellence over the other Synthetics is razor-thin. Despite the vast difference between the civilizations, the design of all space ships is essentially the same. The critical design factor is that humans cannot endure long periods of weightlessness. Freed of gravity, muscles atrophy, and biochemistry go awry. While some of the effects of weightlessness can be countered by regular exercise and diet, it has been found that crews perform much more efficiently in a gravity environment.

When Billy Lynch went to Alpha Centauri, it was not difficult to create gravity on a spaceship. All that was required was to have the ship accelerate at 1 g. The problem is that occasionally warships must stop. Since one cannot have objects, including personnel, suddenly floating away, all spaceships rotate, so that centripetal force substitutes for gravity. The net result is that the two accelerations perpendicular to one another cause a vector that varies according to the respective strength of the accelerations.

If both accelerations were g, the force of gravity would be 13.87 m/s/s or 13.87/9.81 = 141% of g. [9.81 x CSC 45° = 13.87 or (9.812 + 9.912)½ = 13.87]. In fact, the direction and strength of gravity aboard a spaceship vary according to the strength of acceleration. In order to compensate for the varying direction and intensity of the g forces, all space ships have a weighted, rotating inner hull within the fixed outer hull. The inner hull is called the "cat hull" because it always lands on its feet.

Since spaceships cannot take the required year to reach light speed accelerating at g, a way needed to be found to isolate the crew from g forces. Even at 10g, the point at which even the most highly trained fighter pilots pass out, reaching light speed would still take more than a month. The solution was arrived at by following Archimedes instead of Newton. When space ships accelerate, the crew climbs inside water-filled capsules; inside these capsules, the buoyancy of the water neutralizes gravity.

There are three main types of spaceships in every fleet. The largest is the carrier. Its main purpose is defense, and it carries the fighters designed to destroy attacking missiles. On offense, fighters are usually assigned to protect their missiles from attack from enemy fighters. The second type of ship is the cruiser. Its principal function is defending the carrier from the small spacecraft. It has a secondary function; it can use its acceleration apertures as a weapon.

If its engines are focused on a small beam, the debris from the matter/anti-matter engines functions as a particle beam. At the close range, that particle beam can destroy space stations, ships, asteroids, moon bases, or even surfaces of planets. Because of the size of the particle beam, the cruiser must be large in order to offset the recoil of its particle beam. However awesome is the particle beam; the cruiser is not used much. The particle beams travel just under the speed of light and must be close to the enemy to be effective. Missiles are the principal weapons because they can be programmed to track the target after launch and thus are effective at a longer range.

When not in battle, the cruiser carries huge hydroponic gardens where food is grown under artificial light to feed the fleet. This, arguably, is its most important function.

The third type of ship is the destroyer. Aptly named, it is both the workhorse and pawn of the fleet. It carries the most useful of the fleet weapons, the missile. The destroyer is also the first line of defense of the fleet. During the battle, the destroyers form a concave shield in front of the more valuable carriers and cruisers in order to protect them. The destroyer, like the cruiser, also carries a particle beam, but its beam is necessarily much smaller than that of the cruiser.

Other than their size and function, the workings of the three ships are all similar. All ships rotate at the same rate. On the outside of all ships, beyond the armor of the ship, are non-rotating scaffolds for the defensive laser cannon that is the last line of defense from attacking missiles. This scaffold is always stationary. If it rotated with the ship, the laser cannoneers, even with computer assistance, could not get a bead on the attacking missiles. Because the ship rotates and the scaffold doesn't, at least when it is occupied, the scaffold must be rotated to line up to access ports in the ship's hull before the laser gunners can access their positions. Since the scaffold is only occupied in battle, this presents little problem. After the crew enters, the scaffold is slowed to stationary.

Since attacking missiles must attack below light closing speed, if the combined speed of the missile and target ship exceeds the speed of light, they become invisible to each other. All laser cannons are aimed by computers and put out thousands of laser bursts every second, each of which is capable of detonating a missile. If the missile is detonated too close to the ship, the laser cannoneer will be killed by radiation even though the ship is unharmed. The laser cannon actually has very little to do with the laser cannon's operation. He is actually a technician assigned to the laser cannon to make sure it functions properly and especially does not fire on returning friendly fighters. His principal function is to decide upon which targets to fire.

At the center of both the front and back of all ships are the acceleration or deceleration apertures. All ships are powered by matter/anti-matter engines.

When matter and anti-matter meet, they destroy each other, and the resultant explosion powers the ship. No other engine could possibly supply the forces required to accelerate huge space ships at the 1000 g required to reach the speed of light in a few hours. Since the ships travel at hyper-light speed when they are blind and where even a collision with a pebble would cause damage and probably loss of life to the ship, the ships can only travel at the light speed at those distances that they can accurately scan ahead of them. Thus, the ships must make a series of hyper-light speed accelerations and decelerations in order to complete a single voyage. Naturally, it is much easier for the crew to decelerate without doing a somersault at hyper-light speed. The ships do not have a bow and aft. The front and back of all ships are identical.

Because the carrier carries fighters, it also has to launch ports to launch and retrieve fighters. These ports are electrically powered and located towards the center of the ships just outside the acceleration/deceleration apertures. There is no problem launching the fighters. The fighter merely sets up an electromagnetic field around itself opposite to that of the port, and when the electromagnetic field of the port is turned on, the fighter is immediately expelled. The fighter cannot expel itself by its chemical thrust. Repeated such expulsions would damage the port. Retrieving the fighters is much trickier. While the same system of electromagnetic repulsion is used to overcome the fighter's forward momentum, if the electricity does not turn off at the proper millisecond when the fighter's momentum is overcome, it will be expelled back out of the same port. This timing is done by computer.

Besides the ships, there are three forms of craft: shuttle craft, fighters, and missiles. Shuttlecraft are carried by cruisers, are much larger than fighters, and are used to land on surfaces of planets and to ferry material and personnel among the fleet. They, like all craft, are chemically powered.

The second type of craft is the fighter. It is designed to carry a crew of one and to be highly maneuverable. In order to accomplish this, it is kept as small as possible, thereby severely limiting its range. The interesting thing about fighters is that they are manned at all since computers take up less weight. Unmanned fighters do not require life support systems and react much quicker. The explanation is that the commanders do not trust computers to make tactical decisions. Almost none of the flying is done by the pilot; all he does is tell the computer if and when to attack or defend. The weaponry carried by fighters is a laser cannon. This laser cannon is much smaller than the large millisecond burst cannon used to defend ships. This cannon only fires a single burst at a time and requires a few milliseconds to recharge. It is the responsibility of the computer to get the fighter into position so that the one burst does not miss. If the fighter is too close when the missile is detonated, he will be destroyed by the nuclear blast.

The third type of craft is the missile, which is not manned. Since it does not carry a crew and needs no life support systems, it is smaller and more maneuverable than the fighter is. All missiles carry miniature nuclear warheads. One direct hit by a missile will put out of commission even the largest carrier.

Having read all he could learn about Synthetics, Admiral Flango knows that while Synthetics are smarter than the average human, they are not as smart as the smartest human. Therefore, they are not as smart as he. Moreover, if they lack creativity and imagination, they may react poorly to sudden, unexpected maneuvers. Admiral Flango develops plans to do unorthodox and even dangerous maneuvers hoping to take the Synthetics by surprise.

The first trick Admiral Flango uses is to cast thousands of hollowed asteroids in between Synthetica and Primea. Inside these asteroids are electromagnets that are attracted to anything magnetic. Inside the asteroids are large hydrogen warheads designed to explode on contact. Some of the warheads are so large that if they explode even close to a ship, they will immobilize the ship.

The Synthetics detect the asteroids when they plot their hyper-light jump from Synthetic to Primean space. The location of the asteroids is noted because the fleet has to slow to sub-light speed before passing through the asteroid belt. Striking an asteroid at hyper-light speed always causes severe damage to the ship.

It is never done!

As the column of Primean ships proceeds through the asteroids at a sub-light speed, no particular attention is paid to them except that a couple of ships are required to make slight adjustments in their course. A couple of ship captains notice that the asteroids seem to be following them, but only when one collides with a synthetic ship and explodes does an alarm go off. By then, it is too late for a dozen ships because a large number of other mines go off in quick succession, destroying those ships. Henry sends out a warning that the asteroids are mined. It is unnecessary; the ships' captains have already deduced that.

The ships' captains quickly order their laser cannons manned. The laser cannoneers open fire on any asteroid even remotely close. When they do, a couple of other ships are damaged by the hydrogen bombs going off in close proximity. The damaged ships return to Synthetica for repairs. Not many of the huge number of ships have been destroyed, but the odds for the Primeans have been improved slightly.

The Synthetics proceed slowly and carefully through the minefield. Thanks to the laser cannoneers, no other mine gets close enough to cause any damage.

Located in the path of the Synthetic fleet is an uninhabited solar system on the edge of Primean space. In the solar system, Primea has outposts with planetary-sized particle beams hidden deep within moons and asteroids. It just so happens that near one of the moons, the Synthetic fleet materializes out of a hyper-light speed jump.

As the Synthetic fleet passes, Commander Kotlarek of Moon Base VII waits. From the time the Synthetic fleet materializes, he has had a destroyer within range, but he doesn't fire or disclose his position. He doesn't want a destroyer or a cruiser. He wants a carrier. He knows it will be a difficult shot into the middle of the Synthetic column, but he is determined to try even though such a shot into such a large column means certain doom. Although he is deeply embedded into the planet's surface and has numerous laser cannons for missile defense, he knows a fleet of this size can easily overwhelm him. Yet, he is determined to do his part for his civilization no matter the price. However, he can exact a high price for himself and his base.

Finally, when a Synthetic is almost perpendicular to his base, thereby offering him the closest shot possible, he begins to take aim. Not only will his aim have to be true, but the distance, speed of the target, and its vector all have to be allowed for, and the target must be led.

Simultaneous to the firing, bright light is emitted that attracts the attention of the destroyers even while the beam is passing by them on its way to the carrier. Without waiting for orders, the destroyers turn to attack.

Commander Kotlarek has led the carrier perfectly; the beam strikes the carrier amidships. The beam, however, has expanded over the huge distance it had to travel and lacks sufficient concentration to penetrate the ship's armor. Instead, a huge circle on the side of the carrier suddenly glows white-hot and then gradually dims to red. Within the large circle, the thick armor plate cracks and buckles, no longer useful. Beyond the armor plate, there is little physical damage except to flesh. The Synthetics in the personnel areas Just behind the armor are fried almost immediately. However, as the now substantially weakened particle beams travel further toward the center of the ship, it does less damage. When it reaches the next level, there are only what appear to be mild burns. These burns are still fatal, and death will be slow in coming. Beyond the second level, the particle beam does no damage except for the few who were looking the wrong way when the particle beam hit and was blinded.

Synthetic medical personnel is quick to arrive at the scene, but there is little they can do. Those on the outside of the ship are already dead and cooked. The synthetic doctors knowing there is no hope for those on the second level, relieve their misery with a lethal injection. Even the blinded who are recoverable but no longer useful are dispatched. Though the carrier remains operational, the casualties on board are heavy. The bodies of three thousand Synthetics are brought to the cruisers that day as fertilizer. Personnel is shifted from other carriers to make up for the loss, but the carrier remains operational.

It takes 30 seconds for the beam to cool after the first firing. Each successive firing takes longer, up to a maximum of 2 minutes. The distances are such that the beam is ready to fire again before the first beam has reached the destroyers. Knowing that the carrier may be out of range for a destruct hit, Commander Kotlarek decides that with his second shot, he will be certain of a kill. Knowing that such is the distance to his target, the destroyer aims at my turn to attack before the particle beam arrives, and he will miss; he waits until the destroyer reacts to his first shot. When they do, they come straight at him. He cannot miss it!

When the particles of the particle beam strike the destroyer, they instantly vaporize the steel atoms in the destroyer's hull. The power is such that it burns through one side of the destroyer's hull and exits out the other side. The steel atoms instantly heated to vaporization expand with explosive force, ripping the destroyer apart.

It takes a full minute for the particle beam to cool sufficiently to be fired again. By this time, the Synthetic destroyers have turned on him and have fired their own particle beams. One small destroyer particle beam is insufficient to knock out the deeply embedded Primean particle beam that retracts inside the moon each time it fires. However, dozens of particle beams from the Synthetic destroyer arrive simultaneously. What they cannot do singly, they can do in mass. They do not knock out the Primean particle beam, but the heat generated from the mass particle beam attack fuses the heavy doors that allow the Primean particle beam to retract inside the planet. Before the Primeans can force their doors open, a barrage of missiles from the Primean destroyers arrive. The particle beam is defended by laser cannon, but they are not enough to defend against the hundreds of attacking Synthetic missiles. It only takes one nuclear missile to blast the Primean particle beam doors open and destroy the particle beam. Several breaks through. Commander Kotlarek knew when he attacked a large fleet that his fate was sealed. He is only unhappy that he didn't get his carrier.

Before the Synthetic fleet reaches the home planet of Primus, it must pass through an asteroid belt that is wide and deep but not very high. It can be easily avoided by going over or under it. Admiral Flango has considered trying to ambush the Synthetics by placing his fleet inside it but has given it up as too risky. It is too difficult to camouflage an entire fleet, and if discovered, the fleet would be sitting ducks. Still, he can put a small detachment in the asteroid belt with the hope that a successful ambush can reduce the odds.

The Synthetics are suspicious now of any asteroid belt and carefully scan it for shapes similar to the space ship, propellant resides, or any unusual magnetic readings. The Primeans have carefully camouflaged their ships with materials that do not give unusual readings of any kind and disguise the readings a spaceship should give. The radar search beams do not show anything, nor does telescopic examination show any familiar configurations, nor any there any deviances in the normal magnetic or gravimetric fields of the area. As the Synthetic fleet approaches, the Primean does not return the scanning. Such probing would certainly alert the Synthetics. Strict electromagnetic silence is maintained.

The Primean fleet within the asteroids is very small, with only about 100 ships consisting solely of destroyers. Only destroyers are needed for what Admiral Flango has in mind.

The Primeans watch the Synthetics in awe. Never have they seen so many ships before. Their column stretches seemingly to infinity. The column passes directly beneath them, yet they wait, desiring to ambush the column in the center.

Admiral Barker, the Primean commander, becomes anxious as he watches the Synthetics pass. If he allows too many synthetic ships beyond him, they can cut off his escape. He decides to attack but just as quickly belays his order. It occurs to him that having part of the Synthetic fleet follow him dividing itself is exactly what Admiral Flango wants. Admiral Barker waits even though with each passing moment, his and the chances of his detachment escaping diminish.

As the Primean crews wait while the infinitely larger Synthetic fleet passes silently and ominously beneath them, they do not think about the coming battle. Such thoughts are too unpleasant; the terror about to befall them is more than their reverie can bear. Instead, their minds go to pleasant thoughts. They don't think of gunnery, their training, what they will do, or think they will do when the battle starts. They think of wives, girlfriends, picnics, and family members, anything pleasant and happy. For some, it will likely be the last such thoughts in their lives. Admiral Barker thinks of his family reunion, the first time in many years that the whole family has been together.

Admiral Barker has no way of knowing where the middle of the Synthetic fleet is. After several scores of Synthetic ships pass beneath him, he ceases to care. Feeling that this is close enough to the center of the column, he orders the attack. Primean sailors in space suits with rockets attached strip the camouflage. The well-rehearsed process takes less than a minute. Admiral Barker orders acceleration after a minute; the sailors will have to finish on time or be left behind.

Admiral Barker's plan is to attack only one side of the column. The width of the column is too great, and if he tried to break through the column, he would be trapped inside. Admiral Barker hopes he can make his attack and get away before the Synthetics can react. Even though heavily outnumbered, his destroyers are so tightly grouped that they will enjoy local numerical superiority. He has considered attacking the center of the column where the more rewarding targets, the carriers, are but has decided against it. His mission is to get the Synthetics to chase him, dividing their forces.

The Synthetics are not caught entirely unawares. While they did not detect the Primeans initially, they do detect them just as soon as they begin removing their camouflage. However, by the time the Synthetics are turning to aim their particle beams, the Primeans have already fired theirs. Almost simultaneous with the bright light emanating from the bows of the Primean destroyer, the particle beams traveling just below light speed arrive, and the Synthetic destroyers start exploding.

No sooner have the Primeans fired than they commence maximum acceleration away from the Synthetic fleet. In fact, that particle beam is the beginning of acceleration.

The Primeans have an excellent chance for escape since all the nearby Synthetic destroyers have been destroyed. It is the Primeans fondest hope not merely to obliterate some Synthetic destroyers but to lure large numbers of them away where they cannot participate in the main battle.

The ambush proves only partly successful. A number of Synthetic destroyers are destroyed, but the bait is not taken. Not a single Synthetic ship chases the escaping Primean ambushers. With a single mind, the Synthetic captains unanimously realize that they are needed by the main fleet and not off chasing some Primean ambushers. How wonders Admiral Barker, when he sees that the Synthetics are not pursuing him, did they all unanimously understand the folly of pursuit. There wasn't time to receive a radio message from the command vessel.

Do they have mental telepathy?

When Admiral Barker is sufficiently far away from the Synthetic fleet that he is out of danger, he turns his fleet towards Primus and accelerates to hyper-light speed in order to join the main Primean fleet. In so doing, he passes invisible through the Synthetic fleet. A dangerous maneuver must be taken. Such is the dispersal of the two fleets that there are no collisions. The Synthetic detects his passing only after he has passed. As he rejoins the main Primean fleet, Admiral Barker wonders: Have I survived one battle just to perish in another?

Chapter 19

Victory or Death

The asteroid belt is the last obstacle between the Synthetic fleet and the Primus, the home planet of Primea. After the asteroid belt, the Synthetics assume battle formation; the point of the column slows, and as it does, the rest of the fleet catches up. The destroyers form a large semi-circular concave shield. Behind them are the cruisers forming a second shield of the same shape. Behind them are the carriers in the same formation. The fleet ships are a bit closer now than when in the column. They are as close as possible to get overlapping fields of fire but without being in danger if a nuclear missile hits an adjoining ship.

The Primean fleet is already waiting in battle formation in front of Primus. As soon as the Synthetic fleet clears the asteroid belt, the Primean fleet starts to meet the Synthetics. Admiral Flango does not wish to be backed up against his own planet where he cannot maneuver. The two fleets close upon each other at light closing speed, the maximum speed they can travel where their combined speed will not exceed the speed of light and become invisible to each other. Compared to the speeds they normally travel, the speed at which they close upon each other is like a slow crawl. As they close upon each other, they randomly change their course so that their future positions cannot be calculated. If future locations can be calculated, missiles will be sent to those locations at hyper-light speed, and the missiles will be on them even before their launch is detected.

The Primean sailors grow tense as the battle nears. They know that this is no mere skirmish; it is all or nothing, victory or death. The Synthetics expect no quarter and give none. Each sailor knows that even if Primea is victorious, the odds are still against his survival. Every Primean sailor knows that he will come home victorious or not.

As the fleets draw closer, Admiral Flango mulls battle tactics repeatedly in his mind, fighting phantom Synthetics. Self-doubts assail him constantly: Will I prevail? Will I make a tactical blunder? Will my whole civilization perish because of my incompetence? Constantly he reminds himself that overconfidence and complacency are a commander's worst vices. Always respect your enemy, be vigilant, and pay attention to detail; good execution is more important than brilliant planning.

He wonders briefly if the Synthetic commander is suffering as is he. He knows that he must relax. He must not tire himself; he cannot perform at his best if he is tired. He keeps hypothecating; if he uses this tactic, what will the Synthetic do to counter it, constantly reminding himself never to plan too far ahead. To plan too far ahead is to assume how the enemy will react, and the enemy seldom reacts as one assumes. Each tactical decision must be made on its own merits and only fit the tactical situation.

The object of space tactics is to get the enemy within the range of your missiles but outside the range of his. This is done by firing your missiles at him while he is moving at high speed towards you, and you are moving slowly so that you can overcome your momentum and reverse direction so that you are moving away from the attacking missiles when they arrive. Since the attacking missiles cannot exceed the speed of light or become blind, this gives your laser gunners more time to destroy them. Merely slowing down does not help because all missiles are programmed to attack at light closing speed, and if the enemy fleet slows, the attacking missiles proportionately increase their speed.

The problem with the tactic is that the enemy is as aware of it as you are. The easiest way to get the enemy within your effective range and stay out of his is to slow your speed.

Unfortunately, if you slow your speed, the enemy will also.

Another tactic is to calculate the enemy's course and direction and fire missiles at the hyper-light speed at the calculated location. This is why, as the two fleets approach, they constantly and randomly change course and speed so that their future positions cannot be calculated.

In actuality, the admirals use all of the tactics, yet none of them. What they do is a combination of them and anything they can think of at the time. The one thing that all admirals fear is getting too close. Since it takes several minutes for the first salvo of missiles to reach the enemy, several salvos will be fired before the first salvo arrives. Once the missiles are launched, they operate independently; they continue to attack even If their fleet is destroyed. If, after destroying the enemy, the winning fleet cannot escape, it too may be destroyed.

Hour after hour, the two fleets maneuver closer to each other, zig-zagging constantly, their speeds steadily diminishing. Finally, after hours of maneuvering, the two fleets come within range. Yet, neither launches because neither fleet is within effective range. Effective range is the point at which the first salvo of missiles will reach the enemy before he detects the launching of missiles and reverse direction. Should one launch too early, the other could reverse direction and be speeding away when the attacking missiles arrive. Thus though both are within range, the two continue to close upon each other, still zig-zagging and still slowing until just before they are within effective range, Admiral Flango begins launching his missile and fighters.

As soon as the Synthetic fleet detects the Primeans launching missiles, they immediately begin the emergency reversal of their engines. How foolish of the Primean Admiral to waste missiles, thinks Henry. His intuition might have warned "him" of impending danger if Henry had been human.

Henry knows that by the time the Primean missile carriers are close, "his" fleet will have overcome its forward inertia and move in reverse. Reasoning that the Primean missiles should be easy to destroy, "he" decides to take a risk and launches "his" fighters with instructions to ignore the missiles and go exclusively after the fighters. Henry knows if "he" can destroy these Primean fighters, "he" can gain fighter superiority, which will give the Synthetic fleet an overwhelming tactical advantage both offensively and defensively.

Commander Pierre Rukavina is the commander of the first wave of Primean fighters. He has little to do as he closes on the Synthetic fleet at barely sub-light speed. The computer flies the craft; he is there only to make the tactical decisions. As he approaches, he stares at his radar screen, looking for the Synthetic fighters that he hopes will be there. He sees them first as two diffuse clouds, waiting motionless, unable to move ahead because any forward motion will break light closing speed and make the attacking enemy invisible.

Two groups say Commander Rukavina to himself, one for the fighters and one for the missiles. Joy fills Commander Rukavina's heart, for he knows that Admiral Flango's tactic is working; so simple, so brilliant, so devoid of unnecessary risks, so typical of Flango.

At last, under magnification, he can pick out individual fighters that appear as tiny dots on his screen. Just after the Synthetic fighters attack, Commander Rukavina's preprogrammed fighter wave simultaneously dives into and through their own missile salvo. So abrupt is the maneuver that Commander Rukavina passes out when the G forces caused by the dive cause his blood to leave his head. When he awakens, his craft is gracefully dancing among his own missiles as the craft's computer guides the fighter delicately through them. Once through the salvo Commander Rukavina and all of the Primeans engage in emergency acceleration in order to gain as much speed as they can before what is to happen next. As he does, he bends forward so that all of his body is protected by the rear of the fighter. Like Lot's wife, he does not look back.

The Synthetics close on the tails of the Primeans and destroying them in droves are now among the Primean missiles. Suddenly there is a blinding flash as all the preprogrammed Primean missiles simultaneously detonate. The result is exactly as Admiral Flango had hoped. The pursuing Synthetic fighters are wiped out. The fighter superiority hoped for by Michael now favors Flango!

The Primean fighters are close to the source of the nuclear explosion, too close to survive under normal conditions. However, their speed favors them. As they emerge from their own salvo, they are accelerating. When the deadly radiation from the explosion reaches where the Primean fighters were, they are still farther away... When the radiation reaches that point, the Primean fighters are still farther. The radiation eventually overtakes the Primean fighters, but by that time, radiation, which decreases in intensity by the square of the distance from the source, is no longer deadly!

Even the thin metal of a fighter is sufficient to protect them. In the blackness of space, there is no indication to the Primean pilots that the radiation has passed them. Only when the pilots know that enough time has passed for the radiation to reach them do they look in their rear view mirrors to see what is behind them. What they see is a billowing cloud of space dust.

"Hurray," cheer the surviving fighter pilots into the silence of space, thinking they have won the battle, that without sufficient fighters, the Synthetics must surely withdraw. Commander Rukavina turns his fighter wave back to the Primean fleet.

Loud cheers go up from the Primean crews when news of the explosion arrives, and they realize that a Synthetic fighter force wave has been eradicated. The senior officer on the Admiral's bridge congratulates Admiral Flango, and he breaks into a wide smile. Each one of them is convinced the battle is over, much of the Synthetic fighter force and its main defense has been eliminated, and there is no longer enough to escort its missiles and protect the fleet from the missile as well. They have to withdraw. Admiral Flango makes plans to follow them, pin them to their home planets, and decisively defeat them.

Henry, surprised by the annihilation of "his" fighters, shows no emotion. Mentally "he" congratulates "his" opponent for a brilliant tactical move. "He" never considers withdrawing, "he' still believes "he" will prevail, though at a far greater cost.

By this time, the Synthetic fleet has overcome its forward momentum and is receding from the Primeans. Henry again orders "his" direction of travel reversed - towards the Primean fleet!

The Primeans detect the change of course by the Synthetics. Immediately the mood of joy empties from Primean heart as the news speeds like lightning through the fleet as the Synthetics overcome their rearward inertia, the Primeans who have been accelerating brake abruptly so as not to give the Synthetics a tactical advantage. Admiral Flango's intuition tells him there is something wrong; the Synthetics should be fleeing! It is stupid to give battle with inadequate fighter protection, and he doesn't believe that Synthetics are stupid. However, he tries to understand, but his intellect does not tell him why it is the Synthetics are advancing. Deep within Primean space, Admiral Flango has no choice but to give the Synthetics battle.

The two fleets close upon each other, and when they come within effective range, they commence launching missiles and fighters. It is now too late for both fleets to overcome their forward inertia before the first wave of enemy missiles is upon them. Admiral Flango orders his fleet to come to a dead stop. He wants to give himself a chance to escape if victorious. However, the Synthetic fleet does not slow, increasing its speed instead. There is a tactical advantage to this. When the fleet advances, it has the effect of compressing the missile salvos. The faster the fleet advances, the more compressed are the missile salvos, and the less time the enemy's fighters and laser gunners have to destroy them.

The Rukavina fighters now arrive back and rejoin their carriers. The fighters are landed and, without the pilots leaving their cockpits, are refueled and relaunched.

The first salvo of both missiles passes each other in space. They are blind to each other; their combined speed exceeds the speed of light.

As the Synthetic missiles reach the Primean fleet, Primean fighters descend upon them like locusts. Then the unexpected happens, that which Admiral Flango's intuition revealed to him, but his intellect didn't. The Synthetic missiles turn to meet the fighters and return fire. The Synthetic missiles are piloted, their pilots on suicide missions. The Primean pilots expecting to have it easy are taken by surprise and decimated. Those that survive turn away. The Synthetic missiles then turn to attack the Primean fleet. However, they have had to slow their speed to dogfight and have been thinned as well. They are easy targets for Primean laser cannons.

When Admiral Flango sees this happen, he immediately orders emergency acceleration away from the Synthetics. He also orders his fighters to quickly engage and disengage the Synthetic missiles, long enough for the Synthetic missile to deviate from their' attack. The order is flawed, and the tactic only works one time. The third Synthetic salvo of missile pilots, seeing what happened to their predecessors, takes a page out of Flamingo's book, and before the Primean fighter can disengage, the Synthetic pilots detonate their warheads. Now it is the Primean fighters that are destroyed.

Meanwhile, the Primean missiles have arrived at the Synthetic fleet. The remaining Synthetic fighters engage the accompanying Primean fighters, leaving the missiles open for attack. As the missiles approach, a few Synthetic destroyers advance in front of the shield, and the remaining destroyers close the gaps behind. As these ships advance, Primean missiles target Primean ships closest to them. These few ships attempt to defend themselves but are overwhelmed and destroyed. All are hit, and when the first missile hits, a chain reaction occurs that detonates all the other missiles in the vicinity. Such is the explosion that each ship is completely vaporized. What remains of the first Primean wave of missiles is easily destroyed by Synthetic laser gunners.

For each succeeding salvo of missiles, Henry deliberately sacrifices more destroyers. By this sacrifice, "he" avoids much more abrupt destruction of "his" fleet. With each salvo, the weakened defensive fires require a steadily increasing sacrifice.

Due to the distance between the fleets, it took time for Admiral Flango to be informed of the Synthetic tactics. When he is, he immediately grasps their significance. The initial advantage he gained by destroying the Synthetic fighters has been more than offset. It is already too late to win the battle, but he resolves at least to keep the Synthetics from winning it. Admiral Flango orders his fleet to close at maximum acceleration with the Synthetic fleet. He has to repeat his order twice because his bridge crew doubts their ears.

Closing with the Synthetics by Admiral Flango creates the impossible, the ridiculous, the absurd. With both fleets closing on each other at close range, neither has time to overcome inertia and break free. The forward speed of both fleets causes each new salvo of missiles to be compressed. The impossible has happened, that most dreaded by all tacticians, the possibility of utter annihilation of both fleets. The remaining battle does not last long, Henry sees the acceleration of the Primean fleet and tries to slow it, but it is too late. The respective missiles of both fleets overwhelm the defenses of the other. Both destroyer shields are exploded into space dust with the cruiser following with the next salvo and then the carriers.

The Synthetics have won if you can call having a dozen ships left out of more than a thousand victory. Henry's emergency deceleration saves a few of his carriers. It must be victory, and the Primeans are completely gone. The Synthetics proceed to the home planet of Primus and demand the surrender of the civilization. The Primeans know that even though their fleet is gone, the Synthetics have no means of forcing them to surrender or refuse. Admiral Flango, true to his military code to the end, has deliberately sacrificed himself and his entire fleet so that his civilization might be saved. By such sacrifice, the Primeans are saved from the Synthetics. Who will save them from their fellow humans?

Chapter 20
Vultures Descend

The Synthetics have won; the Primean fleet has been destroyed down to its last warship. The victory is Pyrrhic; the pitiful remnants of the Synthetic fleet cannot seize the fruits of their victory. The only thing Henry can do is return to Synthetica.

Evonia and the Federation have not been oblivious to this war. Both civilizations have had scout ships watching the battle. At the end of the battle, they return to give their civilizations the news.

Evonia is delighted with the outcome. It is the largest civilization in the galaxy, and its fleet is in complete readiness. With the Primean fleet destroyed, it immediately declares war upon Primea and commences annexing Primean planets. The treachery of this action is lost upon the Evonian leaders. They justify it on the grounds that if they don't, The Federation will. Soon Evonia will take her rightful place as the leader of the galaxy. It never occurs to the leaders of Evonia that these thoughts are inconsistent.

The Federation, nothing more than a loose alliance of independent planets, content till now to have Primea and Evonia war against each other orally with one of the other to maintain the balance of power, has been engaged in a bitter political struggle since the discovery of Synthetica. The Constitutionalists, who want a constitution with a strong central government, argue that the discovery of Synthetica upsets the balance of power and that the central government needs the power to do such things as tax, declare war, and make treaties. The Federalists, wishing to maintain the traditional sovereignty of their planets, do not want a strong central government and argue that all a strong central government will do is involve their planets in unwanted wars.

The political battle is still raging when the Primean fleet is destroyed. When the politicians discover that Evonia is annexing Primean planets, the power of the Federalists is broken. Immediately the Federation fleet is sent to annex as many Primean planets as possible. In the meantime, a constitutional convention is called, where the central government is given a constitution with the power to assess taxes, make treaties, declare war, and conscript for war.

While the Federation is debating, the Evonians are annexing one Primean planet after another. The process is slow since the Evonians must arrive off the planet with a large enough fleet in order to subdue the planet if necessary. Though the Primean planets are all well defended with planetary particle beams and could give a good account of themselves, none do. They realize that to resist would cost millions of lives, leave radioactive residues, and be futile. If they don't surrender to the Evonians, they will have to surrender to the Synthetics. Without exception, each time the Evonian vessels arrive in orbit around the planet, the planet surrenders. It is only the terms of the surrender that are discussed. The one request is that the Primeans be allowed to keep their religion. The Evonians immediately agree but add that the artificial uterus can no longer be forbidden. This is a bitter pill to the Primeans, but as long as they can practice their religion, they agree.

Though the Evonians have a much larger fleet and have a long head start at annexing Primean planets, the Federation fleet commander, Marie McDonagh, reasons that she does not need to keep her fleet as a unit to force the Primeans to surrender. Instead, she reasons that the Primeans would naturally prefer to surrender to the Federation rather than the Evonians, who they detest. Therefore she orders her fleet to break up into squadrons and annex Primean planets several at a time. She hopes to catch up on the head start that Evonian has on annexing planets.

It is not long before the Evonian fleet arrives at a Primean planet that has already surrendered to the Federation. The Evonians heavily outnumber the lone Federation squadron, easily defeat it and take the planet for itself; there is no battle. The Evonians do not want a fight; they are interested in expanding their civilization, not starting a war. Greed is always stronger than bloodlust. The Primean planet is delighted with the surrender to the Federation, and anything is better than the hated Evonians, women who think they're men and men who think they're women.

After the Evonian fleet departs to the next Primean planet, the Federation squadron, unlike the Evonians who leave a squadron to enforce order, leaves only one ship. The Federation squadron then leaves to the second nearest Primean planet, knowing that the Evonians have already departed to the next. A cycle develops with

Evonia and the Federation leapfrogging to annex Primean planets. When all the Primean planets have been annexed, there is no clearly defined boundary between the two civilizations.

When Henry arrives back at Synthetica to freshly completed warships, "he" returns to Primea at once to claim the fruits of victory. When "he" arrives back, there is a Federation squadron in orbit around the planet. Henry doesn't need to demand the planet's surrender or ask what has happened, "he" already knows. Nor does "he" attack the Federation squadron though "he" could easily defeat it. Attacking the Evonian squadron would mean war with the Evonians, which Synthetica cannot afford. There is only one thing to do, return to Synthetica and rebuild the Synthetic fleet for the inevitable war with Evonia.

After the process of annexing the Primean planets is complete, the much longer and more difficult process of consolidating power and pacifying the population begins. Millions of Evonian occupation troops are brought in to enforce the edicts of the military governments. All Primean military units are disbanded.

Janet Karf is the apple of her father's eyes, a shy, demure Primean girl, always obedient, the personification of the ideal of Primean femininity. Janet is awaiting the most important day of her life, the most important day of any Primean girl's life, her wedding day.

Janet knows that her civilization is at war, and while she hopes it will win, she hardly ever concerns herself with warlike things.

Wars are far away, her fiancé is not in the space fleet, she has no male relatives in the space fleet, and the events of galactic politics do not affect her. She has more important things on her mind, things that affect her in a most personal way, things that will shape and form the rest of her life.

Everything is going well for Janet; her world is beautiful, for she is in love. Then she hears the terrible news - the Primean space fleet has been completely wiped out! The only good thing about it is that the Primean admiral made sure that the Synthetic fleet was destroyed or almost destroyed with it. It is terrible news, and Janet feels sympathy for the men who died and their families, but she knows no one who died. The loss is remote and while other people talk about it, the shock, for her, passes quickly, erased by happy plans.

Then something does happen that bursts Janet's private little world; the Evonians seize the planet and occupy it. The hated Evonian, the she-men who dress and act like men, who have no concept of the dignity and purity of femininity. Even though this will affect her world, it does not diminish her sanguine outlook on life, for she is in love and will soon be married.

As her marriage approaches, Janet begins hearing stories. Stories that shock and appall her, stories about sexual liaisons, even orgies between Primean men and Evonian occupation troops. It is hard to believe that a Primean man would so lower himself as to fornicate with an Evonian, yet the stories are so persistent that Janet begins to believe them.

As she begins to believe them, she wonders if her fiancé. Larry has ever been propositioned by an Evonian. Then, horrified at the thought, she wonders if he would accept her proposition. No, no, certainly not, she tells herself. No self-respecting Primean male-like Larry would ever allow himself to be seduced by such a masculine female. Besides, he loves me too much!

Then it happens, just a few days before the marriage, Larry comes to her and says, "J - Janet, I have to speak to you."

"What is it, Larry? What's wrong?"

"I — I — have changed my mind. I don't want to get married."

"You don't want to get married," she repeats in disbelief. "What's wrong? Is there someone else?" she asks, bile welling up in her throat.

"No, there's no one else. I - I've just changed my mind. I don't want to get married anymore." With that, he turns away from her wanting to avoid the unpleasantness he has caused her. As he leaves, he despises himself, despises himself for being weak, not wishing to admit even to himself the real reason he is abandoning her, for succumbing to the temptation that changed his mind against marriage.

Once Larry has left, Janet recovers her composure enough to go home. Upon the sight of her mother, she bursts into tears and sobs, "Mother, Larry has broken off our engagement."

"There, there, Janet," her mother says, consoling her, "it's for the best."

"What do you mean it's for the best Larry has left me? He's not going to marry me. I'm going to be an old maid!" exclaims Janet through her tears and sobbing.

"That's all right, Janet. Larry's not good enough for you anyway," says Mrs. Karf, holding her daughter and comforting her.

"What do you mean he's not good enough for me, you've always liked Larry?" asks Janet, her mother's words finally sinking in. that her mother knows something that she doesn't.

"I did like Larry."

Her mother's choice of words is not lost upon her this time, "What do you mean did?" she asks, the sobbing stopping.

"Well, you've heard the stories about Primean boys and the Evonian troops."

"You mean Larry."

Her mother nods her head in silence.

"Why that rat, the rotten filthy rat, throwing me over for some Evonian trollops! Mother, why didn't you tell me this before?" asks Janet, her tears turning to anger.

"I couldn't - I just couldn't. I hoped he'd stop, that once he had his fill or got married, he would stop."

"Who, who knows about this?"

"Nearly everyone, it's common gossip,"

"Oh no, now he's made me a laughingstock. How will I ever show my face again?" With that, she runs to her room, throws herself on the bed, and dissolves into tears.

Larry is not the only Primean male who finds the Evonian troops a delight. They have never met women like this before. They do not exist on Primean planets; the Evonian women are so aggressive, so wanton, so abandoned. There is nothing coy or demure about them. They do not play games or insist upon being pursued, and they state exactly what they want! When the first Evonian troops first proposition Primean males, they are as shocked to be accepted as the Primean males are to be asked. What's more, the copulations take place almost on the spot.

As delighted as the Primean males are, the Evonian men are narcissistic, regarding themselves as the alluring sex to be sought after and pursued. The Primean males regard the female as the alluring sex, something that the Evonian women cannot get over. Dramatic changes take place almost immediately among the Evonian troops. They become exceptionally fastidious about their appearance. Even those that were sloppy become neat. What the Evonian girls like best about the Primean men is their aggressiveness, their eagerness, and their blatant lust. The couplings are hot, quick, and violent!

The Primean people are shocked at such immorality-taking place and complain to the Evonian military government. The Evonians are delighted by the relationships and desire intermarriage so that the two cultures will merge, turning a deaf ear to such protests.

Eventually, the newness of easy sex wears off, and the Evonian troops begin to desire something more meaningful. When they try to extend their relationship with the Primean men, they discover the Primean men aren't interested in them; they are only interested in the easy sex. Moreover, to the Evonian's amazement, the Primean men despise them for copulating with them.

After they fornicate with the Primean males, the Primeans want nothing more to do with them. Yet, if the Evonians offer themselves to them again, the Primean males, even though they despise the Evonians for doing so, will eagerly copulate with them. It makes absolutely no sense to the Evonians at all. Why would men want to make love with us and then despise us for doing what they want? How can you hate someone you want to love?

One of the hopes of the occupying Evonians is that their troops will intermarry with the Primeans, and pacification with the Primeans will thus take place. The Evonians hope when the Primeans marry the Evonians, they will see the superiority of Evonian customs, and Primean customs will fall away. After only a short time of occupation, it becomes clear that this is not taking place. Despite the enormous amount of fornication, there are virtually no marriages between Evonians and Primeans, and those that do take place are always with the lowest element of Primean society, the few Primeans who want their wives to support them.

The Evonians decided to adopt a pacification program so that the two cultures could merge. This Is not done for mere abstract reasons; until the Primean culture is absorbed or merges with the Evonian culture, the Primean planets cannot be trusted to support the military efforts of the civilization. The Evonian government decides upon a director before deciding on a program. The new director is none other than Winnifred Wiffer, the wife of Ron Rutter. She is a natural pick. She alone, due to the prodding of her husband, has shown any interest in elevating the status of Evonian men.

Winnifred immediately decides against forced marriages. Such marriage wouldn't work and would only alienate the Primean population more than it already is. If pacification is to work, it has to be because the Primeans embrace it. Someway has to be found for them to willingly embrace Evonian customs or for the customs to merge and do so quickly.

The Evonian occupation troops soon discover something else they had forgotten, these men are fertile, and the Evonian occupation troops find themselves pregnant by the millions. The Evonian commanders who should have anticipated the problem quickly complain to Winnifred, who orders the immediate sterilization of all Primean bachelors. When the Evonians attempt to enforce the edict, there is a violent revolt. The badly outnumbered Evonian troops are attacked by angry crowds and are forced to take refuge in their barracks. The only thing that saves them is the threat of reprisal by Evonian spaceships. Winnifred cancels her edict, and all Evonian troops are confined to the base until they can be taught contraceptive practices.

While the Evonian occupation troops like the industrious Primean men, they detest the submissive Primean women. Winnifred makes it her first priority to raise the consciousness of Primean women, to teach them that they are superior to the male. Indoctrination classes are begun on every formerly Primean planet, and all young women are required not only to attend but must repeat the courses until they pass. One of the first priorities is to teach the Primean women the advantages of the artificial uterus. The Primean women realize that they will have to repeat until they pass study and virtually all pass. However, none of them, except those who can bear children in no other way, opt to use the artificial uterus.

Larry Beve, Janet Karf's former fiancé, eventually tires of the hot, steamy sex with Evonian soldiers and, desiring a more meaningful relationship, asks Janet to take him back. Still smarting from his abandonment and her humiliation at his hands, she refuses. Larry leaving dejected, knowing it is his own fault, is intercepted by Janet's mother, who encourages him to persist, that Janet will eventually change her mind, and takes that advice. Eventually, Janet's hurt fades, and she becomes convinced that Larry really does care for her after all and takes him back. After all, he is just a man, and men can't help themselves in such things. Thus having reassured herself of her moral superiority, a new wedding is planned. Janet will come to regret all of her life not taking him back sooner.

Winnifred is disappointed at the progress of her pacification program and angry as well. Nothing she has done has worked: the numerous sexual fraternizations have come to naught, and the Primean women have completely resisted indoctrination. The Primean people seem determined to frustrate her in her attempts to pacify them. Winnifred determines upon an action that is harsh but irresistible. Sufficient troops are brought in to enforce the edict, and then the edict is promulgated. Marriage between Primeans is forbidden. All Primean bachelors over 18 are forcibly taken to Evonian planets. In their place, at a ratio of 1 to 5, Evonian Vasecta is brought in. Larry's and Janet's wedding is the day after the edict is promulgated. Since he is a bachelor over 18, the marriage is not allowed to take place, and he is deported to an Evonian planet.

When Larry is deported to an Evonian planet, he despises himself for the fool her had been. If only he had realized earlier what a wonderful girl Janet was. If only he hadn't succumbed to the pleasures of the flesh and married when he had the chance. However, there is nothing that he can do. He cannot return to his own planet. All there are on this planet are Evonian women who he despises. At first, he refuses to accept them, but as time goes by and he becomes more and more lonely, they begin to look more appealing. Eventually, he accepts a relationship with one of them that leads to marriage. When his first wife asks him to take another wife in order to improve family finances, he obliges her, but unlike an Evonian man, he refuses to be vasectomized and also refuses any more wives. When he finds how difficult it is to mediate between two wives, he does not desire any more. Unlike the Evonian men, he continues to work.

Naturally, since he is a member of the sect, he would prefer to have his wife bear their own children, but his wives will not even discuss it. Since there is nothing he can do about it, he accepts it. The one thing that he can do, however, is insisted that the children really are his and that half of them at least are males. This is a matter of minor importance to his wives. When his boys are born, he naturally insists they be primarily responsible for their discipline. He also insists that his boys be given at least the same educational opportunities as his girls. As a result of this interest, his sons follow their father's example and grow up with the same values. Distinctly out of step with the rest of Evonian society except those families of Primean fathers, Janet Karf knows this time that Larry will not be coming back to her. She despises the lazy, narcissistic Evonian males. She waits a number of years, hoping against hope that the Evonian occupation government will change its mind and somehow return Larry to her. When she turns 30, she realizes that her biological clock is running down, and she can no longer hope for a miracle.

One day when she finds her boss looking at her in a certain way, she realizes she has caught him looking at her this way many times before. This time, however, she flashes back a quick, shy smile and holds it long enough so that she knows he has noticed. When he asks her to accompany him to lunch, she accepts even though she knows this is immoral. Later, when he asks her out on a date, she again accepts. Gradually their relationship cements until he is helping pay for the rent on her apartment. When she finds herself pregnant, she feels guilty but is not displeased.

When her boss discovers she is pregnant, he abandons her and has her fired. Having no employment and no means to support the child, she sues him and her employer. Much to her surprise, in the Evonian-dominated court system, she wins. Her former lover is forced to support their child, and the company that employed her is forced to take her back with back pay and attorney's fees. With child support and employment, again, she meets another Primean married man. This time she makes sure his wife is aware of her relationship. By this time, such liaisons have become commonplace. The first wife is not happy, but she understands Janet's predicament and does not blame her. When Janet becomes pregnant for the second time, her new lover does not abandon her. She, however, is not the first wife and the first love. A greater amount of her lover's time is spent with his first family. Janet learns to be content with what she has; sharing a Primean husband is still better than being married to a useless Evonian.

When a couple asks the clergy to validate the second marriage, the clergy of the Sect refuses. When the same arguments are put forward, they resulted in the independence of Plicker many years before, and those arguments fall on deaf ears. The clergy is familiar with the arguments and knows what happened on Plicker. They are determined not to make the same mistake again. Notwithstanding the clergy's refusal to legitimize the marriage, the practice of taking mistresses continues, and many children are borne of such relationships. When Winnifred becomes aware of what is going on, she has no objection.

While the Primean girls have suffered the Evonian bachelors deported to, Primean planets have it much worse. The women there totally despise them and won't have anything to do with them. In order to make a living, they must take jobs, and since they are not qualified for anything, they must take the most menial. The Evonian men who the Primean women might accept, the Paterna, are not brought. They are too much in demand on their own planets.

Of the groups affected by the changes, the Evonian women clearly have benefited the most. Though the Primean men are homely compared to the Evonian men and inartful lovers, they are certainly more aggressive, dependable, harder workers, and something unheard of for men, providers. The Primean men prove far more popular for husbands than do the Evonian men. The Primean men accustomed to working for a living, despising the idea that their wives should support them, continue to work after marriage. The presence of these able, hard-working men on the Evonian planet presents quite a culture shock to the Evonian women who are accustomed to lazy and shiftless Vasecta. As the number of the Primean men on Evonian planets increases, their presence changes the Evonian society. After a few years, the sex ratio for everyone, not just for the Primean fathers, is changed to 1:1.

When the sex ratio changes, they realize that the amalgamation of the two societies is finally taking place. The two societies are moving to common cultural standards. However, the Evonian government realizes that something totally unexpected has happened. Rather than the occupiers pacifying the occupied, the opposite has happened. Evonian society has been changed more than the Primeans. The change in the sex ratio affects profound changes in Evonian society, especially the role of men. The only major change to Primean society is the availability of the artificial uterus.

Still, there is a problem yet to be faced. The continuous deportation of bachelors from Primean planets will, if continued, depopulate them. The solution is simple when the new generation of Evonians males raised by Primean fathers come of age, and these men are Imported 1:1 for every Primean male exported. The new Primean males born of Primean fathers are naturally accepted back by their relatives and willingly accepted by the young Primean women who by this time are desperate for young men. Finally, the Evonian government knows it is succeeding in amalgamating Primeans.

Even though it is Evonian society that has been changed, Evonian leaders are pleased.

The shock to Primean society by Federation occupation is not nearly so stressful but is less successful. Like the Primeans, the basic Federation institution is the monogamous family. The constitution of all Federation planets guarantees freedom of religion, and most planets are pluralistic. Primean religion is left intact, and Primean society is almost left intact, the only change being the Federation's insistence upon equality of treatment for girls.

However, despite how close the Federation society is to Primean society, the Federation is still an occupying power. Their presence is deeply resented by the Primeans. In every way they possibly can, they resist amalgamation and preserve their identity. When the artificial uterus is made available on Primean planets, no one uses it. When Primean women are encouraged to insist upon equality, the Primean women ignore the Federation. When both Primean males and females are conscripted for military service, they prove so useless that they are exempted. The Primean males resent taking orders from women, and the Primean girls are more interested in preserving their femininity than in being military.

Like Evonia, the Federation encourages intermixing between the two civilizations, especially marriage. The Primeans, however, want none of it. To them, the Federation is the enemy - to consort with the enemy is treason!

Chapter 21
Diplomatic Entanglements

After the destruction and annexation of Primea, the Federation and Evonia held diplomatic talks to see if they could agree on an alliance and unified action against Synthetica. Evonia is the largest civilization in the galaxy and, despite her size, is worried about the Synthetics. She knows that the Synthetics are capable of more rapid expansion than they are and that Synthetics are dedicated, brilliant, and ruthless.

The Evonians urge a pre-emptive strike against Synthetica. They argue that if Synthetica can be attacked before its space fleet can be rebuilt, victory will be easy. They say that there can't be much of a space fleet in Synthetica, and it should be easy to destroy. Once that space fleet is gone, if they beat the orbiting dry docks, the means of building another will be gone. Synthetica will cease to be a threat.

The Federation is indecisive and vacillates. Though it cannot refute the cogent Evonian arguments, the Federation has never started a war. True, it has made war but only after being first attacked. However ruthless the Synthetics are, they have done nothing to provoke the Federation, to justify the Federation making war upon them. Evonia is urged to proceed against the Synthetics without them. Furthermore, deep in the minds of the Federation leaders is a suspicion of Evonians. If Synthetica were destroyed, what would stop the Evonians from turning on us. As long as

Synthetica exists, there is a balance of power, and no one civilization can single-handedly defeat the other two.

The Evonians cannot believe their ears, and they cannot understand such logic. They know that the Federation scout ships witnessed what happened at the battle of Primus. They know the Federation knows how the Synthetics used suicidal tactics to defeat a superior and better led Primean fleet. Unable to grasp the arguments of the Federation and convinced of the obviousness of their own logic, the Evonians are confident that the Federation is not being honest. It is confident that the Federation has something else up its sleeve. Could it be, they wonder, that the Federation has plans to seize our newly acquired Primean planets when our fleet is away. Of course, that's it, they tell themselves, that has to be it; it is the only thing that makes any sense. The talks stall and eventually move in a new direction. Both civilizations sign a non-aggression and mutual assistance pact.

Thus Synthetica is given time to recover and rebuild. Nor is it just satisfied to rebuild its fleet. Even while the battle rages against Primea, Synthetic colonists are being landed on new planets, and new keels are being laid for Synthetic warships. As dedicated and hardworking as the Synthetics are, they cannot build a new fleet overnight. They expect the two remaining human civilizations, or at least one of them, to move against them, but it does not happen. The time given is put to good use. Enough time is given not only to build a newer, more modern space fleet but also for the civilization to expand enough in size to become the galaxy's largest civilization. A space fleet is constructed that is much larger than the previous space fleet, larger than both fleets that fought at the Battle of Primus. While this fleet is more than twice the size of the last Synthetic fleet, the other civilizations have also been building, and their combined fleets are still larger.

This time Michael does not need any provocation. By war, by custom, the Primean planets belong to the Synthetics. To steal the spoils of war from a victor is an act of war by international law and anyone's understanding. This time as the Synthetic fleet departs for Evonian space, it does not leave in a single column. The fleet is too large, and it will take too long to get into battle formation if the battle is imminent. Instead of a single column, the fleet forms in three columns. Each column is under the control of a different admiral, with another admiral in overall command. The name of the admiral is Pedro, a young synthetic just out of the military academy. Having exceeded Henry in his studies and later by war games against each other by Synthetic custom is felt to be the best qualified and is naturally appointed admiral of the fleet. Henry is given command of one of the columns.

When the Synthetic fleet departs, Michael feels that "his" plans this time have not been discovered. While the building program has gone on, many spying attempts have been made but

Michael has put his ships in an interlocking pattern on the borders of Synthetic space so that no boat could pass without being detected. While these probes are constant, they do not increase as plans for attacking the humans come to completion.

Pedro knows that as soon as "he" completes his first hyper-light speed Jump outside of Synthetic space, the humans will discover 'his" presence and assemble their fleet. Pedro knows the emotionalism of humans, "his" plan is simple, "he" will systematically annihilate Federation planets without mercy because he knows it will take some time for the Federation to assemble their fleet and that of Evonia. "He" hopes that "his" tactics will cause the Federation to give combat before they are completely assembled, divide and conquer.

When Pedro decelerates to sub-light speed some distance before Primus, now a Federation planet, where the previous Battle of Primus had been fought, he finds only a few Federation ships defending. Pedro knows hundreds more will soon be en route.

Just as soon as the Synthetic fleet decelerates to sub-light speed, it assumes battle formation. The battle formation has changed slightly, and there are now so many ships that Pedro has a double destroyer shield and still has a third of his forces in reserve.

Slowly the Synthetic fleet moves on Primus. As they do, the Federation squadron is protecting its yields. Synthetic cruisers move in which the orbiting dry docks and space stations. These installations put up no defense. Their crews escaped to the plant's surface as soon as the Synthetics appeared. As the Synthetic cruisers open fire on the orbiting dry-docks and space stations, they are taken under fire by planetary particle beams that take a toll on cruisers before they can destroy their targets and move out of range. Then the Synthetic destroyers standing outside the range of planetary particle beams fire missiles into the planet's atmosphere. The defenders of Primus have an easy time destroying these missiles moving slowly through the atmosphere. As each one explodes, more radioactive debris is cast in the atmosphere until it reaches lethal proportions.

The bridge personnel on the Federation squadron are horrified and sickened by what they see. There is no demand for surrender, no attempt to spare the planet or keep it from being ruined for habitation for thousands of years, just a simple, blatant effort to wipe out every living thing on the planet for no apparent purpose. The senior Federation officer present, Lara Peterson, is sickened by what she sees but still grasps its cold, ruthless logic. The Synthetics aren't interested in Primus or its population and couldn't care less whether it lives or dies. The Synthetics only want to enrage the Federation fleet so that they attack prematurely. The people of Primus are mere pawns.

She understands the cold brutality of Synthetic strategy and cannot allow herself to fall into their trap. She still finds it impossible to watch while billions of people, a whole planet, are exterminated.

After due consideration, Admiral Peterson decides there is indeed something that she can do; she can feint, she can fake an attack to cause the Synthetics to break off their attack long enough to gain time for the rest of the Federation fleet and their Evonian allies to arrive. Even if she cannot delay long enough to save this planet, perhaps she can delay long enough to save the next hapless planet. Whatever she does, she knows that she cannot allow herself to be tricked into open combat with this huge force, for she will surely be destroyed without doing any harm to the enemy.

Admiral Peterson accelerates her fleet towards the Synthetic fleet until she reaches hyper-light speed, and both fleets become invisible to each other. As soon as their images disappear off her scopes, she veers away from them. It is her hope to react to her threatened attack and break off their bombardment.

Unfortunately for Admiral Peterson, Pedro expects the Federation to try something short of open battle with a numerically superior foe. When "he" sees her coming toward "him," instead of breaking off his bombardment of the planet, he commits "his" reserve and orders the reserve destroyers to fire their missiles at likely points where the Federation fleet will decelerate to sub-light speed.

After veering away from the Synthetic, Admiral Peterson decelerates to sub-light and looks to her scopes to see if she has caused the Synthetics to break off the bombardment of Primus. She is disappointed when she sees that the tactic did not work. As she is cursing her failure, Synthetic missiles commence materializing just outside her formation - the Synthetic have guessed her plans.

Now she is in deep trouble, for there isn't time to launch fighters. The laser gunner immediately takes the missiles under fire, but the synthetic missiles are too many or too close to escape. Unless she can think of something quick, her fleet will surely be destroyed without even harming the Synthetics. Out of desperation, she does the only thing she can think of the order her missiles launched against the attacking missiles. She also orders her fleet to stop decelerating and accelerate at the maximum rate.

Launching missiles at missiles is considered a foolish tactic and a waste of missiles. The attacking missiles attacking at high speed can easily outmaneuver the defending missiles that must stay at a slow speed in order to detect them. The attacking missiles make slight course corrections, and their speed makes them easily past the defending missiles. When the Federation missiles pass the Synthetic missiles, they harmlessly explode. Only a few Synthetic missiles are damaged.

As foolish as the tactic is - it works! The one thing that Admiral Peterson had going for her was that she had just decelerated from hyper-light speed. The course deviation taken by the Synthetic attacking missiles is just enough for her to gain the protection of invisibility at hyper-light speed. The Synthetic missiles still attack through her formation, but since she is blind to them, they pass through her formation harmlessly.

Now that the Federation fleet has been driven off, Pedro completes the bombardment of Primus until the radioactive waste on the planet's surface is well past the lethal point. "He" considers brief laying waste the surface of the planet with particle beams but decides against it. The population of Primus has to be underground by now; attacking the surface will just destroy things. There is no terror in just destroying things. Besides, planetary particle beams are well underground, and they can still fire back upon the cruisers. Pedro gathers "his" star charts, plots the course to the next Federation planet, scans the intervening space for obstacles, accelerates to hyper-light speed towards intervening space for obstacles, and accelerates to hyper-light speed towards that planet.

Chapter 22

Lost in Space

Admiral Peterson watches the Synthetics leave, and she is not happy. She knows they will soon be on another Federation planet, turning it into a nuclear wasteland. She wants to follow them but knows better, and there is nothing she can do if she follows. She must wait here for the rest of the fleet. Only a few destroyers are sent to follow, shadow the fleet, gather intelligence, and report on their whereabouts.

Soon after the Synthetic fleet is gone, the bulk of the Federation fleet arrives. With it arrives the fleet admiral Barbara Hudson. Like the brilliant Primean Admiral. Larth Flango, Barbara Hudson was an exemplary scholar in school - always standing at the top of her class. Like Admiral Flango, she has always performed her duties brilliantly and consistently received outstanding fitness reports. Like Admiral Flango, she is universally respected, but unlike Flango, she was not a universal choice for the fleet admiral. She was, in fact, a very controversial choice. Her criticism is that she is insufficiently aggressive, inclined to be overly cautious, and unable to recognize decisive tactical opportunities. Despite her outstanding academic performance, there is some basis for this feeling. In her past battles, and especially in mock battles, she has shown a preoccupation for defense, a concern for detail, and a fear of error rather than boldness, decisiveness, and aggression.

Admiral Hudson's supporters, mostly female but including many males, castigate this criticism. These critics, the women most vociferous, argue that she is the obvious choice for the fleet admiral given her outstanding record. The criticism leveled against her is a flickering vestige of anti-female bias.

Admiral Hudson believes her detractor's criticism unfounded. She acknowledges that she is cautious but believes a certain amount of caution is crucial. She has never obtained decisive results in mock space battles, but neither has she ever suffered a debacle. More importantly, she has always won and always defeated those aggressive commanders suggested over her in those mock battles.

In the end, Admiral Hudson wins. She is indeed the obvious choice as fleet admiral. She is the only admiral to be undefeated in a mock space battle is not the only reason for her choice. She will not be the first female fleet admiral, but she will be the first female fleet admiral to take a fleet into battle.

Admiral Hudson's background is very different from other senior flag officers; neither parent had been an officer in the space fleet. Moreover, Admiral Hudson's mother is something of an anachronism in Federation society, even an atavism. Admiral Hudson's mother was a housewife. Although her father was a successful businessman, both of her parents belonged to a rare religious cult that taught female subservience to the male. Although it wasn't forbidden for a woman to work outside the home, it was indirectly discouraged because when a wife worked, it was recognized within the cult that her husband was unsuccessful. Admiral Hudson's family was a member of the few members of The Way who did not emigrate to Primus or one of its colonies.

Barbara Hudson had never gotten along with her mother. It was her father that she admired and respected. As a young girl, she had always disdained maternal behavior. She had never played with dolls or even played with the other neighborhood girls. She had only played with the boys. Barbara Hudson sensed the estrangement between herself and her mother and tried to interest her daughter in the archaic female pursuits she cultivated. The effort served only to alienate her even more from her mother.

While in her teens, Barbara secretly repudiated the religious beliefs of her parents and resolved when she could, she would openly repudiate them. This finally took place when she announced that she had been accepted to the Space Academy. Acceptance in the Space Academy was not inconsistent with the principles of The Way, but it certainly was inconsistent with the lifestyle of its adherents. Barbara had been estranged for many years from her mother, and it did not bother her that her mother objected, but she somehow hoped that her father might accept it. Her hopes were in vain. The thought of a daughter being other than submissive was alien to her father, who detested such women and could not accept it. Barbara had always wanted to be a man, but this was impossible. She knew that no matter how she loved her father and wanted him to love and respect her, she could never adhere to his expectations of her. She had known deep inside that he would not accept her choice of lifestyle and was not surprised at his reaction even though she was still hurt. Even though she ostensibly had a choice between staying within The Way or going to the Space Academy, in fact, her choice had long been preordained. The price she had to pay for her entrance was ex-communication from her religion, which she didn't care about, and rejection by her father, whom she did care about. Yet, there was really nothing she could do.

Upon taking command from Admiral Peterson, Admiral Hudson received a full report of the feint attack. Despite the feint's failure and the subsequent obliteration of the population of an entire planet Admiral Hudson commended her predecessor. She believed the feint had been tactically well-conceived, had a high risk of success at a minimum of risk, was well executed, and showed initiative and courage. Admiral Hudson believed the feint had failed only because Admiral Peterson did not have enough forces at her disposal to have it taken seriously. It had been only through Admiral Peterson's diligence, alertness, and quick thinking that the devastation of her forces had been prevented.

As the last of The Federation fleet assembles, a battle plan begins to form in Admiral Hudson's mind. The most important consideration is the survival of the civilization, not the survival of a single planet; the survival of the civilization depends on the space fleet to defend it. Whatever happens, Admiral Hudson must wait until the Evonian reinforcements arrive before committing to battle; only then will the odds be favorable.

Yet Admiral Hudson knows that she can't just stand by and let another planet be annihilated - she has to at least try something. If she can't faint and can't try an all-out attack, there is only one thing she can do, try a diversionary attack. She considers another feint but decides against it; it has already been tried and has failed.

Materializing from hyper-light speed well away from Largess to avoid any chance of materializing within range of the Synthetic fleet, Admiral Hudson is sickened to see that the poisoning of the atmosphere of the planet Largess has already begun. Having already formulated her plans, she issues them to her fleet and begins closing on the Synthetic fleet.

Pedro is immediately advised of the materialization of the Federation fleet and, bored with the slaughter "he" has ordered, devote "his" complete attention to the Federation fleet. As "he" sees the enemy gather into battle formation and move forward, a battle plan emerges in "his" mind, and as it does, "he" does nothing, waiting for the most propitious moment to act.

As Admiral Hudson closes, she expects the Synthetic fleet to break off their attack upon Largess and form into battle formation - but they don't. They seem to ignore her as if they were invisible. Unlike most commanders, Admiral Hudson, instead of growing aggressive, grows even more cautious and slows the approach of her fleet, wary of trickery by the Synthetics.

Pedro detects the change of speed and is disappointed but does not alter "his" plan. Though "his" plan has less chance of success, "he" believes it is still capable of working but perhaps less decisively that originally conceived. He orders the calculation of when the Federation fleet will come within range of his missiles and how long it will take the Federation fleet to detect movement at that range. "He" also ordered "his" fighters readied for launch. Just as the Federation fleet reaches maximum missile range without moving into battle formation first, the entire Synthetic fleet simultaneously commences maximum acceleration and launches long-range missiles. The Synthetic fleet will assemble during maximum acceleration, a battle maneuver always considered too difficult to attempt.

On the Federation flagship, Admiral Hudson is just about to order her first salvo when she notices the simultaneous acceleration of the entire Synthetic fleet. Her intuition has proved correct. She has lured the Synthetics into battle but has she taken them in, or have they taken her. Without waiting for a calculation to be ordered, she instantly orders emergency deceleration and the launching of fighters. Her next order is the calculation of how soon the Synthetic missiles can conceivably reach her fleet. This calculation takes only a few seconds. When the calculation is made, the fighters are ordered to that calculated point in space. Only when the other orders have been given and accepted does she finally order her own missiles to attack the Synthetics.

Bob Jones, the second Federation fighter wave commander, is presented with a command decision. A decision of grave importance has to be made immediately and without advice. Bob Jones knows his mission: to protect the fleet and destroy the attacking missiles. He, therefore, orders his comrades to ignore any accompanying Synthetic fighters and attack only missiles. The result is foregone. While the Synthetic missiles are decimated, so is the Federation fighter wave that can't defend itself.

With the first salvo of Synthetic missiles decimated, the Federation fleet gained time to increase its speed to defend itself and approach hyper-light velocity and freedom. When the remnants of the first Federation fighter wave break through the first salvo of Synthetic missiles, Bob Jones is saddened when he looks around himself and realizes how few survived. Instantly he is faced with another command decision. If he continues with his decision to ignore the Synthetic fighters, not only does his wave face certain death, but succeeding waves of fighters will face cumulative waves of Synthetic fighters. Bob Jones decides to break off his attack of Synthetic missiles and concentrate on dog fighting the Synthetic fighters to protect succeeding Federation fighters. He only hopes the sacrifice of his wave has given the fleet the advantage he hoped.

Pedro, with Synthetic characteristic aggressiveness, has sent most of his fighters to help the missiles break through the Federation fighters. Only a few fighters remain to protect the Synthetic fleet. When the Synthetic fighters move in to thin the Federation missiles, they are in for a surprise! The Federation missiles are equipped with laser cannon! Instead of being easily destroyed, the fighters the missiles open fire upon the Synthetic fighters. The Synthetic fighter pilots are caught by surprise, and hundreds are destroyed before they realize what is happening. Not only is the Synthetic fighter screen decimated, but the Federation missiles breakthrough in unexpected numbers.

Pedro knows that his destroyer screen cannot handle this large number of missiles and orders twelve of "his" destroyers to advance and draw the missiles to them. The advanced destroyers do not draw the Federation missiles to them. The Federation has learned from the Battle of Primus and has programmed its missiles to hold their position and not congregate to attack the sacrificial destroyers. Pedro Instantly recalls the fighters assigned to accompany the missiles. Only they have any chance of arriving in time, and there isn't time to launch more fighters. They do not, however, arrive in time to stop the first Federation salvo. Large numbers of the destroyer in the outer destroyer shield are hit by Federation missiles and destroyed.

The Synthetic fighters do arrive in the middle of the attack of the second salvo of Federation missiles. Their arrival is propitious. Without their maneuverability and extra defensive fires, the outer defensive perimeter of the Synthetic destroyer screen would surely have been obliterated. As it is, many more destroyers are hit but just as many survive. Pedro orders the deceleration of "his" fleet.

Admiral Hudson has only launched three waves of fighters. She has only done so because that is all she knows she can recover before the fleet reaches hyper-light speed and become invisible. After reaching hyper-light speed, the fighters cannot be recovered because the ships and their fighters cannot find each other. She now faces the most difficult command decision of her life. Despite the sacrifices of the three waves of fighters already launched, the Federation fleet is still in trouble. The fleet has successfully managed to defend itself against a thinned Synthetic missile salvo, but the successful missile salvos have compressed the range of the laser canons. Unless something is done, the Synthetic missiles will soon be breaking through her defenses.

Admiral Hudson orders out another wave of fighters. The fighter pilots waiting already in their fighters receive their orders with cheerless silence. They, too, understand the danger to the fleet. They, too, understand the choices faced by their commander. They, too, know who is expendable and who is not. Despite their melancholy, there is no disobedience, not even any griping.

The Federation fighter pilots arrive even while the laser gunners are defending the destroyer screen, something that is done only in the most perilous of circumstances. With reckless abandon, they attack the missile salvo knowing that they are doomed anyway. Each is secretly hoping to suffer the quick and painless death of an errant laser cannon blast and not the slow terror of waiting in empty, vacant space for one's oxygen supply to run out.

The battle rages on the Federation fighter pilots desperately trying to thin the Synthetic missiles to protect their fleet even though they will not benefit. Finally, a Federation pilot, Jill Miller, makes an important discovery. She penetrates the last salvo of Synthetic missiles; there are no more. She has somehow - against all odds survived! Only then does she realizes how those few moments of combat have drained her and how her fuel has been depleted by wild maneuvering. Only when there are no more missiles to destroy does she look around and realize that she is the only pilot from her wave to have survived. Immediately she radios the fleet command that there are no more missile salvos.

Admiral Hudson rejoices. She has lured the Synthetic fleet away from Largess, saved her fleet, and now she can rescue the fighter pilots she thought she had doomed. Only a few Federation destroyers have been hit, but the losses are acceptable. Noting now that the Synthetics have commenced deceleration, she orders acceleration stopped. When she is sure that it is not a trick, she orders the launching of shuttlecraft to find and rescue her fighter pilots.

The shuttlecraft's first priority is the first wave of fighters, those low or out of fuel but with sufficient oxygen reserves, are noted but passed by. As the shuttlecraft proceed farther, they come upon fighters who, despite the fact that there are others even farther on, cannot be passed by. Due to the quick action of Admiral Hudson, all known surviving fighters are saved, save one. She is known to have survived only because it was she who reported the last salvo of Synthetic missiles, Jill Miller.

Jill Miller has used up nearly all her fuel in the wild maneuvering that enabled her to be the sole survivor of her wave. Unbeknownst to her, as she commenced her turn back to her fleet, she did not have enough fuel to complete the turn. Halfway through the turn, her fuel runs out, and she drifts in a direction perpendicular to the rescuing shuttlecraft.

When the rescuing shuttlecraft reach the position from which she broadcast back to the fleet, she is too far away from them to detect on radar, and her weak battery powered distress call. When destroyers with their more delicate receivers arrive later, she is further away yet, and they too are not able to receive her.

Jill Miller desperately tries to stave off her terror of impending death from lack of oxygen. She knows somehow if she can control her emotions, she can conserve her oxygen and stretch her chances of surviving. Desperately she tries to calm herself, reduce her metabolism, reducing the amount of oxygen required.

Finally, the oxygen delivered to her through her gas mask sputters, and she tries to suck more out, desperately trying to draw in the oxygen that she knows isn't there. It is then that terror overwhelms her, and she knows she is going to die. As panic overcomes her, she tries to suck harder and more often to get the oxygen that is no longer there. She passes out and dies from oxygen deprivation.

Deprived of fuel and heat, her cabin cools, and she freezes solid in the cold vacuum of space. Her fighter suffering no friction in the vacuum of space, speeds on at the same speed for millennia until finally, her trajectory on the other side of the galaxy passes too close to an unnamed sun. The gravity of the sun captures her, and she spirals in until the sun's heat consumes both her and her craft.

The first Federation-Synthetic encounter has been inconclusive. Admiral Hudson feels gratified because not only have the Synthetic lost a substantial number of destroyers, but the systematic annihilation of Largess has been delayed. Pedro is not gratified because his object of destroying the Federation fleet has not been accomplished, yet he still believes that he has gained in the encounter. "He" has gained invaluable intelligence of Federation tactics and capabilities. The Federation missiles have been armed with laser cannons, and they have been programmed to maintain their intervals in space. Advancing destroyers for sacrifice will not work. This information may well prove decisive in the all-out battle Pedro knows will come.

Pedro returns to his brutal work. Sitting outside the range of the planetary particle beams, he sends nuclear missiles at targets on Largess. The missiles never hit their targets. They are taken under fire by Largessian laser cannon and destroyed long before they reach their targets. When the radioactive debris in the atmosphere becomes lethal, Pedro stops. Another planet has been sterilized.

Chapter 23

Procrastination

For the remainder of the Federation fleet reports, Admiral Hudson now has her full fleet. Despite that fact, she decides not to attack. The stakes are too high! The fate of the galaxy and all humanity hangs in the balance! Help is needed before the Synthetic fleet can be joined in an all-out battle. The Largessians will have to be sacrificed.

Good news finally comes! A high-speed communication drone arrives from the Evonian fleet. They are nearly assembled and will soon depart but need to know where to rendezvous.

Quickly recovering from her ecstasy, Admiral Hudson puts her mind to the difficulty. Where will the next attack fall? What planet will the Synthetics next exterminate? There are two planets, each equidistant from Largess, Mecha, originally a Federation planet, and Mordal, a formerly Primean planet. Admiral Hudson's first thought is that it will be Mordal because it is the planet further away from Evonia and will be further for the reinforcements to travel. Then it occurs to Admiral Hudson that the Synthetics are exterminating planets to force the Federation fleet into premature battle. They will go to the planet where the Federation fleet has the most emotional attachment. They will go to the planet where some fleet members have a family.

A concerted attack of two different fleets under two different commands will be difficult. Still, if the enemy can be caught between the two fleets, there will be no problem with unity of command, and the enemy will be trapped. With that thought, a battle plan instantly takes form in Admiral Hudson's mind and simultaneously incandesces! With a little bit of luck, the Evonian fleet will materialize behind the Synthetics and attack before they can turn their defense around.

With her plan thus formulated, Admiral Hudson sends a message to the Evonian admiral:

"Expect full fleet battle in front of Mecha. If you arrive behind an enemy, you may be able to surprise and crush them. I shall delay as long as possible. Please hurry!"

Having completed his deadly work on Largess, Pedro orders his fleet to hyper-light speed. Since he wishes to force the Federation fleet into battle, he does not try to disguise his acceleration in the direction of Mecha.

Admiral Hudson is pleased to see the Synthetic fleet accelerating into hyper-light speed in the direction she anticipated. However, there is still no guarantee for the Synthetic fleet could double back at hyper-light speed. Still, she feels confident she has correctly picked the planet since her fleet is what the Synthetics want, not another sterilized planet. She waits until the Synthetic fleet disappears into hyperspace before ordering her own hyper-light speed acceleration.

Admiral Hudson decelerates her fleet well away from Mecha; she does not wish to materialize too close to the much larger Synthetic fleet. When her fleet does materialize, the Synthetic fleet is a long distance away, already beginning to surround Mecha for its sterilization. There is no reason to delay any longer. The Evonians should have received her message and should now be accelerating into hyperspace. Commencing a full fleet battle before the Evonians arrive is a risk since the Synthetic fleet is much bigger than the Federation fleet. The Synthetic fleet must be taken by surprise from behind to be sure of victory. She must close for battle before the Evonians arrive. The Synthetic fleet must be locked in combat when the Evonian fleet arrives for the tactic to be certain. Admiral Hudson gives the order to close on the Synthetic fleet.

Pedro is made aware of the arrival of the Federation fleet and of the fact that it is now closing upon "him." Keeping one-third of his fleet in reserve, "he" orders the attack on Mecha halted and orders the fleet into battle formation. When the battle formation is completed, "he" orders "his" fleet to close with the Federation fleet.

The two fleets are close to each other. Each side constantly changes its speed and course; zig zags steadily towards each other. Each side waits, not wanting to waste valuable missiles, waiting for "effective range," the point of no return when a sudden course change cannot take the enemy fleet outside the range of its missiles. As the distance closes, the speed of the two fleets is reduced. The slower the fleet moves, the easier it is to overcome momentum and change course. The slower the closing speed of the two fleets, the closer is "battle range." Yet, neither fleet wishes to approach too slowly. If a fleet was at a dead stop, the enemy missiles attacking just below sub-light closing speed would be on them only seconds after their launchings were observed.

Finally, just before reaching "effective range," they launch their fighters. It is a precaution; in case of miscalculation, they do not wish to be caught without their fighters to defend them. There is a difference in how the fighters are allotted between the two fleets. Admiral Hudson hoping that the surprise arrival of the Evonian will devastate the Synthetics, has allotted most of her fighters for missile defense. Pedro, having the larger fleet, has allotted most of his fighters to accompany and protect his missiles.

Suddenly pinpricks of light appear on the rear of the Synthetics on the large viewing screen on Admiral Hudson's bridge. Instantly everyone on that bridge recognizes what that represents. The Evonians have arrived. "Instantly, Admiral Hudson orders fleet speed accelerated, and she wants to lock the Synthetic fleet into "effective range" before they can escape the trap she has set for them. Such is the location of the two fleets that this is accomplished almost immediately, and both fleets commence launching missiles.

Pedro, too, detects the Evonian fleet's arrival but is unconcerned about escape. "He" has not ignored the possibility of the arrival of the Evonians. For that reason, "he" maintained "his" reserve instead of deploying against the Federation fleet. Instead, "his" only concern is how to deploy that reserve. Should he deploy it to meet the threat of the Evonians or maintain it for use as needed? Immediately "he" recalls the purpose of a reserve and maintains "his" reserve to be used as tactics required.

Unlike Larth Flango and Barbara Hudson, Eve Soft, the Evonian commander, was only an average scholar. She did well in the early grades, but her relative performance diminished as she progressed, and competition grew stiffer. She performed well in the military academy, graduating in the top third of her class, but later at command and Staff College, she was in the bottom half.

Despite her lack of academic excellence, she consistently received outstanding efficiency reports due to her intense loyalty and affable nature. Her rise in rank was slow but steady. Although she is known for aggressive offense, it is not for this reason that she is in command at this point in Evonian history. Instead, it is due to an entirely fortuitous event in her career: she had been the chief military negotiator for Evonia with The Federation after the Synthetica/Primea War.

Admiral Zoft detects the Federation and Synthetic fleets simultaneously as they detect her. Having decided to intervene in the battle at the most advantageous time - for Evonia, Admiral Zoft continues to decelerate. Rather than closing with the Synthetic fleet after decelerating to sub-light speed, as soon as possible.

The Synthetic and Federation fleet has commenced launching missiles and fighters. The first salvo of missiles approaching the fleet just under light closing speed is nevertheless beyond light closing speed as to each other and pass through each other's formations without detection. Reaching their destination, both groups of missiles are taken under fire by defending fighters. The accompanying fighters respond by engaging the defending fighters. The laser cannon installed on Federation missiles takes a toll on Synthetic fighters wearing down the Synthetic fighter defenses. While both fleets are successful in defending the fleet, the Federation has developed a new lighter material for their fighters, making them more maneuverable. As the battle progresses, the Synthetic fighters are steadily gaining fighter superiority.

Pedro realizes quickly that the battle is not going well. Seeing that the Evonian fleet is delaying, "he" decides to play his trump card and commits "his" reserve fleet ordering it to swing around and attack the Federation fleet from the flank.

Admiral Hudson, already angry over the lethargy of the Evonian fleet, detects the Synthetics committing their reserve against her. Her anger immediately explodes into a rage she never thought herself capable of. She realizes that she has been had! The Evonians never intended to fulfill the mutual defense treaty - they were waiting until the Federation fleet was macerated before giving combat. Worse yet, there is nothing she can do about it. It is too late to break combat. There is nothing to do but press on and hope that the Evonians will assist before destruction.

When Admiral Zoft detects the Synthetics committing their reserve, she knows this is her time to attack. Finally, she gives the order to accelerate and commences launching missiles. However, she has delayed too long, and it will take some time for the missiles to overtake the Synthetic fleet. She does not launch fighters. Since she is attacking the Synthetics from the rear where they have no fighters, she does not need accompanying fighters.

Meanwhile, the Synthetic and Federation fleets are locked in mortal combat. The greater maneuverability of the Federation fighters is giving the Federation the advantage, but the Synthetic reserve fleet attacking from the flank has almost reached its position. Almost simultaneously, the Federation missile salvos start breaking through as the Synthetic reserve fleet commences launching missiles.

Rather quickly, the Federation missiles overwhelm and eradicate the outer shield of Synthetic destroyers and then commence their attack upon the inner shield of Synthetic destroyers. This defense holds firm for a few minutes, but their ranks have been sacked to make up for the losses in the outer shield at the first confrontation. The laser gunners of the inner shield are successful against the first attack, but when the next salvo of missiles arrives, their sights are compressed, and they do not have enough time to destroy all of the attacking missiles. The second shield, too, is overwhelmed and destroyed. After the destroyer shield is obliterated, the Federation missiles fall upon the interior of the Synthetic fleet; it ceases to exist.

Even as the second Synthetic shield is being destroyed, the missiles from the Synthetic reserve fleet are attacking the Federation fleet. The Federation fleet, still being compelled to face the main Synthetic fleet and use its fighters to defend against their missiles, has no defense against this second attack. The Federation fleet is almost instantly destroyed.

Only the Evonian fleet and the Synthetic reserve fleets remain. The odds greatly favor the Evonians since they outnumber the Synthetics, their destroyer shield faces the proper direction, and they have already launched several salvos of missiles at the Synthetics. However, the Synthetics have one important advantage over the Evonians, and they are already moving away from them. Admiral Zoft has failed to join battle quickly enough; the Synthetics have no intention of giving combat to the Evonians now. Henry launches a wave of fighters to protect the fleet from the Evonian missiles and then accelerates into hyper-light speed, leaving his fighter behind. The tactic proves successful; the Synthetic fighters are able to thin the undefended Evonian missiles enough to allow the Synthetic fleet to escape into hyper-light speed.

Admiral Zoft is only mildly perturbed at herself for allowing some of the Synthetic fleet to escape. Even though the Synthetic reserve fleet has escaped, it is vastly inferior to hers, and she should easily be able to force it into combat in Synthetica and destroy it. Deciding there is no point in waiting, Admiral Zoft orders her fleet into column formation and accelerates into hyper-light speed on a course to Synthetica.

Henry returns to Synthetica with his reserve fleet intact except for a shortage of missiles and fighters. While spacecraft can be manufactured quickly, ships cannot. There are only a couple of ships that have been completed. There are, however, plenty of missiles, fighters, and even fighter pilots. These shortages are quickly replaced.

Admiral Zoft warily follows Henry to Synthetica, and she does not wish to be victimized by any Flango-like traps. Every space obstacle is avoided if possible, and if it cannot be avoided, it is either carefully scouted or blasted. Indeed the Evonian do find many space mines, but all are discovered and blown.

A band of outposts is discovered protecting Synthetic space. This band is carefully probed to discover its strengths and weaknesses. When the probing is finished, the band is attacked and overwhelmed with minimal casualties.

Finally, the Evonian fleet reaches the first Synthetic planet. Unlike Pedro, Admiral Zoft does not waste her time and missiles exterminating planetary populations. Instead, the planet's space station and dry docks are blasted with particle beams in orbit. Without dry docks in orbit to build new spaceships, the planet ceases to be a serious threat to the Evonians. It cannot build new warships to threaten the Evonians.

After the first space station and dry docks are blasted, Admiral Zoft divides up her fleet to do the same with the rest of the Synthetic planets destroying the war-making capability of each of the planets. As she does so, Admiral Zoft wonders why mankind allowed these biological robots to develop so far, much less why they were designed in the first place. As she divides her fleet, each unit is given strict orders to avoid confrontation with the main part of the Synthetic fleet until the Evonian fleet can be assembled.

As the Evonian fleet spreads out over Synthetica, Henry continues to retreat, trying to gain as much time as possible so that the few ships near completion can be completed before being destroyed in dry-dock and so that the Evonians will have to expend as many cruisers as possible destroying the dry-docks. When all but a few dry docks of Synthetica have been destroyed, there is no point in delaying anymore. Henry positions his entire fleet before the next planet and waits.

In a short time, a detachment of the Evonian fleet appears out of hyper-light speed. It does not attack but simply waits out of range. As time goes by, more and more Evonian detachments materialize; the entire Evonian fleet has assembled and formed into battle formation. When in battle formation, the Evonian fleet begins closing with the Synthetic fleet.

As the Evonian fleet closes upon "him," Henry realizes that even with sacrificial tactics, the numerical superiority of the Evonians is such that "he" cannot hope to win. Indeed 'his' only hope to win is by a catastrophic blunder on the part of the Evonian commander. Realizing that such a blunder is unlikely if "he" follows accepted tactics, Henry decides on a bold but foolish tactic that can only work if the Evonians blunder by trying to take advantage of the tactic.

Henry first charges "his" engines up by directing their thrust through both front and rear apertures of "his" ships, thus holding the ships motionless. When the engines reach full operating power, "he" launches a salvo of missiles at extreme range toward the Evonian fleet and directs all the power of "his" engines through the rear aperture. The Synthetic ships, now at full power, slingshot forward, quickly exceeding light closing speed where "he" and the Evonians are invisible to each other.

Admiral Zoft recognizes this ploy as a desperation tactic. Believing that her enemy is using this tactic to get in close where they can do more damage and that they will expect her to change course, slow, and wait for them, Admiral Zoft decides to take advantage of the tactic and win a bold, bloodless victory. She calculates the point at which, based upon her previous location, the Synthetics will materialize, launches missiles at that location, and changes course to put herself perpendicular to that location and out of range.

As Henry waits for the Evonian reaction, he experiences a reaction that is almost unlike a Synthetic - apprehension! "He" knows "his" plan is desperate and easily thwarted. All "his" enemy has to do is change course and wait for the Synthetic fleet to materialize. Eventually, "he" will have to give battle, and Evonian numerical superiority is overwhelming. Even though the Evonian and Synthetic fleets are invisible to each other because their closing speed exceeds the speed of light, the Synthetic missiles are programmed to attack below the range of invisibility and can detect the Evonian fleet. Moreover, because the Synthetic fleet and its missiles are traveling in the same direction at less than hyper-light speed Henry can detect his own missiles. Most importantly, by watching how "his" missiles react, he can guess what their target, the Evonian fleet, is doing.

When Henry sees his missiles changing their course, "he" cannot believe "his" eyes. The Evonians have taken the bait. Their commander has forgotten that the Synthetic missiles will indicate the location of the Evonian fleet. It is a blundering mistake! Henry has the probable destination of the Evonian fleet plotted and commences launching missiles programmed to travel at hyper-light speed to the plotted location, decelerate and attack.

Admiral Zoft has amusedly been watching for the Synthetic fleet to materialize at her point of ambush where she will destroy them, is oblivious to the fact that the Synthetic missiles launched at long range are indicating her location. She is first puzzled and then horrified when Synthetic missiles begin materializing inside her defensive formation. The missiles are immediately taken under fire by laser cannoneers, but they are too many and too close. The

Evonian defenses are smashed, and only a few random ships survive. The Synthetic fleet has not suffered a casualty.

When the Synthetic fleet materializes behind the Evonian fleet, the senior ship captain, Captain Stahl, braces herself for death — but it does not come! Instead, the Synthetic fleet simply waits. Captain Stahl is confused. Why don't they attack? We have no defenses; they have us at her mercy. With that thought, the answer is obvious. As ruthless as Synthetics are, they are even more logical. The battle is over; the Synthetics have won! There is no need to destroy the remnants of the Evonian fleet. Without survivors, who will spread the bad news!

Captain Stahl contacts the other ships and quickly determines that she is the senior surviving officer - she is in command. She takes command, orders the remnants of the fleet into the column, and orders her navigator to plot a course for home. She will give the Synthetics what they want; she will spread the bad news.

Chapter 24

Epoch

When Captain Stahl arrives at Fleet Headquarters with the news that the Evonian fleet has been all but wiped out, the general staff cannot believe their ears. How can a whole fleet be all but wiped out without the enemy force losing a single ship?

When the news sinks in, all the Admirals have the same thought - God help us now!

In order to prevent panic, the general staff tries to avoid the news of the defeat from the public. This cover-up is doomed to failure. Word of the loss leaks out almost immediately and spreads just as quickly beyond Evonian civilization.

The Synthetic fleet waits a few weeks before following Captain Stahl. Henry wants to allow the effect of the defeat to sink in. When "he" arrives at the home planet of Evonia, "he" immediately demands its surrender. There is no refusal, no heroics, the population will be killed if they resist, and their martyrdom will serve no purpose. When Evonia surrenders, Henry leaves behind, transports troops to occupy Evonia, and travels to the Federation's home planet, where "he" demands and obtains its surrender. After The Federation surrenders, "he" dispatches the remainder of "his" transports to the various planets to occupy those planets.

The inhabitants of all the planets fear that the Synthetics will begin a systematic liquidation of the human population. It is an order that does not come. In fact, the regime imposed by the Synthetics is benevolent beyond the wildest imaginings of any humans. Each planet is allowed to keep its government, bureaucracy, social system, police force, etc. The synthetics normally take no interest in human affairs except for scientific developments. The only time Synthetics ever intervene in human affairs is to quell insurrections. Ironically, when the local insurrection is quelled, it is nearly always by siding with the rebels and against the local authorities who have been abusing their power. There is, in fact, only one area that is forbidden to humans, interplanetary space travel, especially space colonization. Interplanetary trade is allowed to go on, except that it is a Synthetic monopoly. There being no further use for interplanetary governments, they are dissolved.

The humans who expected to be systematically eradicated find that they are better off under Synthetic rule than they had ever been before. For the first time in human history, war is obsolete. Gone is the death and destruction caused by war and the tremendous financial burden of maintaining a military defense.

Only after the Synthetic occupation has been well established do the humans realize why they were allowed to survive. As usual with Synthetics, the answer is deceptively simple; there is no reason to eradicate them. While the Synthetics know that humans are emotionally unstable, they also realize they are creative. To eliminate this creative force would be a mistake. Most importantly, there is no reason to eradicate them. It is a simple matter to destroy all the dry docks in orbit around the planets and thus to enforce the prohibition on humans in space. Once this is done, humans cannot expand, cannot build new space fleets, and cease forever to be a threat to the Synthetics.

The millennia have been attained: the best, most prosperous time of human history, free of war, free of want, free of unnecessary suffering. The humans born in this era cannot understand the violent history of mankind and especially why mankind feared and persecuted synthetics.